I0772595

THE LAST DEATH

THE LAST DEATH

Lou Ann Jasinski Book 3

By

Tanya Goodwin

This is a work of fiction. Names, characters, places, and incidents are the product of the author's imagination. Any resemblance to persons, events, or locales is entirely coincidental.

ISBN-13: 979-8-218-37439-6

Dedication

I dedicate The Last Death to all law enforcement within our nation and at our borders, both land and sea, who fight against traffickers of Fentanyl, with its deadly consequences, and all other illicit drugs, including the new ones circulating everyday. I also dedicate this book to all medical staff, particularly, emergency room physicians, nurses, and everyone else who labor to keep those who battle a substance abuse disorder, and those who unknowingly ingest a deadly drug, alive, and unfortunately and ultimately, the pathologists and medical examiners who receive the ones who don't survive.

I would be remiss to not extend my deepest condolences to families who have experienced the death of a loved one from a drug overdose. Because Fentanyl is now the leading cause of death for ages eighteen to forty-five, virtually everyone knows someone or some family who have experienced this tragedy.

In The Last Death, I refer to a fictional drug, "Rocket". Rocket, its chemical properties, its deadliness, including its effects, its elusive antidote, and its trafficking, is purely, as an author, the result of my imagination—my creativity. I pray that a drug such as "Rocket" remains fictional.

Finally, on a bittersweet note, Rae Monet, my longtime graphic artist, is retiring. The front cover of The Last Death is her last of all my novels and novella covers that she has created for me. But, I'm happy to announce that Karen Duvall, who has designed the back covers and the dust jackets for my hardback books, will now be my hundred percent graphic artist!

And, as a double whammy, my editor, Faith Freewoman, is likewise retiring. The Last Death sadly was her farewell edit. I will be announcing my new editor in forthcoming books.

Change is part of life.

Also by Tanya Goodwin

Suspense /Crime Fiction Novels

The Last Known Survivor--Lou Ann Jasinski Book 1

The Last Will-Lou Ann Jasinski Book 2

If Memory Serves- Dr. Tara Ross- Vol 1

The Embalmer- Dr. Tara Ross - Vol 2

Brush With Death- Dr. Tara Ross -Vol 3

Code Pink- Dr. Tara Ross-Vol 4

Cold Case- Dr. Tara Ross-Vol 5

Do Not Disturb

Hidden Obsession

Christmas Novellas

An Evergreen Christmas

An Evergreen Wedding

An Evergreen Baby

An Evergreen Holiday- Boxed Set

The First Star-Dr. Tara Ross Christmas Edition

Snowfall

Contemporary Medical Romance

Roxanne

Fang Hospital- Dr. Gabriella Van Court Book 1

Fang Baby- Dr. Gabriella Van Court Book 2

Fang Vacation- Dr. Gabriela Van Court Book 3

Fang Wedding- Dr. Gabriella Van Court Book 4

About Tanya Goodwin

Tanya Goodwin writes suspense, police procedurals, and crime fiction. Her experiences as a physician are reflected in her characters and in her stories, and her life as a doctor allows her to switch from stethoscope to keyboard. A former New Yorker, she now resides in Florida. Tanya is a member of Sisters in Crime and Mystery Writers of America.

You can reach Tanya Goodwin at:

http://www.tanyagoodwin.com
www.facebook.com/tanyagoodwinauthor
Twitter: @TanyaGoodwinDoc
Instagram tanyagoodwinwrites

1

Joanna eased to the back of the pack during the 7 am shift turn over at Hampton Medical Center's Emergency Department. Although she was wearing the official emergency department's teal blue scrubs, she hardly felt "official". It was her first orientation day as a newly tapped RN, and she was lucky to land her first choice as an ED nurse.

It was a dream come true. She and Kaylee had fought as survivors of trafficking. Once scary look-a-like teens and now young women, Joanna for an instant wished for Kaylee to stand in her place. But Kaylee was in Greece, and she was here.

Joanna sucked in a breath. She'd managed to not only complete high school, but also to complete college with a baccalaureate degree in nursing, graduating at the top of her class.

Joanna exhaled the anxiety that accumulated in her lungs. Her years as a runaway teen crumpled in her head. Yes, she deserved to be here—belonged here.

She took a step forward and intently listened to the outgoing attending physicians' and nurses' handoff to the incoming crew– Joanna amongst them.

Joanna followed along, but the ED was nearly at full capacity. The clear notes of the first ten patients trailed into a series of muddled B flats.

How was she going to remember all this, much less survive the next twelve hours?

Perhaps the ED wasn't the right place for her after all.

The outgoing shift trudged, red-eyed out of the ED, leaving the fresh faces of the next shift to continue where they left off.

Five patients were already dispositioned and discharged, but according to the waiting room Joanna passed on her way in, a throng of people were already waiting to be seen.

Last night's full moon had apparently wreaked its havoc. The superstition was today's reality.

The day crew scattered leaving Joanna in its wake.

Claudia Jackson approached Joanna with a crooked finger.

She recognized the charge nurse, having interviewed with her two weeks ago. Afterwards, Joanna had skipped to her car sure she had nailed the interview.

But by the look on Claudia's puckered face, there definitely wouldn't be any more skipping. Even with Claudia's pixie haircut, she was no sprite.

"Joanna."

Joanna straightened her shoulders. "Yes ma'am."

Should she have called her ma'am? Too late now.

Claudia arched her eyebrows. She was in her forties, and hardly a ma'am. The term flew out of Joanna's mouth, a leftover habit from her stints at multiple elementary schools, courtesy of her mother's failure to pay rent. It was a miracle Joanna had made it to seventh grade. But after her mother's eventual heroin overdose, Joanna's homelessness severed any further education. Her education became one of the Miami streets and then Dr. Gerald Newell, now dead trafficker, popped into her life. She'd never be the same. But no one knew that. Not her GED teachers, not the college, and not Claudia nor anyone else at Hampton, and that's the way she wanted it.

She was a nurse now, and Lou Ann Jasinski and Harry Boxer were her family…and obviously Kaylee. She and Kaylee were bonded for life and no ocean or country could ever change that.

"I have to attend a meeting. In my absence I'll leave you with Shelly, who you'll shadow today," Claudia said.

Claudia held her hand out to a young nurse whose eager brown eyes matched her fresh ponytail. "This is Shelly. Shelly, this is Joanna. This is her first day. I know the place is a zoo, but you know what they say, "Baptism by fire.""

Shelley smiled. "We'll just toss her right in."

Claudia grinned back. "I'll see you two later."

After Claudia was well away from earshot, Shelly approached Joanna. "Yeah, it's a zoo today. But it was that way when I oriented four years ago. I'll never forget feeling overwhelmed, and there are days that I feel the same. And I didn't mean it when I said that we were going to toss you right in. I wouldn't do that to you. Claudia is is an awesome emergency room nurse with fifteen years of experience. You'll see her in action. Learn from her. We all still do."

Joanna nodded. "Thanks, but I don't want to get in your way."

"Well, you're not going to stand against a wall. So off we go. Follow me."

Joanna hustled to keep up with Shelly.

"Rooms one through five are pediatric rooms. There are nurses who are specifically trained to attend pediatric patients from newborns to teens, and that's their wheelhouse. On occasion you may be assigned there in the future, but it's relatively rare. Are you inclined toward pediatrics?"

Joanna shook her head. "Nope."

Joanna adored Lou Ann's and Harry's newborn daughter, Joanna's and Kaylee's namesake. She hated to admit it but it would be hard for her to care for sick babies. It was too close to home. However, if need be, she'd do it. After all, she was a nurse and she wouldn't pick and chose her patients. Dr. Zimmer and Nurse Lynn didn't pick and choose to take care of her.

Shelly continued the quick tour.

"Rooms six through twelve are for adult patients with the first two for minor injuries like sprains, fractures, or anything that needs to be sutured. The remainder are for abdominal pain, rule out appendicitis, asthma, COPD, rule out MI, and the like—except for room twelve which is in that corner. That's the GYN room and includes victims of sexual assault. We have a special team for those who have been sexually assaulted."

Joanna's mouth went dry and her knees suddenly softened. She instinctively halted.

"Are you all right?" Shelly asked.

Joanna inhaled and slowly exhaled.

"I'm okay. I skipped breakfast," she lied. She'd had pancakes of which the remnants had resurrected in her belly.

Shelly dug into her scrub's pocket and pulled out a wrapped candy. "Here, take this. I carry these around when I can't get to lunch or maybe not even dinner. Somedays you realize that you haven't even peed."

Joanna took the candy.

"Thanks."

"Don't mention it."

Thankfully, Shelly pointed out the last two rooms. "These are trauma rooms. Patients arrive either by ambulance or by helicopter for life threatening injuries. Hopefully we won't have any today."

Claudia had given Joanna a quick tour of the emergency department during her interview, but it wasn't nearly as hectic as this morning.

"The triage nurse brought back two patients. Log into the computer and review the notes on rooms six and seven, both classified as minor."

Joanna logged into the computer and read the nurse's triage notes regarding rooms six and seven.

"Room six is a twenty-two year-old man that has a right forearm laceration and room seven fell off his skateboard and sustained a left ankle injury."

"Sprain and laceration. Let's elevate the skateboarder's ankle and place an icepack on it. The attending will order an x-ray to make sure there are no fractures. Then we'll scoot into room six. He'll need his wound cleaned before the attending sutures it."

"Got it," Joanna said.

She let Shelly take the lead and both entered the skateboarder's room.

"Hello," Shelly said. "I'm Shelly and this Joanna, and we're your nurses today."

"I'm Greg," he pointed to his angry, ballooning left ankle, "and no longer able to defend my championship."

"Yeah, sorry about that," Shelly said.

Greg shrugged. "At least I got a tag team today."

Shelly gently elevated Greg's ankle while Joanna reached into a cupboard and took out a packaged ice pack and cracked it into action.

"Cool," Greg said.

Joanna placed the pack on Greg's ankle.

One of the attending physicians sauntered into the room.

Joanna tossed the doctor a quick glance. She'd seen him at morning report from afar. His name tag identified him as Dr. Hottman, and with his chiseled facial features extending to the rest of his athletic body, the name was so apropos.

"Hi Greg. I'm Dr. Hottman."

Hottman approached Greg and quickly assessed Greg's ankle.

"Looks like a bad sprain." Hottman nodded. "Being a skateboarder, I had a couple bad spills myself."

Joanna could see that. She glanced at Shelly, who did a covert eye roll, and mouthed, "later."

Joanna replied with a quick nod.

"I'll order an x-ray in case I've missed something, but I don't think so." Hottman arched his brows. "Looks like your competition days are done for now."

On Hottman's way out of the room, he pointed at Joanna.

"I'll need your assistance in the next room."

"Umm…sure."

Shelly hustled toward Joanna and whispered in her ear, "Watch out for Dr. "Hotty".

Was that what she meant by "later"?

Joanna strode next to Hottman, keeping up with his rapid pace.

They entered room six.

"Hello, I'm Dr. Hottman and this is…"

"Joanna, you're nurse," she announced before Dr. "Hotty" could.

He grinned.

She recognized the kind of guy that he was, and she wasn't going to allow him to push her around. Yeah, he was the doctor, and she, granted the newbie nurse, but she'd make sure early on that they were a team.

"So let's take a look a that nasty gash, Mr. Galen," Hotty said, and then flashed another grin toward Joanna.

Joanna responded with a quick, straight-faced nod.

"We'll take care of that," she said to the patient.

"I was doing some yard work and carrying a bunch of branches and stupidly forgot that I'd cranked the kitchen windows open. I grazed my arm across the corner of the metal frame," he pointed to his right forearm, "and this freakishly happened."

"We're used to freakish things," Hotty said.

He turned his attention to Joanna.

"Nurse, irrigate that wound, get me some lidocaine, and a suture kit. Oh, and he'll need a tetanus shot."

Hotty left Joanna with Galen.

Joanna slid an absorbent pad under his arm.

"This may sting a bit," she warned.

She cleansed his wound with a syringe filled with a normal saline solution.

He didn't even flinch.

"Not so bad," he said.

Joanna had just finished irrigating the patient's wound when Dr. Hotty returned.

She darted onto the exam room cupboard and grabbed a vial of lidocaine, a syringe, needle, and a suture kit. She popped the top off the anesthetic vial and poured its contents into a sterile cup and set the cup on the blue-toweled Mayo stand, a silver metal tray on a likewise silver metal stand, and carefully dumped the contents of the suture kit on the field.

"What size gloves?" she asked Dr. Hotty.

"Eight, please."

Joanna grabbed a pack of size of eight sterile gloves and deposited the gloves on his field and then grabbed a pair of size sixes for herself and donned them.

"Ready," she said.

"Well, goody," Dr. Hotty," replied.

"Thanks, nurse," Mr. Galen said.

"Yes, thank you, nurse," Dr. Hotty said. "Let's get Mr. Galen fixed up, shall we?"

"Absolutely," Joanna answered.

Hottman injected the local anesthetic around the patient's wound and waited a minute.

"Let me know if you feel pain, and I'll stop and give you more numbing medicine."

"Will do, Doc."

Dr. Hotty began to suture the patient's laceration.

"All good, Doc. Don't feel a thing."

"Good to know I got it just right," Dr. Hotty said, proud of his technique.

Arrogant jerk!

Joanna had to admit that Hotty's needlework was perfectly straight.

Once finished, Hotty held up the suture.

"Cut, please, and don't cut my knot," Hotty ordered.

Joanna crisply cut the suture just right.

"Good work, "Hotty said.

"The nurse will dress your wound, give you a tetanus shot, and a copy of wound care. Do you have a primary physician?"

"Yes, I do," Galen answered.

"See him or her in a week. Your doctor can remove the sutures in the office."

"Take care, Mr.Galen," Hotty said.

"I will, Doc."

Hotty exited the room leaving Joanna to clean up.

"Thank you for taking care of me, nurse."

"You're welcome," Joanna said.

A pleasant warmth filled her chest. Mr. Galen was her very first patient, and she survived Hottman.

Jackass!

2

Lou Ann walked the hallway while cradling Joley Kay against her shoulder and gently bounced the red-faced crying baby, trying to comfort her.

"I know your poor little gums hurt."

Joley Kay baby-snorted and stopped wailing.

Lou Ann sighed. Her soft lulling voice had worked—for ten seconds—and then back to cranky baby.

Harry came out of the bedroom and held out his arms.

"Here, let me take her so you can take a shower."

Lou Ann surrendered Joley Kay.

"Thanks. I know you've been up all night too."

"I'll go get the whiskey," Harry said.

"Harry!"

"It's for me. The baby gets the cold teething ring and baby pain reliever. Want to share? I mean the whiskey."

Lou Ann chuckled. "Maybe after my shower."

Joley Kay settled in Harry's arms and blinked a few times before falling asleep

"I hate you, Harry."

"Beginner's luck. The whiskey is still on," he joked.

"Sounds inviting."

Harry laughed and then hushed when Joley Kay stirred.

Lou Ann and Harry held their breaths, and Joley Kay blessedly returned to sleep.

Figures, since the baby and they were up most of the night.

But there was no more sleeping for Harry and her.

Harry was due at the FBI field office this morning and she at the sheriff's office to review homicide cases, now that she was the lead homicide investigator.

Both Harry and she had been able to take twelve weeks parenting leave of absence. Joanna was a huge help. But that had come to an end since Joanna had her new nursing career, and she and Harry had to return to their own jobs.

Her heart always ached when her neighbor and best friend, Suzy, came over to sit with Joley Kay. But today she welcomed a break.

A soft knock came at the door.

"Suzy to the rescue, and right on time," Lou Ann said.

Lou Ann answered door while still wearing her baby-stained nightgown.

"Bad night, huh?" Suzy asked.

Lou Ann sleepily nodded.

Harry luckily appeared with his robe covering his boxer shorts. But his mussed hair gave his sleeplessness away.

"Teething?" Suzy asked.

"Me, no. The baby, yes," Harry responded.

Suzy grinned.

"Hand her over to me so you two can shower and have breakfast."

"Sure, now that she's quiet."

"Go," she ordered Lou Ann and Harry.

Lou Ann and Harry looked at each other and rushed away.

"Race you! "Harry challenged Lou Ann.

He bolted toward the shower.

Lou Ann laughed while she passed him.

Harry grabbed the hem of Lou Ann's nightgown.

"Cheater!" she called.

"Every parent for himself!" he called back.

Lou Ann flung her nightgown over her head leaving Harry with it in his grip.

"Ha! Ha!"

Lou Ann beat Harry to the shower knowing full well that they were going to share the cleansing water.

Lou Ann cranked the faucets and leaped under the blessed spray.

Harry dumped Lou Ann's stained gown and his baby spit up T-shirt and his boxers into the hamper.

"Every parent for himself, huh?"

Harry walked into the shower, joining Lou Ann.

"You won," he said.

Lou Ann hugged Harry and kissed him beneath the spray of the shower.

"No. We both won. We need to stick together if we're going to survive parenthood."

"Well, we did right by Joanna and Kaylee, so we've got that."

Lou Ann and Harry bumped fists.

Lou Ann smiled. "Yes we did."

Lou Ann and Harry dressed for their respective duties.

"I feel semi-human after that shower," Lou Ann said.

"Yeah, some semblance of functionality."

Lou Ann sniffed. "I smell breakfast!"

Harry waggled his eyebrows. "May it not be an olfactory mirage."

"No, I think it's real. Let's follow that heavenly scent to the kitchen."

"Right behind you," Harry said. "I'm too tired to race you."

"Ditto."

When they walked in Suzy was setting two plates on the table.

"Have a seat," she said.

Lou Ann and Harry grinned at each other and scooted into their chairs.

Suzy loaded each of their plates with two sunny-side-up eggs, and buttered toast with jam. Then she poured a cup of coffee for each of them.

"Eat up while the little one is still asleep," she said.

"Suzy..."

Suzy waved her hands. "Nuh-uh."

"You're a lifesaver," Lou Ann said.

"I couldn't have said it better," Harry added.

Breakfast nirvana settled in her stomach, and Harry rolled his eyes upward as he joined her in savoring this slice of heaven.

"Have a seat and eat this delightful breakfast that you've gone to such lengths to provide," Lou Ann said.

"Oh, I already ate while you two were in the shower."

Isabelle let out a happy bark and Pinky, Suzy's Frenchie puppy, ran around in joyous circles.

Lou Ann smiled. "Looks like they enjoyed their breakfast too."

"Thanks for letting me bring Randy with me."

"No problem. Isabelle couldn't be happier."

It was much easier for Suzy to come over with Randy rather than carting Joley Kay and Isabelle over to her house.

"I have the baby's car seat and two doggy safety seats if I have to go anywhere. So off you go."

Lou Ann and Harry peeked into the spare back bedroom they'd converted into a nursery and grinned at each other at Joley Kay's baby snores.

Harry kissed Lou Ann.

"Let's get going before she wakes up," Harry whispered.

Lou Ann hesitated.

"Come on, Mama. She'll be just fine."

"I know."

Lou Ann blew Joley Kay a kiss.

"Bye-bye, baby. Mama and Dada love you so much," she whispered. "We'll be home soon."

Lou Ann took a deep breath and she and Harry headed out the door.

3

Joanna walked out of room six after reviewing wound care instructions with Mr. Galen, nearly bumping into Claudia Jackson.

Shelly approached the two of them.

"Looks like you've been busy," Claudia said.

"She has," Shelly said. "She's tackled a sprained ankle, and she assisted Dr. Hottman with suturing a laceration. She got all the appropriate equipment and the patient was grateful to have Joanna as his nurse. The patient left very satisfied and I'm sure he'll turn in an A-plus review."

Joanna tried to stifle a blush, but felt the heat spread across her cheeks.

Joanna tossed a raised-eyebrow glance at her exaggeration.

Shelly grinned at her.

"Good job, Joanna," Claudia said. "You two break for first lunch."

Shelly tilted her head, inviting Joanna to follow her into a room with a long table with a number of chairs, a full-sized refrigerator, and a microwave.

Joanna had seen the break room while touring the emergency department during her interview with Claudia. But it was empty at the time. Now the room buzzed with nurses and another attending physician who Joanna recognized from this morning's shift report.

Joanna's presence was lost in the hubbub of a fast and furious lunch, making way for the second and third shift lunch periods.

Shelly reached into the refrigerator and pulled out a sandwich and a can of flavored carbonated water.

Dang! Joanna didn't bring any lunch. She'd bring one tomorrow, but today she'd have to rely on one of Shelly's candies.

"Oh, I can share my sandwich with you," Shelly offered.

Joanna shook her head. "That's okay. I'll survive. Maybe I'll have some coffee."

Joanna looked at the black slick at the bottom of the coffee carafe. "Or maybe not."

"I'll brew a fresh pot. Meanwhile, the cafeteria is on this same floor. Go out the door, then turn right and then left, and then follow the signs leading to the hospital cafeteria. Actually, the food there is pretty good. But you'll have to bring your lunch back here instead of staying in the cafeteria, because if the ED goes crazy, we'll have to respond. I'll save you a seat."

"Okay. I'll be right back."

Joanna took the elevator to the second floor up, followed the signs leading to the cafeteria, and walked in, joining the end of a long line. This could take a while, and by the time she got food she'd have to gobble it down when she returned to the ED. The lunch shifts were only thirty minute long since Hampton ED was massive. Maybe she'd back out and be better prepared tomorrow.

She'd turned around—and ran smack-dab into Dr. Hotty.

"Oh, I'm sorry!"

It was all that popped out of her mouth.

"That's all right. Don't apologize. It's a zoo in here during peak lunchtime." Hotty beckoned to her. "Follow me. This is the visitor line. The staff line is over there. It goes a lot faster out of necessity."

Shelly didn't tell her about that.

Joanna had no choice but to follow Hotty.

"After you," he said.

Joanna inched ahead of him After all, he did get here after she did.

She assessed her choices. Whatever she picked, she'd have to devour it in a hurry.

Then she spied macaroni and cheese. She grinned while thinking about Harry's macaroni and cheese. Although this wasn't the boxed kind, which she loved because it was Harry's version, it was still mac and cheese.

She plopped a scoop of macaroni and cheese in her to-go carton and moved forward.

Joanna noticed that Hotty chose a salad, but she refused to apologize for her macaroni and cheese.

Although she did add a scoop of green beans so she'd seem more nutritious-conscious.

She laughed to herself. Kaylee detested green beans. Then she grew a bit sad because she missed her. There was an unbreakable bond between them because they were both survivors of sex trafficking. But that was her secret now.

Joanna grabbed a bottle of lemonade, her favorite drink, and proceeded to the cashier. She presented her hospital badge. But even with the staff discount, she was short a dollar.

She started to put the lemonade back when Hotty said to the cashier, "I'm paying for hers."

Joanna shook her head.

The cashier waited and eyed the line forming behind them, so she accepted Hotty's money.

"Let's head back," he said.

"Thank you, Dr. Hottman. I'll pay you back tomorrow."

"Not necessary. It's not like this is going to break me financially."

He had a point there. He must make a lot of money. However, she was a proud of making a descent living, even as a new nurse, and although money wasn't her primary objective in becoming a nurse, the benefits did matter. Joanna always dreamed of being self-sufficient in an honest way, and she did put in all the hard work to be where she was today. So she decided that whether he liked it or not, she was going to pay him back to the penny. It might not be important to him, but it was to her.

Hotty broke their silence while they were on their way back to the break room.

"By the way, my name is Dr. *Ian* Hottman."

No way was she going to call him by his first name, inside or outside of the hospital—should they happen to meet outside.

"And you can call me Nurse Joanna."

Ha! So there!

Hotty, aka Ian, chuckled. "Okay, Nurse *Joanna*. We should hurry back so we can wolf down our lunch. And, by the way, I was also eyeing the mac and cheese," he added.

"Really?"she asked, eyebrows raised.

Hotty grinned. "Really. No lie. I like mac and cheese."

There was hope for him yet—aka Ian.

4

Lou Ann settled into her new office on the fourth floor of the Sheriff Department's headquarters, right next to Assistant Chief Glenda Martinez's office.

She leaned back in her desk chair and grinned.

Gone was her third-floor office as a former sergeant and under the hawk eyes of her nemesis Lieutenant Dan Mathews.

Dan was below her now, not only in terms of floors, but more important in rank, since she'd been promoted to Chief Homicide Investigator.

Her smile turned into a yawn.

She was about to call Suzy about Joley Kay when someone rapped on her office door.

"Come in," Lou Ann called and quickly stifled a yawn.

Glenda stood at the opened door, her normal in-command demeanor replaced by a grim face with glistening eyes.

Lou Ann popped up from her desk chair and hurried to Glenda, who hesitated in the doorway.

Then with a sigh, Glenda stepped in and closed the door.

"Glenda, what's wrong?"

In private she and Glenda were on a first-name basis.

Lou Ann took Glenda's trembling hand. Something was terribly wrong.

"Come sit down."

She led Glenda to a chair and Glenda sat zombie-like.

"I'll get you some water," Lou Ann offered.

Glenda shook her head.

"I need your help," Glenda said, with pain saturating every word.

Lou Ann knelt at Glenda's side. "Anything."

"My niece is dead and I need you to find out what happened."

"What?"

Questions collided in Lou Ann's head as she desperately tried to process what her boss just said.

Then Lou Ann got to her feet and hugged her.

"I'm so sorry."

Lou Ann's world once collapsed at the frightening realization that Kaylee, her niece, could be dead. But by God's grace, she wasn't.

But Glenda's niece was never coming back—a wound that would never heal.

Glenda melted into Lou Ann's arms and then pushed away, sniffling and wiping her eyes while she regained her composure.

"I'm sorry," she finally said.

"Don't be. You have every right to feel the pain. And besides, it's just us right now."

Glenda nodded.

Lou Ann plucked a tissue out of the box on her desk and handed it to Glenda, who dabbed her eyes with it and then blew her nose.

"Where is your niece? I need to get to her."

Whether it was suicide or homicide, that answer would be between Lou Ann and the medical examiner.

"My sister went to Gloria's apartment. They were to go shopping and then to lunch. When Gloria didn't answer the door, or then her cell, my sister, who had a key, opened the door and found Gloria lifeless in her bed. My sister called 911 and then me. Between sobs she told me Gloria was cold." Glenda shook her head with a shaky breath. "I knew right away."

Lou Ann's phone buzzed.

"Jasinski," she answered.

"We need you immediately at 611 Flower Lane, apartment 2D. We've confirmed by Rescue Response a dead young female. We've secured the scene. ME is on the way," the responding deputy sheriff reported.

"Gloria Perez."

"Yes, ma'am, confirmed by her mother. Another deputy has her, apparently and unsurprisingly distraught."

"Assistant Chief Martinez and I are on the way."

"Yes, ma'am."

"Let's go, Glenda. We're going to see to your niece, and I won't rest until you and I, and your sister, find out what happened to Gloria."

5

Lou Ann ducked under the yellow and black crime scene tape, then turned around to see Glenda hugging her sister while she sobbed.

Lou Ann lowered her head, and then turned back around and strode forward with clenched teeth, intent on solving the circumstances of young Gloria's death.

A deputy sheriff guarding the scene nodded briskly. "Investigator Jasinski."

Lou Ann acknowledged him with a nod, donned a footed white, jumpsuit with shoe covers, rubber gloves and surgical cap before proceeding into the apartment complex. She passed two other deputies before ascending the elevator to the second floor, and went straight to apartment 2D, where another deputy stood guard at the open doorway while also keeping neighbors well behind the crime scene tape.

Lou Ann ignored Gloria's sympathetic neighbors and walked into the apartment.

The crime scene unit outfitted in the same standard garb as Lou Ann's, had already arrived and was milling about the apartment, scrutinizing everything.

Lou Ann noted that there didn't appear any forced entry into Gloria's apartment.

"ME's in the bedroom with the victim," one of the crime scene unit members said, and then pointed Lou Ann in the direction of the bedroom.

"Thanks," she replied and proceeded to Gloria's bedroom.

Please, not sexual assault, she begged to herself.

"Hi, Barb," Lou Ann said to the medical examiner, who probed Gloria's body while Gloria lay lifeless on her bed.

"Hi, Lou Ann. From my initial gathering, this young lady didn't appear to die a violent death, but I reserve any final judgement. I found her curled up and lying on her side. CSU and I already took photos and you should receive copies promptly."

Lou Ann met Barb's gaze.

Gloria was barefoot, but wearing a black cocktail dress, aka "clubbing attire."

And she still had full makeup on, including smudged red lipstick with further smudges on her pillowcase. And a layer of white foam lined her lips. Rigor mortis and lividity had already set in. Gloria died at least six hours ago. Barb would be able to narrow down time of death, but determining the time of death wasn't an exact science. Lou Ann's investigation could further close that window.

"No evidence of strangulation," Barb said, acknowledging Lou Ann's silent question.

"We'll be checking for any DNA around the bedroom, bath, and the rest of the apartment," Lou Ann said. She paused. "Toxicology screen."

"Yes," Barb replied then arched her eyebrows. "There's vomit in the bathroom sink and toilet bowl."

Gloria, or perhaps someone else, or both, was sick as a dog last night.

Lou Ann zeroed in on the yellow plastic band around Gloria's wrist that read, SPARK.

Barb nodded.

Clearwater's Spark nightclub overflowed with clubbers on weekend nights.

"Voluntarily or involuntarily, Gloria most probably died of a drug overdose," Lou Ann said.

"My suspicions, exactly."

Lou Ann had a lead to start.

"I'll start her autopsy right away," Barb said.

It was standard for Barb to examine Gloria's body for sexual assault or sexual activity proximal to her death.

Lou Ann sucked in a breath. How to begin to tell Gloria's mother and Glenda about what she'd witnessed? And to add to their pain, the investigation surrounding Gloria's death was just beginning.

Damn!

6

Joanna and Dr. Hotty were both swallowing the last bite of their lunch when Claudia rushed into the break room.

"Rescue's on the way with an unresponsive female."

Hotty tossed his napkin on the table and bolted out of his chair. He pointed to Joanna. "You're on. Let's go!"

"Me?"

"Yeah, you."

Hotty took off, leaving Joanna in his wake.

Claudia jabbed her hands into her hips. "Are you waiting for another invitation?"

Joanna shook her head.

"Come on. You're needed."

"Yes, ma'am."

Claudia waggled her eyebrows.

Joanna's heartbeat banged in the back of her throat because she was clueless about how to proceed. She was bound to fail her first day.

Shelly beckoned to her.

Thank God she wasn't going to be alone. They wouldn't do that to a trainee. But then Shelly did say that her first day was hell.

Joanna tailed Claudia and Shelly to trauma room one, nearly stepping on their heels.

Shelly tossed a yellow paper gown and goggles to Joanna.

"Put these on and grab some gloves and a cap. We never know what will roll in."

Joanna recalled the infection control and the PPE garb required and how to put it on and did it.

Step one done. Now for the patient.

She'd hang back and do as she was instructed while making sure she didn't get in the way. She'd aced basic life support and advanced life support, but this was reality and not a test.

Joanna's breaths hitched while the team stood waiting for Rescue to arrive, shepherding the patient clinging to life. Could the others hear her anxiety? See her panic?

The patient could die despite all measures. Was she ready for that? Since she nearly died herself would that make her a better nurse? Or make it harder for her?

Joanna pushed her nightmares aside. It was time to help another person to live.

Rescue raced into the ED while pushing an unresponsive young woman strapped on their gurney, straight into trauma room one.

Joanna blinked and looked again. This woman appeared to be her age!

Dr. Hottman, along with Claudia and Shelly, aided the Rescue team in transferring the unresponsive woman from the gurney to the trauma bed, taking care not to dislodge the woman's breathing tube taped to the woman's mouth. An IV tube snaked from her left elbow.

Claudia grabbed the bag of solution that was infusing into the young woman's IV and hung it on an IV pole while Shelly attached the woman's cardiac leads to the ED's monitor.

A member of Rescue summarized the situation for them. "Patient's roommate found her collapsed and called 911. Upon arrival, patient was unresponsive. V-fib confirmed and we shocked her times three and we were able to elicit sinus bradycardia at 42 beats per minute, but no spontaneous respirations. She was intubated and received Narcan twice as without responsive with the first. Epinephrine times one with sinus bradycardia with increase to 62. We've continued ventilation and and fluid resuscitation with lactated ringers infusing in an 18 gauge in left antecubital. BP's have remained 80 over 50." Then he added, "We found a pill on the patient's bedside that according to the roommate, the young lady received from an unidentified person on campus."

"Fentanyl, I presume?" Hottman asked.

"Sadly, it appears to be, " the Rescue member replied.

The patient's heart rate plunged to 40 beats per minute.

"What the hell?! Atropine!" Hottman called.

The drug that was to immediately raise the patient's dangerously slow heartbeat failed.

Right before everyone's eyes, the patient flatlined with a 60 over palpable 0 blood pressure.

"Not today! Not today!" Hottman yelled, commanding the patient to live.

Joanna stood helpless against the wall of the trauma room. Hottman's frustration pierced her gut. Despite multiple rounds of resuscitative drugs and measures the patient died.

Hottman's exhale reverberated through the room.

"Time of death, 12:51," he said.

He tossed off his PPE and walked away.

Claudia acknowledged Joanna.

Damn, she was absolutely no help in this situation. Claudia was surely going to tell her that.

"Help us take all the IVs, monitors off this young lady, but leave the endotracheal tube in place. Then we'll send her to the morgue, where the pathologist will care for her," Claudia said.

Claudia, Shelly, and Joanna dismantled the last evidence of the young woman's life.

With a lump in her throat, Joanna worked alongside Claudia and Shelly while the three prepared the woman in silence.

When everything was finished, Joanna followed Claudia and Shelly out of the room where they took off their PPEs.

Shelly left, leaving Joanna with Claudia.

Joanna met Claudia's gaze. "I'm sorry, Claudia," Joanna said softly.

Sorry for the patient and her inability to respond.

Claudia rested her arm across Joanna's shoulders. "We learn from experience, both the fortunate ones and the unfortunate ones. There will be times that, despite everything we do, we'll fail. That just happened. We'll all have a debriefing." Claudia pulled Joanna closer. "You included."

Joanna nodded, holding her breath so she wouldn't squeak in a response.

"That's how it is in the ED," Claudia added.

Only six and a half hours left for Joanna to finish her first shift as an ED nurse.

Tomorrow would be another day.

7

Lou Ann left the building and walked toward Glenda and Daisy, Gloria's mother. She couldn't avoid Daisy, or Glenda, and she wouldn't because it was what she'd need if it were either Joanna or Kaylee who'd been found dead. They were changed forever, victims of trafficking. But they were alive and despite their nightmare pasts, Joanna and Kaylee were succeeding.

Daisy shook uncontrollably, while Glenda was wearing her best stoic demeanor, covering for a quivering mass beneath her duty facade.

"I'm going to take Daisy home and stay with her," Glenda said.

"I think that's a great idea. I'm going to continue my canvas."

"As you should. Keep me abreast."

"Will do."

Glenda escorted Daisy to her vehicle.

Lou Ann recognized that Glenda was hurrying her sister away before Gloria was gurneyed out of the building and into the waiting ME van. Daisy's painful journey was only beginning. Plus, funeral arrangements would be delayed until a full autopsy was completed.

That was thing about funerals—the business of the whole matter. It wasn't until your loved one was buried, that the unavoidable pain smacked you so hard that it left a forever scar.

Lou Ann's brother Lyle's and Melinda's tragic deaths left Lou Ann —and even more so, Kaylee, who'd survived the car wreck—with deep wounds. Plus, what happened to Kaylee afterwards cut her to the bone.

Lou Ann shivered.

She watched Glenda drive away with Daisy pressing her forehead against the passenger door window until Lou Ann could no longer see the back of the car.

Now Lou Ann's whole focus needed to be on piecing together Gloria's death.

Lou Ann went back inside the apartment building and knocked on the first floor door with the "MANAGER" sign.

The door opened and a ruddy-faced, middle-aged man with his eyes glistening with tears stood in the doorway.

She'd remembered seeing him outside of Gloria's apartment and thought he was just a lingering neighbor, but apparently he was more than that.

"I'm Lou Ann Jasinski, a homicide investigator with the Sheriff's Department."

"I knew you'd come."

He beckoned her inside his apartment and closed the door behind them.

"My name is David Montgomery, and I'm the building manager. Come in. Please sit."

Lou Ann's attention roamed from the plastic-covered sofa and chairs to the coffee table's polished sheen with the TV remote the sole item lying perfectly parallel on it. A flat screen TV hung on the otherwise hungry white walls. There wasn't a hint of a woman's touch anywhere in the too-strange, sterile bachelor abode.

A crunching groan shot through the apartment when Lou Ann sat on the unforgiving plastic-covered chair that was closest to the door.

David sat alone on a sofa facing her, oblivious to the creaking cover beneath him.

He shifted on the sofa. "I didn't hear or see anything last night. Two girls down the hall were having a party, and the music was a bit loud and another tenant called to complain about the late hour noise."

Lou Ann took a notebook and pen out of her back pocket.

"And what time what would that be?" Lou Ann asked.

"Just after 9 pm."

"Did you leave the apartment?"

"Yes. I went down three apartments and knocked on the door and asked them to tone down the music—which they did, so I returned to my apartment, where I stayed the rest of the night."

Was this an alibi?

"Did you happen to see Gloria or anyone who didn't belong in the apartment complex?"

"Just the party guests that I have on a security camera."

Lou Ann jotted down David's responses, not only for timeline purposes, but also because of his odd demeanor. But then again, he was odd.

"May I see the footage from last night to noon today before Gloria's mother arrived?"

"Absolutely. I have that in my office. Come, I'll show you."

Lou Ann glanced at her side arm while she followed David.

Although there wasn't any obvious evidence of a forced entry into Gloria's apartment, David would have a master key into her apartment. And he did hang around the scene without identifying himself as the apartment manager. Double odd.

Lou Ann widened her eyes upon entering David's office. Damn! And she thought his living room was weird!

Behind his (of course) glass-covered desk and shiny leather desk chair, a mounted buck's antlered head stared at her.

David arched his thick eyebrows.

"Oh, you like my five-point buck? Took him down first shot."

"Mmm."

"You hunt?" he asked.

"Nope."

"Yeah, I guess not with that gun. Your husband, he hunt?"

He'd apparently noticed her firearm and her wedding ring.

"No."

Lou Ann eyed David's office bookshelf tidily arranged with all the books' spines flush. A gray cat sat on the top of the bookshelf.

"Hi, kitty," Lou Ann cooed. "I didn't hear your cat," she said.

"That's because she's dead."

"And, uh, how long has she been dead?"

"A year since last Tuesday," David chuckled. "She was my baby. I didn't want to have her buried or cremated, so I had her stuffed. That way she's always with me. You got any pets?"

"A dog."

"Well, I'm a cat person."

"I see that."

David opened the laptop on his desk, entered a password, and a split screen security cam opened, showing the first and second floors of the apartment complex, including showing a female and male couple on the first floor carrying grocery bags to their apartment.

Lou Ann leaned over David to view the footage.

"That's Milly and Josh in 10 D. Nice couple."

No one else appeared on the first-floor screen. The second-floor screen likewise remained quiet. Gloria's 2D apartment door still had a "Do not Enter. Crime Scene" posting.

David sighed. "Gloria was such a fine young lady."

"You knew Gloria well?"

"I know everyone who lives here well. That's my job."

"How about the party last night? What apartment was that?"

"16 F. Kelseigh and Jade, 21 year-old roommates, off-campus. They're going to graduate next year, Kelseigh with a business degree, and Jade with a major in chemistry."

"You know a lot about them."

"It's my job to screen applicants."

"At least they turned downed the music."

"Yeah, they take direction well."

"How long have they had a lease?"

"Two years. Generally good girls. Good students. Minor music complaints, mostly from Mrs. Stanko, in 15 D, who's a bit of a cranky old bird. She's been here since my parents owned the place. I took over when they died." David laughed. "Mrs. Stanko came with the place."

Lou Ann redirected David's litany.

"Can you start from 6 pm last night?" Lou Ann asked.

"Sure."

David rewound the security files to 6pm and hit play at an increased speed. He knew they'd be there for hours, and every precious hour counted for her investigation of Gloria's death—foul play or not.

Nothing noteworthy thus far with tenants seemingly returning home from work.

From 7:00 to 7:30 pm a swarm of guys and girls ducked into apartment 16 F. The party that night was just beginning.

"Stop," Lou Ann burst out.

David halted the files for the first and second floors at 7:32 pm.

Gloria exited her apartment, alone, wearing the same black cocktail dress she was wearing when they found her. Lou Ann zeroed in on Gloria's right wrist. She wasn't wearing that yellow wristband yet. Had she been on her way to Spark nightclub? Although Lou Ann was beyond clubbing,—except for the brief time in an Athens club where she chased the real murderer and exonerated Kaylee from a Greek jail—leaving for a nightclub at 7:30 pm seemed early. Had Gloria stopped somewhere else before she arrived at the club?

Lou Ann's answer came four minutes further into the files.

Gloria was now on the first floor and knocking on 16 F, Kelseigh and Jade's apartment.

A young woman opened the door, hugged Gloria, then they both went inside the apartment.

"Who is that?"

"That's Jade," David answered.

"Did Gloria hang out with Kelseigh and Jade?"

"Yeah, they were friends, even though Gloria was no longer a student. She graduated last year with a degree in architecture and was doing an internship with Wells and Farnworth, a well-known architectural firm. Gloria was going to be a success despite those arrogant asses who didn't recognize her talent but instead made her their gopher."

"And you know this this because…?"

This guy was frickin weird.

"I saw how she used to drag back home, sometimes as late as 7 pm. I would ask her if she was okay, and she would say yes, but was tired from a long day at that firm."

"How did you know she was interning at that firm?"

"I saw her briefcase with their logo, so then I asked her if she worked there—you know, to update my files—she said yes, but as an intern. She was to be brought on as an employee within the month. She deserved that."

David was clearly obsessed with the tenants' lives. Were they aware that he was spying on them?

"Start the files again," Lou Ann ordered.

David restarted the security files.

While David's eyes stayed focused on the running files, Lou Ann focused every few seconds on David's increasingly, sweaty forehead.

The files sped by.

"Whoa! Slow it down," Lou Ann said.

"I figured you wanted to get to the 'meat' of things."

David stopped the files and lowered his head. Then he lifted it and turned to Lou Ann.

"I hesitated to tell you that I did see Gloria at 1:30 in the morning." David quickly went on. "But I ended up not saying anything because I saw her briefly, but only because I saw on my security file that she looked a bit tipsy and was having trouble inserting her key her into her door. I figured she must have had too much to drink at the party so I went to the second floor to help. I opened the door for her and asked if she was okay. She was giggling, but her speech made sense even though she was a tiny bit wobbly."

"You mean slurred."

"Not slurred-slurred."

"Why didn't you tell me this earlier, especially it was obvious from our presence that she was dead?"

David shook his head. "Honestly, I had no idea she died. I think she may have been drunker than I thought, and that she drank more after I left."

"How long were you in her apartment?"

"No longer than five minutes. I made sure she didn't fall. She lay down on her bed and waved me away. I left. I thought she was still sleeping off from the aftermath from the night before, but then her mother arrived and you know the rest."

"Why are you telling me now? I saw you among the crowd," Lou Ann pressed.

"Gloria was dead, and I swear I don't know anything that could explain it. I knew you would eventually seek me out, and I didn't want you to think I had anything to do with her death. I should've stayed."

Lou Ann glared at him.

"I'm so sorry. I have to live with this guilt that I tell you at the scene."

"Continue the tape."

"Okay."

David quietly slowed the files to regular speed.

At 9:36 pm Gloria left Kelseigh and Jade's apartment, with Jade. Bother were giggling and both walked normally.

Jade hadn't been with them, though. *What's wrong here?*

Lou Ann examined every second of the first and second files.

Between 7:30 pm and after Gloria left the party with Jade, partygoers were seen leaving between 9:00 pm until no more left after 1:00 am. But then Jade appeared without Gloria at 1:12 am. *Where was Gloria? What does Jade know?*

At 1:32 Gloria returned, her gait unsteady. As David described, she tried unsuccessfully to insert the key into her door.

David left the file running and it showed him unlocking the door for her. He went inside and the door closed. He was correct when he said he only stayed for five minutes. Actually, he left her apartment 4 minutes and 6 seconds later.

Lou Ann examined his demeanor on the tape. He didn't look anxious or panicked. He didn't look around to see if anyone saw him. He went to the stairwell and reappeared on the first floor and entered his apartment.

After that there was no activity until 6 am Monday when tenants appeared to be leaving for work.

"Didn't you wonder why Gloria didn't leave for work?"

"Based on how she came home obviously drunk, I figured she probably called in sick."

That made sense, even for David.

"Continue with the files."

Lou Ann widened her eyes and stared at the screen.

Daisy arrived at Gloria's apartment at 11:30 this morning and knocked on Gloria's door. Then she pounded harder and more frequently.

Lou Ann's heartbeat sped up when she saw Daisy's expression, and watched her get a key out of her purse and unlock her daughter's door.

And the tragedy unfolded in Gloria's apartment where the videotape was unable to record what happened.

Lou Ann already knew that Daisy called 911 and then Glenda, prompting Glenda to seek Lou Ann.

"You can stop the tape," Lou Ann said.

David nodded.

"I'm so sorry," he said.

"I'll need you to come to headquarters and to my office for a complete interview."

"Will do."

"Here's my card and phone. I have other pressing matters to attend to today, so come at 4 pm."

"I'll be there."

"All right."

Lou Ann drew a deep breath.

"We'll talk later," she said.

It was 1:45 pm, and she had a long list on her immediate agenda, and it didn't include lunch.

8

The ED slowed, and the patients were all evaluated and waiting disposition, which made it a rare and optimal time to gather for a debriefing. Hottman had pronounced the young woman dead an hour and a half ago and Joanna, like the rest of the team, remained quiet. The team's distress over failing to resurrect the woman was palpable.

Meanwhile, Joanna was silently berating herself. How could she have been so useless during the whole code? She could have at least helped. Done something. Anything. But where she failed, so did everyone else, especially Hottman, who hadn't said a word or even looked her way.

She knew he didn't do it out of anger or disappointment with her, and she figured his avoidance was more about confronting his own sense of failure.

No one gave up on the woman, but circumstances, and ultimately death, won.

Claudia gathered the team into the break room and closed the door.

Two hours ago they were all enjoying lunch, including the fun banter between Joanna and Hottman. And then they were all summoned and the remainder of the shift wouldn't be the same.

And now they were all sitting around a bare table.

A final chair squeaked across the tiled linoleum floor.

"Looks like everyone's present," Claudia announced.

Joanna sat next to Shelly and kitty-corner to Hottman, who for the first time since the young patient coded, glanced in her direction. No smile. No scowl. Only a momentary acknowledgment.

He tipped his chair back until the front legs were off the floor, leaving him balanced on the back ones. He challenged gravity in that

29

position for a few seconds and then without a flinch, returned upright.

Surely they'd seen him pop a wheelie, but no one commented on his stunt. It probably was "classic" Hottman, and she'd have to get used to it.

Claudia summarized from the young woman's arrival to her death.

The room exploded with silence.

Hottman took a swig from his bottle of water and recapped the circumstances surrounding the now deceased young patient. "The rescue squad acted appropriately and as expeditiously as possible. The patient also was ordered additional Narcan doses. We were able to convert her fromV-fib to ultimately an encouraging sinus bradycardia, which unfortunately rapidly decompensated to asystole," Hottman paused, and then continued, "which despite our efforts proved ultimately fatal for the young woman. Fentanyl, as we all acknowledge, is epidemic and we all have unfortunately seen that here. I can't conclude that it was Fentanyl. It could be a combination of substances or not at all. The Medical Examiner should tell us more. The deceased woman will be transferred from our morgue to the medical examiner's office. I've spoken to our pathologist, and he is in agreement. That's all I have to add."

Hottman gulped the remaining water and stood.

"I have patients to take care of so please excuse me. I'm available if anyone has any questions or concerns. Just remember that patients can and do die despite all our attempts, even the young."

Hottman walked out the door without looking back.

"We've reviewed the mechanics of the code and everything was done appropriately and expeditiously as Dr. Hottman said," Claudia continued. "But after every code that results in death, there are abundant feelings. Anyone want to speak up?"

"Codes are intense, no matter the outcome," Shelly said. "It's the tragic part of being a nurse, or a doctor, and even the lab and respiratory who respond. We might all go home tonight physically, exhausted, but more so, emotionally spent. It won't be the first time, and unfortunately it won't be the last."

Claudia nodded. "True. Anyone else?" she added.

She glanced at Joanna.

Joanna shook her head. Claudia and Shelly had already reassured her.

"All right. Let's get back out there," Claudia said.

The team stood and filed out of the break room.
Claudia tapped Joanna's shoulder. "You too."
"Will do."
Hottman pointed his finger at her.
"Nurse Joanna. I need you to discharge rooms 7, 12, and 14."
"I'm on it."
"Great. Thanks."
Joanna widened her eyes.
"Uh…you're welcome."
One battle was lost. But the war continued.

9

After leaving David Montgomery's managerial apartment, Lou Ann walked along the first floor hall and stopped at apartment 16F where Kelseigh and Jade lived and where Gloria was seen entering last night and even more important, leaving with Jade.

These might have been looky-loos at the scene, but they would've been surrounded with others' curiosity. David, however, stood out.

Lou Ann rapped on their door.

No response.

She knocked harder, and waited.

Still no one came to the door.

Lou Ann leaned closer to the door and listened.

No footsteps. No breathing.

She tried again.

No one answered.

Perhaps Kelseigh and Jade had gone to class.

Or maybe they're sleeping off a hangover.

She'd move on and revisit the apartment later.

Lou Ann turned away from 16F when an old woman poked her head out of her open door.

Must be Mrs. Stanko.

"Pssst," the woman called, and then beckoned to Lou Ann.

Lou Ann smiled and accepted the woman's invitation.

"Hello. I'm Lou Ann Jasinski, homicide investigator with the Sheriff's Department.

"I'm Lillian Stanko. Please come in, Ms. Jasinski. Is Ms. okay? How should I address you?"

Mrs. Stanko hardly seemed like "the cranky old woman" David described. But then David was weird.

A beige upholstered sofa stood against a cream-painted wall and a

32

colorful granny square crocheted afghan was draped across the back of the sofa.

"Took me forever to crochet that."

"It's beautiful."

It reminded Lou Ann of her own grandmother's creative nature.

"Thank you, dear. I mean, Ms. Jasinski."

Lou Ann smiled. "Not a problem."

Lou Ann settled on the comfy sofa. No plastic covers!

Lillian sat on the sofa, leaving a respectful distance.

Lou Ann's stomach growled.

"Pardon me."

"You must have missed lunch or not had a filling one."

"I'm fine," Lou Ann insisted.

Lillian got up from the sofa."Make yourself comfortable. I'll be right back."

Lou Ann waited on the sofa while listening to Lillian rustling around in her kitchen, returning shortly with a glass of iced tea and a club sandwich.

Lou Ann's mouth watered and her stomach said "take it."

"Thank you."

"You're welcome."

Lou Ann bit into the heavenly sandwich and followed it with the best iced tea she'd ever tasted.

"This is awesome."

"I'm happy you like it. I know you must have a long day ahead. You'll need the energy."

"I'll definitely be busy."

"I noticed all the commotion earlier this afternoon and then I heard about Gloria. She was such a sweet girl. She and Kelseigh and Jade would come over for lemonade or iced tea. They admired my crochet and asked me to teach them how to crochet. And they were doing really well."

"David Montgomery said you had complained about the music coming from Kelseigh's and Jade's apartment party last night."

"David pokes his nose into everyone's business here. He's not anything like his parents. They were wonderful people. Anyway, I didn't complain. Perhaps somebody else did." Lillian laughed. "It was probably David, himself, who was bothered by the music."

"Have you seen Kelseigh or Jade since Gloria's body was discovered?"

"No. News of what happened to Gloria traveled fast. The whole complex buzzed with people talking about it. Then crime scene tape went up." Lillian sniffled. "Unbelievable. I saw Gloria in the hallway on Friday. She was her way to work. She smiled and waved to me and said she was working on her crochet project. She was happy and bouncy, and now this…"

Lou Ann took out her notebook and pen.

"Did Gloria mention that she was seeing someone? You know, romantically involved?"

"Her boyfriend, Tyler, broke up with her about two weeks ago and Jade, Kelseigh, and I tried to comfort her—try to keep her mind off him. Hard to do. I believe they dated about six months."

"Had you met Tyler?"

"Only in passing. I knew about him through Gloria, and whatever Kelseigh and Jade told me about him."

"Was he coming over frequently, or was she mostly going to his place?"

"I knew he came here, but from what Jade told me Gloria spent more time at his place than he spent here. Seemed a bit arrogant to me, but that's just my opinion. Jade and Kelseigh felt the same way. We wanted her to find someone better for her. She was going out more often. I told her a nightclub wasn't the best way to find a new guy. Hmm. She told me not to worry about her. But of course I did, and so did the other girls."

"Had you seen Tyler around since the breakup or recently?"

"No. But nosy David would know."

Lou Ann finished her sandwich and tucked away her notebook and pen.

"Thank you for everything, Mrs. Stanko."

"My pleasure. I hope you find out what happened to Gloria."

"I'm doing my best. Here's my card with both my cell, and office numbers. Call me if you think of anything else. I may contact you again as well."

Lillian took Lou Ann's card.

"Anything to help out."

"Thank you again for your kindness."

"You're most welcome."

Lillian walked Lou Ann to the door and waved as Lou Ann sauntered down the hall.

"Godspeed, Ms Jasinski."

"Yes, I could use God's speed. Goodbye."

Just as Mrs. Stanko's door closed, Lou Ann's cell rang.

"Jasinski here," she responded.

"Hey, Lou Ann. It's Tim Farmer."

She'd trained Tim and he, as she expected, turned out to be one of the best sheriff deputies.

"Hey, what's up?"

"I was on my way out of headquarters when I encountered two young ladies who were visibly upset. They said they were looking for you. They're in the lobby."

Had to be Kelseigh and Jade.

"Keep them there. I'm on my way."

10

Joanna finished discharging the patients as Hottman had requested of her. She completed discharge teaching, answered the patients' concerns and questions, and forwarded all the electronic prescriptions. The patients' gratitude despite the unexpected wait time due to the earlier complex code situation, and the debriefing, gave her a needed boost. Yes, she was essential.

Hottman leaned over the ED counter while Joanna completed her electronic notes in the computer.

She looked up at him.

"Yes?"

Hottman grinned.

"Good job, Nurse *Joanna*, with your timely discharges. All the patients gave a five-star review which in my lengthy experience, we don't see that often enough. I'll certainly let Claudia know."

"Thank you. I appreciate that. But I wasn't out to impress anyone. I was doing my job and treating patients as I would like, or my family would like, to be treated. No one wants to spend hours in an emergency department, but I know that it happens sometimes."

"Yes, it does."

"I've got another laceration in room 8, and I'll need your help."

"I'll be right there, Dr. *Hottman*."

Joanna signed her notes, logged off the computer, and then joined Hottman in room 8. She'd already assisted him earlier in suturing a laceration, and now she knew exactly what and where to find what he needed.

Joanna prepped the woman's wound and then perfectly cut Hottman's suture while he approximated the woman's accidental kitchen knife slice.

"All done," he said to the patient.

"Thank you, Doctor, and Nurse," the woman said.

"You're welcome," Hottman and Joanna replied at the same time.

Joanna dressed the wound while Hottman disposed of the sharp instruments and even cleaned up after himself.

"I would've taken care of that," Joanna said.

Hottman shrugged. "I was here anyway."

"You certainly did a good job. I approve."

Hottman grinned. "Good to know."

Joanna turned back to the patient. "I'll be back with instructions and any prescriptions," she said.

She and Hottman left the room.

"Are you always this tidy?" she teased.

"Nope."

"Good to know," she parroted.

Joanna returned to the ED workstation and printed out wound care instructions and then returned to the patient with the discharge instructions.

"Here you go," she said to the woman. "I'm going to give you a tetanus shot before you leave, and Dr. Hottman would like you to take an antibiotic, so shortly I'll forward the prescription to your pharmacy."

Joanna injected the shot.

"The local anesthetic should wear off in about an hour. I'd recommend an over-the -counter pain reliever of your choice. That's all there in the printed instructions. If you have any concerns or problems, call us. You can follow up with your primary doctor, or you may return to the emergency department."

"Thank you."

"You're welcome. Take care."

Another laceration, and another discharge. I'm really getting the hang of this.

Joanna returned to the station and sat next to Shelly where Shelly was entering her own notes.

"Wow! You're on a roll!" Shelly said. "And Hotty has never before cleaned up after himself. He usually leaves a big mess."

Joanna shrugged. The last thing she wanted was to be seen as his favorite or for other staffers to think that something was going on between them.

"Given everything that happened today, and that I'm a neophyte, I think he's just being easy on me."

"Okay."

"What okay?"
Shelly smiled. "I mean it's okay."
"Okay."
"Okay."
Was there a hidden thing between her and "Hotty" Hottman?
Nah.

11

Lou Ann entered headquarters and walked straight over to the two bleary-eyed young ladies sitting on the bench. They stood while Lou Ann approached.

"Hello, I'm Lou Ann Jasinski, investigator with the Sheriff's Department."

She left off that she was also a homicide investigator. It wouldn't heal what were heavy hearts, hers included.

"I'm Jade. And I'm Kelseigh. We live in the same apartment complex as Gigi. I mean Gloria. We call her Gigi because it's short for her full name Gloria Grace," Jade said. She sniffled. "I had no idea that was gonna happen."

Lou Ann's thoughts spun 180 degrees.

"My office is on the fourth floor. Let's go there and talk."

Jade plucked a tissue from her purse and dabbed her eyes, while Kelseigh kept silently shaking her head.

They cleared security and then walked with Lou Ann to the elevator bank. Jade's sniffles penetrated the silence of the elevator car.

"Hi, Ilene," Lou Ann said to her office receptionist. "I'll be in my office with these young ladies."

Ilene looked at the wan young women and offered them a tissue box.

Jade blew her nose. "Thank you," she managed to squeak out.

Ilene nodded.

Then Jade and Kelseigh followed Lou Ann into her office.

"Please have a seat, girls" Lou Ann said. She winced. They weren't girls. They were young women. But Jade and Kelseigh didn't seem to care, because their friend was dead.

"I understand you had a party last night. Can you tell me about that?" Lou Ann asked, not addressing either one in particular, but aiming for Jade to respond, which she did.

"We—Kelseigh and I—decided to throw a party kinda at the last minute."

Kelseigh interrupted, "It wasn't really last minute because we sent out text invites Saturday night, plus we told whoever we ran into that night…Saturday."

Last minute or planned, Gloria left that party with Jade.

"Did Gloria, or, uh…Gigi, come to the party?"

Jade and Kelseigh looked at each other as if asking each other whether they should answer honestly.

"Yes," Jade volunteered.

"Do you know approximately what time she arrived? If you can't remember exactly, then did she arrive at the beginning, middle, or near the end of the party?" Lou Ann asked, giving them an out because she knew the exact time from David's security tapes.

"Mmm?" Jade mused and again eyed Kelseigh. "I'd say…sort of beginning…like maybe 7:30-ish."

"Yeah, that's about right, because we already had some people show up around 6:30, but the party didn't get going until like 7," Kelseigh added.

"Had you seen Gloria, or had you texted her?"

"Texted," Jade said.

Kelseigh nodded.

"Did she reply right away?"

"Of course," Jade answered. "Umm, I didn't mean it like that. Sorry."

"It's okay. I didn't take it that way."

Lou Ann needed to keep them talking. But truthfully, she wasn't offended.

She smiled inwardly, recalling how difficult it was to communicate with her own once-estranged niece, Kaylee. They had some knock-down-drag-out fights. But now Kaylee was back in Greece, and she and Kaylee were on more than speaking terms. They'd hit the sweet spot of family, and Kaylee visited often. Lou Ann and Harry and now Joanna, would have to bank vacation time so they could visit Kaylee. For the first time, Lou Ann looked forward to being a tourist in Greece rather than going there to rescue Kaylee, *twice*. And they all knew how that turned out. But she and Kaylee reached a final, blessed, peace treaty.

Lou Ann continued. "Did Gloria arrive alone?"

She already knew the answer, but then again David's tapes might have missed something, or someone at the party who was waiting for her. There weren't any tapes of what went on inside the apartment.

"Yes," Jade answered.

"Did Gloria meet anyone at the party?"

"She pretty much knew everyone there," Jade said.

"How about her ex, Tyler? Did he show up, perhaps uninvited?"

"How do you know about Tyler?" Jade asked

"The apartment manager, David Montgomery."

"Phfft !" Kelseigh and Jade vocalized their opinion of David at the same time.

Lou Ann felt the same way.

"David sticks his nose in everyone's business!"

"Yeah!" Kelseigh concurred.

Apparently, so did Lillian Stanko.

Jade rolled her eyes. "That's a big, emphatic, no! Tyler is *persona non grata!*"

Kelseigh elbowed Jade.

What was that all about?

Lou Ann made a mental note about Kelseigh's gesture. She'd definitely return to it later.

"When did the party break up" Lou Ann asked.

"Most people left well before midnight, probably by 11 pm, with a few stragglers afterwards. Last three people left at around 1 am. I was tired, so I basically kicked them out. Then I went to bed," Kelseigh explained.

Lou Ann stared at Jade, who wiggled in her chair and blurted, "I left at 9:30 with Gigi. We decided to go to Spark because a couple of people from the party were planning to meet us there."

"I stayed behind to clean up and go to bed. I'd been studying that whole weekend because I enrolled in the summer semester, and I have a final exam coming up this Wednesday," Kelseigh said, "so I begged off going to the club."

"So you and Gloria, Gigi, went to Spark around when?"

"Around 9:30."

That was right.

"Did you go in separate cars?"

"I drove, but I had no idea!" Jade cried.

"Easy, now," Lou Ann reassured her.

Lou Ann was positive Jade knew what had happened last night at

Spark.

Jade swallowed.

"Would you two like some water?"

"Yes, please," Jade said.

"Me too, please," Kelseigh said.

Lou Ann picked up her desk phone and punched in Ilene's extension.

"Hi, Ilene. Can you bring us three bottles of water?"

"Sure."

A minute later, Ilene knocked on Lou Ann's office door.

"Come in."

Ilene brought three cold bottles of water as requested.

"Thanks, Ilene."

"No problem."

Ilene exited, closing the door behind her.

Lou Ann gave Jade and Kelseigh each a bottle, and then uncapped hers and took a swig. Lillian Stanko's iced tea had long since worn off.

Jade's fingers trembled while she gulped hers. Kelseigh only sipped.

"You were saying that you drove to Spark with Gloria. Were there any others in the car?"

"No. Just me and Gigi."

"Were you both drinking before you went to the club?"

"God's honest truth, I had a beer around 7:30 and Kelseigh and I were busy entertaining, so nothing more than a cola. Gigi had a glass of wine. But she and I were snacking a lot. We knew we were going to go out later on."

Lou Ann had seen both Jade and Gloria leaving the party on the tape. They were giggling, but their gait was normal.

"You and Gloria went to Spark. Did you stop anywhere along the way?"

"Nope."

"How far is Spark from the apartments?"

"About a fifteen-minute drive, and then there's parking to deal with. The club is really pumping on a Sunday night. I ended up parking about a block away."

"You and Gigi walked a block to Spark?"

"Yes."

"Do you still have that yellow wristband you had to wear to get into the club last night?"

"I cut it off before I went to bed."

"What time did you and Gigi get home from the club?"

Jade hesitated. "I got home a little after midnight."

"Was Gigi stumbling when you both returned?"

"Gigi didn't come home with me."

Now Lou Ann hesitated.

She made direct eye contact with Jade.

"Why didn't she come back with you? You had the car. How was she planning to get home?"

"I begged her to come with me!" Jade blurted. "I took her hand and she slapped it away. That's not like her at all."

"What do you mean that she wasn't like that?"

"Tyler was at the club last night. Both Gigi and I were shocked. He for sure got wind of the party and was pissed off because he wasn't invited—and to make it worse—some of his friends were there. He must have found out that Gigi and I were planning to go to the club. He has a big ego, but Gigi is lovestruck when it comes to Tyler, and she knew I didn't approve of him. I think she wanted to get back together, and I think he regretted breaking up with her even though in mine and Kelseigh's opinion, he wasn't a good match for her. But I guess neither could really quit the other. Then this hot guy scooted up to our table and scoped out Gigi, who returned his attention to make Tyler jealous.

"By then I could tell no good was going to come of this. Our mutual friend, Cassie, said she would take Gigi home because Gigi wanted to hang out some more. She told me 'bye and that she'd see me later. The last thing Kelseigh, Cassie, and I wanted was for Gigi to go with Tyler."

"So you left her there?"

"You make it sound like it was all my fault! I told you that I even grabbed her arm."

"Tell her the rest," Kelseigh urged.

Lou Ann looked straight at Jade.

"I got home, and then I called her at work this morning and they said she called in sick. No surprise. I texted her around 11:30 this morning because I thought she was sleeping. She didn't answer. Jade clutched her head. "I was so wrong. I should have gone up and checked on her!"

"Jade, it wouldn't have made a difference," Lou Ann said. "She died during the night."

"Oh, my God!"

Lou Ann gave them a few minutes to process what neither could change. After the sniffling calmed and the tissue box emptied, Lou Ann continued. "Do you know Mrs. Stanko?"

Jade and Kelseigh nodded.

"Mrs. Stanko is awesome," Kelseigh said.

"We were over at her place a lot. She'd make us sandwiches and iced tea, sometimes lemonade. She was teaching us to crochet. Sounds corny, but it was fun," Jade added.

"Did Gigi go over there?"

"Yeah, but after the breakup with Tyler, not as often. Even Mrs. Stanko was concerned. We all agreed that she just needed some time."

"Then Jade and I were so happy when we found out that Gigi was coming to the party."

"Then I was happy when she wanted to go to the club," Jade said.

"Were all of you regulars at the club?"

"Pretty much so," Jade answered.

"Did Tyler and Gigi ever go to the club together?"

"Yeah, a lot."

"So it wasn't unusual for Tyler to be there?"

Jade shrugged. "No. But...from what I heard and then saw, he hadn't been there in weeks. So I mistakenly thought it would be great for Gigi to get back out there and have fun. I wouldn't have taken her to Spark if I'd known Tyler would be there. "

Lou Ann changed the subject.

"Were you aware that Mrs. Stanko complained about the loud music coming from your apartment during the party?"

"No," Kelseigh said. "But David made his way over and told us to 'knock off' the music. We did that. But we thought David wanted it done that, not Mrs. Stanko."

David lied. Lillian Stanko never did complain. Lillian admitted it and Kelseigh and Jade confirmed it. Lou Ann would confront David with that later. But why would he lie, *twice*? Such a head-scratcher.

"Thank you, Kelseigh and Jade. You both have been very helpful, for Gloria's—Gigi's—sake. I'm so sorry for the loss of your friend. We all are."

"You're going to find out what happened to her, aren't you? We need to know," Jade said.

"I'll do my best."

"I know you will."

Lou Ann gave Kelseigh and Jade her card.

"If you think of anything else, let me know."

"We will," Jade said.

Kelseigh and Jade stood.

Lou Ann took them back to the lobby, escorted them to the door, thanked them again, and waved to Kelseigh and Jade, and they waved back.

Lou Ann returned to her office and finished her water.

She tapped her fingers on the desk.

David's interview was next.

LouAnn's desk phone buzzed.

"Yes, Ilene."

"Assistant Chief Martinez is here to see you."

Glenda, already?

Before Lou Ann could respond in the affirmative, there was a knock on Lou Ann's door before Glenda walked in. Her high rank granted her that uncontested entrance.

Lou Ann stood up from behind her desk.

Glenda gestured for Lou Ann to sit and both women sat.

"How's Daisy?"

"Her doctor prescribed a mild sedative. She finally fell asleep. A neighbor is with her until I return. I preferred not to call you." Glenda lowered her head. "I need to keep busy. I need to connect with someone—you."

Lou Ann rested her elbows on her desk and lowered her chin on her folded fingers.

"I understand," she said.

"So."

Glenda desperately needed an update.

"I reviewed the apartment security tapes with the on-site manager, I spoke with a woman, an older woman, because the manager said she complained about a party on the first floor last night. Interestingly, she denied making the complaint. Then two young ladies, college students, who hosted the party last night, arrived at my office. They were good friends with Gloria, who they referred to as Gigi, short for Gloria Grace."

Glenda nodded. "We called her that too."

"Gloria attended that party and then left with Jade, a friend. They went to Spark nightclub. Jade returned earlier, and alone because Gloria wanted to stay at the club. Apparently Gloria's ex-boyfriend was there last night and she, according to Jade, wanted to make Tyler jealous by flirting with an unidentified guy. Gloria was to return with another friend, Cassie, who I haven't spoken with yet. But I've yet to visit Spark or to speak with Casie or Tyler. The apartment manager is due for a more thorough interview in about fifteen minutes. That's what I've got so far."

"I know you have a lot of work ahead of you."

"I also need to reach out to Barb's office, but the final autopsy will take a while, as you know."

Glenda scratched her forehead. "Good job. I know I can trust your thoroughness, as always."

"I'll keep you in the loop every step of the way. Have you eaten anything?"

"No. I'm not hungry."

"You and Daisy need to keep up your strength. I know you may not want to go to the cafeteria, so I'll call for takeout. What would you like, or do you want me to order something for you? You can eat in privacy, and once I interview David Montgomery, the apartment manager, I'll come by."

"Sounds fine."

"Your favorite sub meal?"

"Sounds fine," Glenda repeated.

They both stood, and Glenda exited Lou Ann's office.

"Is Assistant Chief Martinez okay?" Ilene asked.

Lou Ann sighed. "As okay as she could be. Let me know when David Montgomery arrives."

"Of course."

"I'll be waiting in my office."

Lou Ann sat behind her desk and logged into her sheriff department's protected access to a criminal database. She entered David Montgomery. No results. Then she entered Jade and Kelseigh's names, and even Lillian Stanko. Nothing, just as she expected.

She logged off of the database and then googled complaints against David Montgomery. Lou Ann widened her eyes. Although she couldn't completely trust the internet, three young women had posted unverifiable complaints about David Montgomery. One called him inappropriate and one actually called him a "perv."

Wow!

Lou Ann likewise found him creepy and not completely honest.

Her phone buzzed.

"Mr. David Montgomery has arrived."

"Send him in."

He was right on time, to the minute.

Ilene escorted David into Lou Ann's office.

Lou Ann stood and shook David's sweaty hand.

"Please sit."

Unlike the last time she talked to him, he'd smelled of soap and was clean-shaven. Even the part in his hair was straight. He wore a yellow polo shirt, which tucked into perfectly creased tan pants secured with a brown belt. His loafers gleamed. This guy went all out for this interview. What was he hiding? He had no idea she'd caught on in a second. He backed on the first dishonesty that he'd not seen Gloria. But she'd get him on the untruth about Lillian Stanko complaining about the music. Did he think she wouldn't approach Lillian independently?

But she'd wait to see if he dropped any more lies.

David sat, crossed his legs and rested his hands across his top leg, as if he had no idea what do with his hands. But his posture screamed anxiety.

She'd first gain his confidence.

"Thanks again for taking the time to review the security tapes."

David grinned. "You're welcome. I'm here to help in any way I can."

"I appreciate that."

Lou Ann leaned over her desk.

"I want to again clarify your impression of Gloria's state when she returned to her apartment. You mentioned that you noticed on your security system that Gloria was having difficulty inserting her key in the keyhole."

"Yes, I was concerned because she dropped her keys several times. She clearly wasn't able to enter her apartment."

"Yes, I saw that. But then you admitted you entered her apartment with her."

"I couldn't leave the door open so anyone see her in that condition."

"Please, recap for me how long you were in Gloria's apartment."

"No longer than five minutes."

So far he hadn't changed his story.

"Walk me through exactly what happened in her apartment."

David took a deep breath. "I'm sorry. It's just hard to talk about. I'm still in shock about Gloria's untimely death."

He cleared his throat and continued, "After I opened her door and let her in, and as I mentioned, I then closed the door. I led her to her bed. But then she bolted out of it and rushed into her bathroom, slamming the door shut. When I heard her throwing up I called to her to find out if she was okay. She didn't answer, so I got concerned. The bathroom door was unlocked, so I went in there. I found Gloria leaning over the toilet and vomiting. Too much to drink, you know. I got a washcloth, wetted it, and wiped her mouth. Her forehead was hot and sweaty. So I got a separate clean one, and ran it under cold water and pressed it to her forehead. Gloria stopped vomiting. I noticed she was even more unsteady on her feet, so I got her back in her bed. She was less hot, but I didn't pull up her covers. She rolled on her side, and then she began to snore. I waited a bit. She didn't stir. Then I left her key on her bedside stand and used my master key to lock her door behind me."

This version had a lot more detail. Plus, Lou Ann questioned David's reported time in Gloria's apartment.

"David, you said that you spent no longer than five minutes in Gloria's apartment. But with everything you just recalled, I don't see how you could do all that in five minutes. Are you sure about how long it took?" Lou Ann probed.

"I told you it was an estimated time. I didn't look at the clock."

"Let's back up a bit. According to your surveillance, you saw Gloria stumbling in front of her door at 1:30 this morning. You happened to be awake at this time?"

"Yes, I'm a night owl, plus I have insomnia. It's an ongoing problem for me."

"Did you have to change out of your nightclothes before you went to help Gloria?"

"I don't wear traditional nightclothes. I sleep in shorts. But I did have to throw on a T-shirt."

"How did you get to the second floor—to Gloria's apartment—which is at the end of the hallway?"

"I took the stairway."

"So your apartment is at the beginning of the first floor, and Gloria's apartment is at the end of the second floor."

"I can move pretty fast. And when I saw her struggling in the wee hours, I double-timed to reach her. I didn't want her to fall and hurt herself."

"Okay. I understand that you were concerned."

"That's my job. Plus, I did what any decent person would do."

"So you left your apartment at 1:30 am. What time did you

return?"

David winced. "No, it couldn't have been five minutes. I was off. I didn't put it all tougher until now. It honestly really seemed like no longer than five minutes, but clearly that's not the case. When I eventually looked at my apartment clock it was 1:56."

"You returned twenty-six minutes later?"

"I guess, yeah."

"When you left Gloria, you mentioned that she was lying on her side. Do you recall which way she was facing?"

"Gloria was facing her nightstand which was to her left. I remember that because I left her key on the nightstand."

"You said she was snoring. Loudly?"

"Loud for a girl."

"You said she felt hot. What was her skin color?"

"She was hot to the touch, but pale."

"What about her makeup?"

"Smudged. Poor girl must have had way too much to drink. What kind of bartender would keep pouring her drinks?"

"How do you know Gloria went to a bar?"

"She was dressed like that."

Judgement.

"Plus, she was wearing some kind of yellow wristband."

"What was written on the band?"

"I just noted the bright color. I didn't read it because I was too busy taking care of her." David shook his head. "Some bartender kept feeding her drinks. He didn't care about her like I do…did."

"Thank you for coming in, David."

"I hope I helped."

"You have."

Lou Ann walked David out of her office and gave him her card.

"Call me if you think of anything else."

Like whatever you're not admitting.

"Absolutely."

David grinned at Ilene before he left.

Ilene slid back in her desk chair. "Ew!"

"Yeah. Double ewwwww!"

Lou Ann returned to her office and sat behind her desk. She tapped her pen on her desk.

Jade and Kelseigh called David a "perv". Would Gloria have said the same?

Lou Ann's desk phone buzzed Ilene's extension.

"Yes?"

"I have Dr. Barbara Kent,"on the phone.

"Put her through."

"Hi, Barb," Lou Ann greeted the medical examiner.

"Hey, Lou Ann. I've started Gloria's autopsy, but apparently I'm going to be extra busy because I just received another young woman from Hampton ED who was unsuccessfully resuscitated after a drug overdose. Here's the kicker. That young woman from the ED was wearing the same yellow Spark wristband that Gloria was wearing."

Silence.

"Are you still there, Lou Ann?"

"Yeah. Spark is on my list of stops. Now it's number one on my agenda. I'll see you later."

"I'll be here."

Lou Ann hung up the phone.

Her day just hit overtime.

Lou Ann cradled her forehead against her palm.

She'd be late to pick up Joley Kay from Suzy's. Joanna would be ending her shift at 7 tonight and surely would need rest, especially since it was her first shift. Harry was at the field office tonight, and she had no idea when he'd be back. Suzy was a good friend and neighbor. And she loved both Joley Kay and Isabelle, Lou Ann's dashound. She had no choice but to call Suzy, which she'd actually planned to do earlier, but Gloria's death had taken priority.

Lou Ann picked up her cell and tapped in Suzy's number.

"Hi, Lou Ann." Suzy's cheerful voice somehow relaxed Lou Ann's shoulder muscles.

"I wanted to call earlier, but tragically my boss's niece died sometime during the night and I'm investigating what happened to her."

"Oh. My! How awful!"

"I hate to ask, but can you…"

Suzy interrupted her. "Say no more. You do what you need to do. Joley Kay is napping after a busy day playing with Isabelle and Pinky. We're all good. Don't worry."

"Thank you."

"You're welcome."

"Harry might be able to pick her up and Joanna might, but it'll be after 7 pm when her shift ends."

"We'll all be here. It will work out. Plus after they all leave, I'm all alone."

Suzy's husband had died last year after a long fight with cancer. She loved having Joley Kay and Isabelle over to join her new puppy, Pinky. But Lou Ann couldn't help feeling like a bad mom.

After she ended the call with Suzy, she dialed Harry's personal cell. If he was on a case or in a meeting, he wouldn't have his personal cell handy, only the work one, which she'd never call.

Harry answered on the first ring. "Hey, babe."

"Oh, thank God I got you on your cell."

"What's up? You sound stressed."

Being an FBI agent, Harry could automatically interpret the undertone in voices. That was a good problem today. But it could also be challenging at times because she couldn't fib her way around him.

"Glenda's niece died last night."

"Shit! I'm so sorry. You're working on who killed her?"

"No. Homicide is my strong point, but she appeared to either die of intoxication or a drug OD, which doesn't make sense."

"Yep. So who killed her?"

Lou Ann sighed into her cell.

"I'll be here late. And I just called Suzy and let her know. I wasn't sure about your status and Joanna won't be back until after seven."

"Rest easy."

"That's what Suzy said."

"I'll pick up Joley Kay and a dinner which we can reheat."

"Thanks, Harry. I love you."

"I love you too. So go solve your case."

"If only it was that easy."

"Tell me about it. I'll see you later tonight."

"Hold my spot."

"You got it."

Lou Ann ended her call with Harry, feeling relieved, and a teensy bit less like a guilty mom. At least Joley Kay had her daddy and Joanna. But then Lou Ann's heart sank. By the time she got home, Joley Kay would be asleep and wouldn't even know her momma came home.

So Lou Ann needed to focus on getting as much as possible done today so she could get home for dinner with Harry, Joanna, and most important, Joley Kay.

Off to Spark!

12

Lou Ann parked in Spark's empty lot. Anxious to find out why two dead young women were wearing a Spark admission wristband, she hadn't considered that a nightclub might not be open in the afternoon.

She was about to leave when a Corvette squealed into the lot and swerved into a space just feet away from Lou Ann's sheriff's vehicle.

A man exited his sports car and glared at Lou Ann. Then the official vehicle grabbed his attention.

He strode toward LouAnn, who left her vehicle idling.

The man walked over to the driver's side but kept his distance.

Lou Ann cut the engine and stepped out of her vehicle, propping her hands on her hips. "Hi there. I'm Inspector Lou Ann Jasinski with the Sheriff's Department," Lou Ann identified herself.

The man stepped back. His facial muscles contracted into a defensive expression.

"I'm Joe Moreno. I own this place. Is there a problem?"

"No. Well, perhaps," she qualified. "I'm investigating the deaths of two young women who were wearing a Spark wristband."

Moreno's eyes got very big.

"I need to talk with you. Can we go inside?"

Moreno hesitated, and then nodded. "Okay."

Lou Ann followed Moreno into the club while neither said a word.

The empty club appeared larger than the outside of it, but then it was empty, which made the size appear even more impressive.

A truck's exhaust echoed into the club.

"Hey, Gino! Tommy!" Moreno called. "Truck's here."

The truck groaned outside while its huge series of wheels ground from the outside to the back of the building.

"Food truck," Moreno explained. "The guys got it. Let's go into my office."

Papers were strewn across the top of his gray steel desk. Not that her desk was neat, but it wasn't tornado-style.

"Have a seat."

He pointed to a black vinyl chair on the opposite side of his desk.

It squeaked as she sat, reminding her of David's plastic-covered furniture. But this chair did have more give, and it was okay comfort-wise.

Moreno sat in a black wheeled office chair behind his metal desk.

He rolled toward his desk, haphazardly pushed his chaotic piles of papers aside, and steepled his hands on the top.

"How can I help you, *Inspector*?"

"I spoke with a young woman who attended your club last night. She said that Spark, quote, 'Really pumps on a Sunday'. I wouldn't have thought a nightclub would be busy on a Sunday. I would think Friday and Saturday nights would be your biggest draw."

"You would think that, yes. But although Fridays and Saturdays are packed, so are Sundays. A lot people want to blow off last-minute steam before the beginning of the work week. We stay open until 1:30 in the morning on Sundays with most customers gone by midnight, but there are still quite a few stragglers. Fridays and Saturdays we're open until 3 am."

"Were all the admission wristbands yellow last night?"

"Yep. We alter the colors. The bands have a date stamp, so when the color is yellow again, they can't use the same yellow band. Plus, there's no smoking inside. They have to step outside to do that."

"Do your lots fill up on a Sunday night?"

Moreno nodded with a smile. "Oh, yeah! Cars are parked for blocks. The crowds have tripled since I bought the club last year. And it used to be closed on Sundays. I resurrected this place."

"How many customers do you usually have on Sunday, and what was your total number last night?"

"Gino's my club manager. He'd know."

"Gino! Come in here," Moreno yelled through the open door.

Gino entered. "Whatcha need, Joe?"

"What were our stats for last night, and were they the usual?"

"Last night we hit 250, which is on a par with our Sunday nights. We don't have any competition because nobody but us are full-scale open, not just some barflies elsewhere."

"That's a crowd," Lou Ann said.

"Tables were full most of the night and the dance floor was

packed. It was like a contact sport!"

"Thanks, Gino."

"No problem." Gino looked at Lou Ann. "Nice to meet you, ma'am."

"She's actually an inspector with the sheriff's department," Moreno said.

"Ooh. Pardon me, Inspector. No disrespect," Gino said while backing away to the door. "Um…I got some inventory to do. You know, the truck."

"Thanks for your help, Gino," Moreno said. "Close the door on your way out, will ya?"

Gino waved. "Absolutely." Gino managed to both text and close the door behind him.

"What else do you need to know, Inspector?"

"A couple of things."

Lou Ann took out her notepad.

"I've met Gino, who's the manager. I heard you call Tommy. What's his role?"

"Tommy's one my cooks."

"Who else do you employ?"

"Tommy's my main cook, but there are four—three guys and gal —who cook the food. I also employ four wait staff, two bartenders, a DJ, and George, the bouncer. George keeps the customers in line, checks IDs, and hands out the wristbands. Everyone helps clean up after closing, but I have a custodial company that does a more thorough cleaning, including the bathrooms. Those are my weekend people. I do the invoices and billing during the week. Plus, we're open for lunch on Tuesdays through Thursdays. Keeps the money flowing in and keeps me in the black. Plus, I'm planning on renovations and maybe even opening another location. But that's a far-off dream. I got one year under my belt. Maybe next year or in two years. Depends."

"How do your bartenders deal with customers who are clearly inebriated?"

"Our policy is to cut off any inebriated customers or not even allow them to get to that point. Cabs or UBERs are called for those clearly at risk of hurting themselves or others."

"I need to review the security surveillance from last night."

"I have a lot things to get done so I can't take the time to review them with you, but I can pull it up for you. We start a new tape every evening, but we keep the prior ones for one week before we write over them."

Moreno reached into his desk drawer and pulled out a memory stick.

"Here you go, Inspector."

Either she'd pegged Moreno incorrectly or he was complying out of fear, or both, or most likely both.

"Thank you. The families of both women will be grateful that every avenue of their last day can be followed. I'm not...*we're* not here to fault you or your club. If someone or someones were responsible for their deaths, you need to know too, to protect your customers, and your reputation. You've built a successful club."

"I initially was suspicious of why you came here, but I understand. I hope you find what you're looking for, and I'm deeply sorry for the two young women, and their families."

"Thank you for your time, Mr. Moreno. I'll get this surveillance tape back to you as quickly I can."

"No worries. I have enough tapes."

Lou Ann and Moreno stood and shook hands.

She left her card on his table.

"I'll let you know what I find."

Moreno nodded.

"Do you need to see anything else?"

"Eventually. But this tape is a good start."

"Okay."

Moreno pointed to a door.

"This door will take you out to the lot."

Lou Ann held up the tape.

"Thanks again."

Another step forward.

Lou Ann glanced at her watch.

It was already 5:30.

She'd go home, kiss Harry, and Joley Kay, and Joanna when she got home. They'd have dinner together and then she'd cuddle with the baby, and with Harry, to be fair. And she'd congratulate Joanna on completion of her first ED shift. She had it all—a family to come home to. But Daisy and the young woman's family wouldn't have that tonight or for a heartbreakingly long time.

And when everyone was settled, she'd stay up and outline her next steps.

13

Joanna shuttled from one exam room to another. Her work already flowed more easily and more efficiently. Her busyness helped keep her mind off of the earlier code. She'd helped wrap the dead woman, and by now the next place in the woman's death journey was the morgue, and on the medical examiner's table.

She'd overheard Dr. Hottman—Ian—speaking with the young woman's mother. His voice was steady and calming. But she knew that on the inside, his heart thudded with every word.

Like her and Hottman, and everyone else, their priorities continued to care for others and save another life.

The oncoming evening shift began arriving.

Wow. She'd come to the end of her first shift.

The troops rallied into a huddle. The remaining patients' care plans and dispositions were reviewed.

This time Joanna didn't hide in the back of the pack. Instead, she stood in the middle—a forward step.

The code was briefly discussed. Even though it occurred earlier, it seemed as if it just happened.

The sign out quieted.

Death would always be part of the ED, but reviewing the mechanics of what and how it happened was beneficial for everyone.

That was it. The next team took over.

She'd see them again first thing in the morning.

Claudia and Shelly patted Joanna on her back.

"Good job on your first day. I'm sure it will be memorable. Mine certainly was," Claudia said. "See you in the morning," she added.

"I'll be on time."

Claudia grinned. "I know you will."

Claudia headed toward the woman's locker room.

Shelly hugged Joanna. "You made it!"

Joanna grinned. "I did."

"Let's head off to the locker room and get out of this place, at least for the next twelve hours!"

"Hey, Joanna," Hottman called.

"Hotty wants to talk to you," Shelly whispered gleefully in Joanna's ear, and then Shelly rushed off.

"I…uh…wanted to say congratulations on your first shift." Hotty grinned. "And you owe me lunch tomorrow."

Joanna winked. "You can count on me to pay up."

Hotty winked back. "I know you're good for it. See you tomorrow morning."

Joanna smiled and nodded. "Tomorrow."

Heat climbed to her face and she gave Ian Hottman a quick wave, turned, and hurried to the locker room before he could see her blushing.

Shelly peeked out from behind the locker room door.

"Ooh! You made Hotty hot!"

"No, I didn't.

"And look at you! I can't wait to see you two tomorrow!

Joanna nudged Shelly.

"Let's get going."

But to tell the truth, Joanna could hardly wait to find out what tomorrow would bring.

Lou Ann pulled into the driveway, next to Harry's car. She leapt out of her vehicle and hurried into the house.

"I'm home!" she called.

Harry came to greet her while carrying Joley Kay.

"Look! Mama's home!"

Joley Kay squirmed in Harry's arms, and reached for Lou Ann with her little outstretched hand.

"Mmmm! Mmmm! Mama!

"She said mama!"

"Yes, I heard."

Lou Ann hugged Joley Kay to her chest and rained kisses on her baby daughter's head.

"Love you! Love you!" Lou Ann cooed.

The baby waved her chubby hand to Harry.

"Da! Da!"

Harry grinned clear to his cheeks.

"Yes, I heard that!" she parroted Harry.

With Joley Kay in her arms, she leaned toward Harry and kissed him.

"I'm so glad to be home."

Daisy would never again be able to hug and kiss Gloria.

Harry met her gaze.

"We're lucky," Lou Ann said.

"Yes we are, babe."

Harry knew how deeply affected she was after discovering Gloria. He too dealt with death and violence. They had that in common.

They tried not to bring their work home, but there were times when they bounced their ideas off each other, and yes, there were times it ended in successes. And when it ended in failure or stagnation, their mutual support was equally if not more beneficial.

While not letting go of Joley Kay, Lou Ann followed Harry into the kitchen.

"Wow! Something smells good!"

Harry grinned. "I've added more than my mac and cheese to my culinary skills."

"I'm impressed. No takeout!"

"Nah. Followed the recipe online."

Lou Ann glanced into the pot. "Real mashed potatoes!"

"Peeled them myself. Lost some of the potatoes with the skins, though.

"A-plus for effort!"

"And I made some peas, from a can. They're easier to smash up for Joley Kay. And chicken for us, and I put some in the blender on puree for Joley Kay. And pardon the mess. I'll clean it all up."

"The sign of a good cook. You're gonna spoil me."

Harry winked. "I thought I already had."

"Now you're doubly talented!"

"I heard a car pull up. Must be Joanna."

"Hey, I made it home!" Joanna called.

"Good ears, Harry."

He waggled his eyebrows. "I've many talents."

Joanna joined them in the kitchen and kissed Joley Kay.

"Hi, my baby. I missed you." She kissed Joley Kay on her cheek and the baby giggled.

"I'm really beat, and I'm starved." Joanna glanced around the kitchen. "What? No takeout?"

"Nope. Home cooking tonight," Harry said.

"Sounds and smells good to me."

Joanna plopped down into a kitchen chair.

"What a day." Joanna's face sagged. "And not all good."

"Why? What happened?"

"Rescue brought in this young women. She was found unconscious. They tried everything, and then we did. Well, not me. Really. Frankly I was in shock. Nothing worked, and she died from a drug overdose. They think it was Fentanyl. I helped wrap her up."

"Don't tell me. This young woman was transferred to the medical examiner's office."

"Yeah. How'd you know?"

"Because I spoke with the medical examiner, who already had Glenda's niece, who died sometime last night from a drug overdose. Presumably. She received a woman from Hampton ED."

"Oh, my God. That was our patient, our young lady who we couldn't resuscitate!"

"What time did she arrive in the ED?"

"It was just at the end of lunch because we all ran out of the break room."

"So around noon?"

"Yeah."

"Did you recall what she was wearing?"

"Rescue had to cut off her clothes, but it looked like it used to be a dress."

"A dressy dress, like a one you'd wear to a nightclub?"

Joanna shrugged. "I don't know. There was so much going on. All I heard was that Rescue was called after her roommate found her unconscious and called 911."

"I don't mean to quiz you."

"That's all right. I feel so bad for Glenda and Gloria's family."

"We all do."

"So are you on the case?"

"Yes. I wanted to find out how Gloria died. She wasn't a drug user."

"Do you think someone poisoned her?"

"It's a possibility."

"Maybe she got a hold of a pain med that was laced with Fentanyl."

"Maybe you could moonlight as a special agent," Harry said.

"No thanks. I'll stick to nursing."

"Let's eat dinner," Lou Ann said.

"I'm for that," Joanna said.

Harry served his meal while still wearing an apron.

"Oh, leave that on! You're so sexy!" Lou Ann teased.

Harry removed the apron.

"I'll put it back on later!" he teased back.

Joanna rolled her eyes.

"What's the matter? You don't think we have a pulse?" Harry quipped.

"I know you do. The walls are thin!" Joanna replied. "I'm joking. I've seen how you two are, and I hope one day I can have one tenth of what you have."

"You will," Lou Ann said.

Harry set Joley Kay's special meal on her highchair tray.

"No, Harry. Give me her plate. I'll feed her."

She couldn't let go of her daughter.

"Okay," Harry said softly.

Joanna nodded with understanding.

They ate without saying a word, but the baby took full advantage and happily babbled on in between tossing her peas across the table.

"Joley Kay!" Lou Ann shouted.

Lou Ann then tossed a spoonful of her mashed potatoes across the table.

"I'll see your spoonful mashed of potatoes and raise you one."

Harry flipped two spoonfuls across the table.

Lou Ann, Harry, and Joanna broke out laughing. Joley Kay snorted a giggle.

"Here! Have some peas!" Joanna challenged and rolled a forkful across the table.

It was a rollicking food fight.

"All right, everybody. Cease fire," Lou Ann interrupted.

The dinner hijinks temporarily put a Band-Aid over her sadness.

Lou Ann grinned at Joley Kay. The baby dug her fingers into the mashed potatoes and brought it to her mouth, responding to her mama's gleeful attentiveness.

"You're such a good girl," Lou Ann cooed.

Lou Ann met Harry's soft gaze.

He'd offer her solace and advice later, as he always did, followed by a lovemaking chaser.

She was truly blessed.

"Have some more of Daddy's mashed potatoes. He worked really hard on those."

"Dada."

"Yes, Dada loves you too."

"And I love all of you, and I'm grateful that, after a long day, I have you to come home to," Joanna added.

"Ditto," Lou Ann said.

They finished their meal with the kind of light, superficial banter that they all needed after the day's tragedies and battles.

"I'll clean up here, and you can clean up our daughter." Harry waggled his eyebrows. "And I'll meet up with you later."

"Deal. And bring the apron."

Lou Ann set Joley Kay into her bathtub baby ring.

"You certainly are a mess, young lady!"

She held onto the baby.

"Joanna, can you please pass me the baby shampoo, washcloth, and baby bath?"

"Sure."

Lou Ann shampooed Joley Kay's fine baby hair.

"She even has potatoes in her hair."

"We egged her on!" Joanna said.

"Yes we did."

Joanna shielded the baby's eyes with the washcloth while Lou Ann rinsed off the shampoo with a cup of water.

"Can I do the rest?" Joanna asked.

"Go for it."

Joanna bathed the baby while Lou Ann supported her baby daughter.

"Babies are like the ocean. You can't turn your back on them."

"You're going to be so clean!" Joanna cooed.

Joley Kay splashed.

"Oh! Got me!" Joanna giggled.

Joanna stroked the baby's soft skin.

Joanna's mother never bathed her. She was always too high, and thankfully didn't attempt it. Joanna shuddered. She could've drowned in the tub and her mother wouldn't realize it. Or her mother could've easily scalded her.

She learned how to bathe herself while her mother and her cadre did drugs in the next room. The locks on her bedroom door were busted, so she'd move her banged-up dresser against the door, crawl into her lopsided bed, and shut her eyes tight until she was too tired to continue, and then fell asleep. And every morning she woke up thankful to be alive. She dressed, hopped out the window, and walked to school. She had no breakfast, and had nothing to bring for lunch. Jason, who lived in a trailer next door, would share his lunch with her, often giving her most of it. He was poor, but his mama loved him.

Joanna dropped out of the fifth school she attended in the seventh grade because kids made fun of her thrift store clothes and stringy, uncut hair. She took off and never looked back, learning how to survive on the streets. That is until she had the misfortune of meeting Dr. Gerald Newell, a sex trafficker. Her life would never be the same.

She wasn't ashamed to be happy when she heard that her mother finally died of a heroin overdose. But the best thing that ever happened to her was Lou Ann and Harry. But she would always be known as Joanna Stemple, as her birth certificate declared.

"Lou Ann, how did you know Harry was the man for you?"

"We crossed work paths. There was some tension between law enforcement and the FBI. But we talked a lot." Lou Ann smiled. "I really liked his sense of humor."

Joanna grinned. "I could see that. I remember that he coined the nonexistent 'mondo fries' at the diner. I really thought that was on the menu."

"Yeah, that was funny. But Harry and I had our troubles, which I won't go into. And even when I hated him, he kept coming back. And after the first time in Athens to track Kaylee, I let him back into my heart. We've grown into a strong relationship."

"So with you and Harry, it was love at first site?"

"Um…in a way. I was attracted to him, but you know that I tend be less flexible—I need to think things through."

"No!"

Joanna and Lou Ann laughed.

"You are more fluid now."

Lou Ann plucked Joley Kay out of her baby tub ring while Joanna held out a fluffy towel and Lou Ann handed her the wet baby. Joanna hugged the clean baby and sniffed Joley Kay's sweet baby scent.

"I may want to have a baby someday. But for now, I have my Joley Kay!"

"Is there something you want to talk about or ask me?" Lou Ann asked.

Joanna shook her head.

Lou Ann nodded. "Okay."

I'll get her ready for bed," Joanna said.

"Let's get you in your PJ's," Joanna softly cooed to Joley Kay in a singsong rhythm.

"Ja-ja," Joley Kay responded.

"Wow! Joley Kay hit the trifecta today!"

"She knows who her family is."

"And so do I," Joanna said.

After cleaning the remnants of the food fight off the kitchen table, Harry set the plates and utensils in the dishwasher, and engaged the cycle. The dishwasher whirred into action.

He laughed to himself. He should've put Joley Kay in there. But a good bath would do just as well.

He removed his apron and was about to put it away, but changed his mind.

Lou Ann's joke was about to come true.

He halted outside the hallway bathroom and listened to Joley Kay, Lou Ann, and Joanna giggling behind the closed door.

He closed his eyes, taking in the beautiful sounds of the women in his life—his baby daughter included.

Yeah, he was a happy man.

They were, and then they weren't, and then they were again—him and Lou Ann.

It was his bravado that did them in—poor choices. Nothing happened with the woman in the bar, or either with his female colleague in Madrid. He'd played with Lou Ann's trust and deservedly got burned. He'd always loved her, and he would love her forever. Joley Kay, though unplanned, was the best thing that ever happened to him and Lou Ann. Warmth pumped from his heart to every inch of his skin while he listened to Lou Ann laughing behind that door. His persistence in pursuing her paid off a gazillion-fold.

Stirring came from behind the bathroom door and the bathroom doorknob turned.

Harry scurried away to the bedroom.

He had to get ready to surprise Lou Ann.

"I've a feeling Harry's waiting for you," Joanna said with a smile.

Lou Ann cocked her head.

"I'll put Joley Kay to bed," Joanna said.

"Aren't you tired after your first shift? And you're on again tomorrow, aren't you?"

"Yes. But I've learned that rocking Joley Kay to sleep is actually calming for me."

"All right."

Lou Ann kissed her daughter on her head.

The baby smiled and then yawned.

"I don't think she's going to hang on much longer," Joanna said while she shooed Lou Ann down the hall. "I got it. Don't worry."

"I'm not worried. I know how much you love her and how much she loves you."

Lou Ann gently closed the door behind her.

"It's just you and me now," Joanna whispered to Joley Kay.

Joanna dressed the baby in the PJs that she'd bought for her.

"Still fits!"

Then she sat in the rocking chair with Joley Kay's head nestled on her shoulder.

Within five minutes, Joley Kay fell asleep in Joanna's arms.

Joanna eased up from the rocker and gingerly lay Joley Kay in her crib. Joley Kay inhaled and then sucked her thumb. Joanna covered her and waited. She was out!

Joanna tiptoed out of the nursery and left the door ajar.

She passed Lou Ann and Harry's bedroom door and grinned.

The ties that gloriously bind.

And those ties reached Kaylee in Greece.

It would be morning there.

Joanna decided to snuggle down in the bed in the same room she'd once shared with Kaylee and she'd call her.

Joanna would ask Kaylee's advice—the same Kaylee who just two years ago convinced Joanna to follow her into teenage trouble.

But Kaylee wasn't the same anymore, and neither was Joanna.

They'd grown into womanhood, and although they pursued different paths, they remained bonded forever.

Joanna connected with Kaylee via FaceTime.

Harry undressed and put on the apron. Then he hopped into bed and waited for Lou Ann to come through the door.

She had a long and distressing day and he had too.

He continued to track and capture sex traffickers, and set free their victims.

Joanna and Kaylee were such victims, and it took months of

therapy to mute what would be forever present in their minds. It wasn't an everyday problem for Joanna or Kaylee, but there remained trigger days and nights—and nightmares.

Joanna, despite her wretched childhood that culminated in the horrors of captivity, fought back against her history and became one hell of a nurse. They'd all proudly attended her nursing degree graduation, including Kaylee. And they'd all go to Greece—including Joley Kay, both Joanna's and Kaylee's combined namesake, and this time they'd travel on pleasant terms to attend Kaylee's law degree graduation.

They flourished despite those dead monsters, Gerald Newell—and Harry refused to call him doctor—and that slime ball, Otto, who Kaylee was blessedly responsible for his demise. And Margo, the groomer, was now rotting in jail where she belonged. Joanna had almost beaten the woman to death. Margo still had the lasting effects of the punishment delivered by Joanna's fists there on Demetrios' mansion lawn.

Demetrios died that day in Greece, shot by that coward, Newell, who got his just desserts in a rain of bullets. But it was Kaylee's first shot that probably killed him. But no one would know if she did because he, Lou Ann, and their colleague and good friend, Brad Jarret, also fired their weapons, riddling Newell with bullets. Who actually fired the killing shot would always be their secret to the grave.

The bedroom knob turned, and Harry posed for Lou Ann.

Lou Ann's eyes went big.

"I'll give you an A+ for creativity."'

"Come over here and kiss the cook."

Lou Ann climbed across the bed toward him cougar-style.

Harry reached to untie the apron.

"Oh, no you don't. You promised me you'd wear that apron."

"Temporarily," he joked.

"No, you didn't say a thing about, *temporarily*."

"No, I did not," he admitted.

She had him there. He mentally shrugged. Okay, he'd play along for the fun of it.

She set her mouth on his.

Every nerve in his body caught fire.

Who knew wearing an apron could spark that kind of wildfire?

He definitely needed to cook more often!

Lou Ann lifted his apron.

Man, he was about to burst into flames—flames of ecstasy.

They both needed the release that was about to rocket them away from the weight of their days.

Their shifting and gyrating exploded them from their launchpad until they lay together, spent and sweaty, their rocket fuel depleted.

Harry took a deep breath and sighed, replete.

"Mission accomplished, babe."

Joanna called Kaylee's international number, engaged FaceTime, and waited for Kaylee to respond.

Perhaps she was busy studying both Greek and US law.

Kaylee was always determined in everything she did: escaping Newell, stabbing Otto in the eye with a plastic fork, smacking Margo on the head with a dinner tray —classic—running for her life with an injured foot, and even when Newell and Margo caught her and punished her, she took it.

And she hated to have been dragged back from Greece to Clearwater and fought Lou Ann, less so, Harry. Although he was beyond pissed off the time, once Kaylee commandeered his car while he slept. She convinced Joanna it would be okay, that they'd be back from their joy ride before Harry woke up. That didn't happen, and yet Kaylee just walked right past him as if it was no big deal. But Joanna was sure that on the inside, Kaylee was trembling. But she wouldn't show her vulnerability. She never did. And that's what kept her going and alive.

Kaylee's face appeared.

"Hey, Joanna. I'm so glad you called. You must've read my thoughts because I've been thinking about you. I know you started your new nursing career in the emergency room."

"It's so nice to see your face! I miss you."

"Likewise. And I miss you. When are you coming to Greece?"

"We'll be there for your law school graduation."

"I know. But I want to know when you're coming to see me. I've gone there a few times. Now it's time to even the visits."

"I'd love to, but I just started my new job, and I'll be in orientation this week, so I can't ask for the time off."

"I get it. I have some finals coming up."

"Am I disturbing your studies?"

"Nah. I'd rather talk with you anytime."

Both paused.

"What's wrong? I can see it in your face," Kaylee said.

"Um…"

"What umm? Tell me."

"I don't know how to bring up what I want, or need to, without you."

"It's fine. You're not going to hurt me by referring to me and Demetrios."

"You're reading my thoughts."

"We have that kind of telepathy."

Joanna hesitated. But she was the one who called. She drew a breath and continued. "Umm, how did you know Demetrios was the one?"

"From the day he took me away from Newell at the airport. He was larger than life and I had no idea what was going to happen to me. But he didn't approach me in the limo or when we arrived at the mansion. He never touched me without my permission. In fact I ended up approaching him, and still he was reticent. And he was gentle."

"I didn't mean to go there, but I need your advice because I can't really talk to Lou Ann. Although I think she guessed because I asked her and Harry. So here's the thing, I'm attracted to Dr. Hottman, the ED attending, and I sense he's feeling the same way. I mean we just met today. The nurses call him, Dr. Hotty, and so I pictured him as having rather loose morals. But that's not how he is."

"Is he hot?"

"Yes."

"Ooh!"

"Maybe he's just being nice to me. But I have to say, he was a bit of an arrogant dick at first. He intimidated me at first, barking out orders."

"Isn't that what doctors do?"

"Yes."

"But then we got on together. I didn't bring any lunch or have enough money for the cafeteria, so he bought me lunch. And we were having fun, talking, when we had to run out of the break room to attend to a young woman who succumbed to a drug overdose despite all efforts."

"How sad."

"Afterwards, Ian, Dr. Hottman—Hotty—was quiet. He took it hard because he did everything he could. She was so young, Anyway, by the end of the shift, I caught him looking at me, and he caught me looking at him. By the end, he was blushing, or maybe he was just feeling hot, but he joked that I owed him lunch tomorrow."

"Are you still there, Kaylee? I rambled on."

"Ramble all you want. I was listening. So you're afraid to get close to a man, a man who's clearly into you."

Joanna sniffled. "Yes." She paused and then continued, "No one at the hospital knows about what happened. Everything came out in Margo's trial in Miami, not in Clearwater. No one has said anything, and I don't want them to know, or treat me differently."

"You and I *are* different, but we have to continue to function in this world. Everyone in Athens and Ekali knows about me. For you, perhaps no one does in Clearwater. So back to your dilemma. If you become involved with Ian Hottman, should you eventually tell him? That's a tough one. You're not dirty. You know that, right?"

"I feel that way at times. I mean, so many men took their turn with me. How do I admit that? And if something did happen between us, or with any man, I can't. I'm afraid I'll freeze, or worse, run away. I won't know how to love, or be sexual when the time comes."

"Joanna, it's normal for you to feel that way. You know you didn't have a choice. You were a captive. Horrible things were done to you. But don't deny what is rightfully yours—to love and be loved. If things develop between you and Dr. Hotty, you'll tell him when it's right. If he's the right man for you, it won't matter. Now he may be hesitant, or extra gentle. That's expected. I didn't have the same thing happen to me because Newell kept Otto and others away because he thought he was responsible for killing you. I was the pot of gold and to be delivered unharmed."

"Virginal?"

"Yes."

Silence.

"What if they, and eventually Ian, and the whole staff, find out about me before I can tell Ian…if it comes to that?"

"That's always a risk. If Administration knows, then I'm sure the news wouldn't travel farther because they could be liable for leaking confidential information. I'm also fairly sure that if they knew, then they'd personally contact you. Has any of that happened?"

"No. But I just started."

"If there were any concerns about your past, then that would have been brought up during your application process, maybe in a roundabout way."

"That hasn't happened."

"Okay then, take a deep breath. Try not to be paranoid. Again, I repeat, you did nothing wrong. You are not the criminal. Keep repeating that. And I'm so proud of you."

"And I'm proud of you," Joanna replied.

"And now that we've done our affirmations for the day, how's the family?"

"Joley Kay is growing by leaps and bounds, and she's starting to talk. And she can be cranky because she has some teeth coming in."

"Aww, poor baby."

"Isabelle is very protective of her. Plus, you already know Isabelle is always there for anyone in need."

"How true."

"Now for the more complex family members—excluding me— Lou Ann and Harry. Lou Ann is investigating the death of Glenda's niece. She was found dead early this morning of a suspected drug overdose, or complications from alcohol inebriation, like aspiration or cardiac or respiratory arrest."

"Wow. That's definitely nurse lingo! But how terrible for Glenda, her niece, and her niece's family. I'm confident Lou Ann can find out what happened. It must weigh heavy on her."

"It does. Harry continues to work on sex trafficking cases, rescuing the victims, and prosecuting the perpetrators."

"Harry and Lou Ann saved us and many others. It's a war out there, but one battle at a time," Kaylee said.

"I don't want to continue to be battle-fatigued," Joanna admitted.

"Neither do I. But let's keep holding each other up. I'm so relieved and happy at the same time to talk with you and see you. And about Hotty, let things play out. Be open to letting him in. Sounds promising."

"What about you, Kaylee?"

Silence again.

"I don't know. I'm not ready."

"That's all right. You'll know when. Then you can call me for advice!"

"You know I would."

"I love you, Kaylee, and I don't want to interrupt your studies any more than I have already."

"Interrupt anytime. Except during my final exam! And I love you back!"

"Goodnight, sister."

"Goodnight, sister."

Joanna and Kaylee ended their FaceTime call. Although their faces disappeared from their screens, their connected souls defied international bounds.

Joanna yawned.

She needed to get some sleep, because tomorrow anything was possible.

14

Lou Ann rested her head on Harry's chest. He kicked the apron that lay crumpled at the end of the bed with his toe, and it landed on the floor.

Harry hugged her closer. "Eh, I'll put it in the laundry tomorrow."

Lou Ann smiled, her cheek pressing against Harry's chest. "So well worth it!" She waggled her eyebrows. "A definite repeater."

"Dinner? Or after dinner 'dessert'"?

"Both."

"Deal. But I'll have to reschedule on the fly when we're both home at dinnertime."

"Hmmm," she hummed, her voice echoing in her head while her ear creased into Harry's extra-warm post sex skin. "Pencil me in."

It had to be a pencil that could be erased at a moment's notice. No pen. And that went for both of their unpredictable work schedules. That very unpredictability was one of the factors that ended their relationship the first time around—that, and Harry's roving eye. But they'd moved past that seesaw, and the second time around now had matured into an affectionate and committed relationship. Joley Kay's birth cemented it further—a little person part him and her.

Lou Ann could've spent the rest of the night blessedly glued to Harry, but solving Gloria's death couldn't wait—if it could be solved beyond what everyone thought was obvious. But the investigative part of Lou Ann's brain bucked the obvious every time, even when her case did turn out to be the obvious. And she hated the obvious.

"I hear the wheels in your head turning." Harry rocked Lou Ann from his chest. "Let me jump onto one of those wheels."

Their marriage was one minute rocket sex, and the next macabre brainstorming, and she wouldn't have it any other way, and she knew Harry wouldn't either.

71

"Let me see what you have," Harry said.

"I'll show you mine if you show me yours."

"Last one to their laptop does laundry for a month," Lou Ann challenged.

They jumped naked out of the respective sides of the their bed, sidestepped each other in the weirdest-ass ballet, and raced to grab their laptops.

How many couples do this, especially on a Monday night?

Lou Ann bounced onto the bed.

"I won!"

"Ha! Mine's already open with an encrypted password!" Harry boasted.

"Nuh-uh. I specifically said 'laptop'," she countered.

Harry's frown deepened. "Okay."

"I'm willing to call it a draw," she said. "We'll split laundry duty."

Which, given assorted baby-stains, was a compromise both could accept.

"Do-able," he confirmed.

They bumped fists and then focused on their screens.

"I can't reveal sources or methods, but Sunday evening we got a tip-off about a boat loaded with Fentanyl set to arrive in a Clearwater marina. It was supposed to be a typical leisure boat. But our paid informant payed off because we got them on 30,000 grams of Fentanyl, and 5000 grams of Cocaine. I know Glenda and you feel for her, but you need to consider that Gloria might have been a secret addict, or that she got ahold of online or chat Fentanyl pills."

"No! I haven't told you everything I know so far, so don't jump to conclusions!"

"Hey, you know me. I don't jump to conclusions. You also know that's not how I or any of the agents work."

Lou Ann shook her head. "I didn't mean that way. I'm still shocked and dismayed. Yes, it's possible that Gloria was involved ,voluntarily or accidentally, with a deadly dose of let's say, Fentanyl. Which gnaws at me. But I also recognize I need to separate myself from the personal and return to the necessarily objective nature of my job. Harry, it's harder than I ever thought. Glenda had no idea. Daisy, her mother, had not the faintest inkling that something was off about her daughter."

"I would bet Gloria didn't share aspects of her party life surely with Glenda, or her mother, any more than Kaylee and Joanna didn't and still don't share some things with us."

Stab in heart! But despite Lou Ann's deepening relationships with Kaylee and Joanna, Harry was right. She recognized that Kaylee and Joanna continued to share secrets—secrets that only Kaylee and Joanna would trust each other with—and Lou Ann was sure there were secrets hidden deep within their brains that neither would release to anyone, not even to each other. *Such is the monopoly of damage.*

"I didn't tell you about Sunday's bust because it was already over with, and once it's processed a limited press release will be circulated. Then I wanted to tell you today but your focus shifted—as it should—to Gloria's death. I thought about the Fentanyl, mostly because, it's the number one cause of death in Gloria's age group, both younger and older to age 45, and I would have to tell you to add that in your top categories as to cause of death, no matter how gut-wrenching. I get it, babe. I…we…need to find a way to halt this, but I don't see that happening. Cartels aren't stupid. They're moneymaking and enabled."

"Fentanyl crisis, yes. But here's the thing. I found Gloria curled up on her side with her makeup smudged and white foam caked around her mouth. There's vomit, too, which I can assume was hers, but could be someone else's.

Which brings me to her final last night's activities. I spoke to her friends, who are college roommates. They are on the first floor and Gloria's apartment is at the end of the hall on the second floor. Gloria attended a party at their apartment and later went on with one of them to Spark nightclub.

The roommate drove them there, but Gloria didn't want to leave with her. Then Gloria's recently ex-boyfriend showed up at the club that night and put her in a tailspin. Another friend promised to bring her home. According to the roommate there was this unknown, hot guy who Gloria flirted with to make her ex jealous. I don't know how she got home, but according to the apartment manager—who's odd and "pervy"—saw Gloria on his security video stumbling up to her apartment alone and couldn't insert the key the door.. He stated he went up there, opened the door for her, and tucked her in her bed because he said he was afraid she would fall."

"How chivalrous of him," Harry snarked.

"You know where I'm going."

"So pervy manager is conveniently not on his security file and did more than put her to bed out of *concern*?"

"Bingo."

"This guy have a record? Let me answer my own question—no."

"Nothing in the database. But I don't believe he gets out much. Very much an odd loner."

"Let me guess agin. Except when he's following the comings and goings of young women."

Lou Ann grinned. "Maybe you should take this case."

"Oh no, no my dear. You put all that together. I just know you and how you think very well."

"You're profiling me."

"Always have. That's my job. But you're not my job. You're my stellar Homicide Investigator wife. I'm only your reflection."

"I went to Spark nightclub and spoke with the manager, who got really nervous when he saw me in his empty parking lot. He was there with two other guys doing inventory and unloading a delivery truck. The owner spoke with the club manager, who agreed to send me last night's CCTV- encrypted footage from last night at Spark where Gloria and another woman, who was found unconscious earlier today and died in the ED on Joanna's first day shift, were last night."

"She didn't mention it to me at dinner. What a first day."

"Yep. But she didn't notice that the woman had the same yellow admission to Spark wristband. Barb called me and let me know. I'm going to the ME's office tomorrow, among the gazillion other things on my agenda. But my homework tonight, other than you, is to review the Spark surveillance video."

"I was going to watch a Netflix movie, but what the hell. This might be more interesting. Let it roll."

Lou Ann opened the encrypted file Marino sent. "Here we go."

Harry leaned closer.

Lou Ann advanced the footage.

"For a Sunday night, that club's busy."

"I thought the same. But the two young women from apartment 16D, Kelseigh and Jade, I interviewed, and then the club owner confirmed, Spark does big business on Sunday nights. Plus it's summer and most clubs don't offer Sunday nights. Jade said she had to park two blocks away because the lot was full. They left the apartment at nine-thirty for the club, and Jade left the club around even-thirty, without Gloria. I've not spoken with Cassie, who agreed to drive Gloria home."

Lou Ann advanced to 9:30 pm. At 9:45, Jade and Gloria entered the club, both with steady gait.

Harry eyed the screen. "That's really clear. Not like the older, grainy VHS tapes I used to slog through."

"Especially for a nightclub," she added.

"So that's Jade and Gloria are at the bar?"

"Yep, that's them. And it's the same bartender I saw at the club this afternoon."

"He's chatting with them, and smiling, but that could be the bartender in him. On the other, I'd seen that look elsewhere. He knows those girls. There'a flirtation going on there."

"Yeah, I also see more there. I'll have to interview the bartender, and Jade, and Cassie."

Jade and Gloria left and were off the screen until they reappeared while scooting to a table.

"Here's something! Two guys pulling chairs up to Jade and Gloria's table. I have no idea who these guys are, but I'm going to find out and track them down. Jade mentioned that Gloria's ex-boyfriend showed up. Ah, when this guy sat, Gloria leaned away from him. I put my money on that one being Gloria's ex-boyfriend, Tyler."

"What's your take on the other guy?" Harry asked.

"Wait for it…ah…Gloria scooted her chair toward him… This must be the mystery guy…I 'd say a pretty hot guy too…that guy Jade told me about. Gloria's flirting with him to stick it to her ex."

"Sounds familiar."

Lou Ann paused the screen and looked at Harry.

"Oh, come on, I never stuck it to you."

"But you did shut the door on my foot."

"You put it there on purpose. You weren't injured. You faker!"

"Got me in the door." Harry leaned over and kissed Lou Ann. "And see? It all worked out."

Lou Ann grinned. "In a circuitous way. But now we've come full circle."

"And you were worth fighting for every step of the way." Harry grinned. "But I digress. Move along. Let's see what goes on next."

Lou Ann squeezed Harry's hand, returned to her screen, and advanced the file.

Gloria and the hot guy stood and disappeared into the crowded dance floor.

"Damn, I can't find them in that crowd."

Harry narrowed his eyes and surveyed the screen.

"Can you get a fix on them?"

"Nope." Harry stared at the screen. "Um...they're back on. You really lucked out. This place was packed. Hmm. She's being watched, Lou Ann."

"That's why I need you, Sir Eagle Eye."

"Thanks. But I've watched tons of these, albeit not many with this clarity unless my perps do it for show, i.e, a kill video."

"So this must be boring for you."

"No, it's actually more challenging because it comes across as just another club night, but there's more to it. Okay, our friends are back from the dance floor."

"She sat down with Jade, next to whom I presume is Gloria's ex, but I could be wrong. Apparently Jade didn't mention everything that went on that night."

"Did she come across as evasive?"

"Between the two of them, Kelseigh and Jade, Kelseigh was nudging Jade at one point, prompting her to elaborate. Strangely, I had them on my agenda to visit, but when I knocked on their door, they obviously weren't home. Then it was Tim Farmer, my former trainee, who noticed them sitting and crying in headquarters' lobby and let me know. I took them to my office and both said Gloria attended their party and then left with Jade to head for Spark at 9:30, which matches the timeline as I know it. Kelseigh didn't go to Spark and stayed behind to end the party and clean up. The question remains who really drove Gloria home, and what was David Montgomery doing in her apartment while she was clearly impaired?"

"I'm betting we're going to get a good glimpse of what went down, when, and with whom."

Lou Ann resumed the footage.

Mystery guy got up from the table and disappeared into the crowd.

"Let's see if he returns," Harry said.

Mystery guy did return, carrying two drinks.

"Jade and the other guy, who I'm considering Gloria's ex, already have drinks on the table. I find it strange that Jade and Gloria didn't go get their own drinks because they're friends who'd come to the club together. I know if I went with a girlfriend to a club, we'd stick together and get our own drinks. Plus, that probably is Gloria's ex, because both Kelsiegh and Jade indicated that they didn't like him and felt he was not the right guy for Gloria. And what's more, they didn't invite him to their party. And I don't think Gloria would have gone to the party if Tyler was there."

"Maybe he's not her ex."

"True. But I find her behavior—her rearing away from him—odd."

"Maybe he made a bad joke, or something he said caused her to pull away."

"Because it's Glenda's niece, and I'm probably pushing too hard to solve a puzzle without sorting through everything. My objectivity is off balance. I need to correct that."

"I'm guilty of the same thing at times. You know, the trafficking cases. I want to leap in and grab hold of every perp and smash them into the ground because of Kaylee and Joanna. But I'd kill my case and my career. So I haul my rage to the back of my brain."

Lou Ann and Harry paused. She heard him swallow and her gulp echoed in her ears. But like Harry, she had to store her sensitivity away so she could approach this case with an open mind.

"Okay, let's keep moving," she said.

Harry nodded.

The unknown guy set the drinks on the table, one for Gloria and one for him.

"Damn! Your so-called ex tosses back his drink and then slams the empty glass on the table. They all get up and look like they're yelling and pointing fingers at each other."

"My 'ex' then shoots a middle finger at the other guy. Jade grabs Gloria's hand to get her away from this scene. Gloria resists like Jade told me. Then 'Tyler' stomps away. Unknown guy goes over and hugs Gloria. Jade again tries to get Gloria to leave. Gloria waves her off. Jade leaves. Five minutes later, Jade is back in the frame, but this time she's with another young woman. Cassie?"

"Cassie?"

"Yeah, Jade said that since Gloria wouldn't leave with her, she asked a mutual friend, Cassie, to take Gloria home."

Jade never reappeared on the file, and that was exactly at 11:30, it consistent with Jade's recollection.

Lou Ann patiently waited.

But then Cassie left the club without Gloria.

"So much for trust," Harry said.

"That leaves Gloria with the hot guy, who bought her a drink. Gloria stands and grabs the table to steady herself. She only had one drink that we know of and yet she's clearly impaired."

"But that guy is steady as a rock," Harry noted.

"It was the drink!" they said at the same time.

"I bet he spiked her drink, or somebody did," Lou Ann said.

Hot guy wrapped his arm around Gloria to steady her, and both disappeared from the rest of file film.

"She probably went home, but he wasn't seen with her at her apartment. She was stumbling all by herself."

"Perhaps he dumped her off on the street and then took off."

"If he spiked her drink, why wouldn't he have gone up to her apartment and taken advantage of her?"

"Don't know. But that's for you to find out. But I gotta say that if it was Fentanyl, she would've dropped and not made it home."

"Unless he gave her a roofie and she took an additional pill as a chaser and…that was the end. But I can't bring myself to imagine Gloria deliberately getting some Fentanyl-laced pill."

"It's everywhere, babe."

"I know, but still…"

"There are some things we don't want to see."

Lou Ann closed the encrypted file. She had only twenty-four hours to review it, and she'd already made her notes. So she was done, except for interviewing the bartender, and she could take as long as she wanted to get to that.

15

Lou Ann tied on her apron and attended to the pancakes sizzling on the frying pan. She smiled at her results. After countless fails, she finally mastered the art of flapjacks.

Harry came whistling into the kitchen.

He kissed her on the cheek. "Are you going to wear that apron tonight?"

She flipped a pancake. "I might."

"Now I'm going to think about that all day."

Joanna carried Joley Kay on her hip. "Look who's awake!"

Lou Ann stepped back from the burner and nuzzled her daughter's squat little neck.

The baby giggled.

"Morning, my sweet pea," Harry cooed.

"I'm making a pancake just for you, my Joley Kay!"

"Smells and looks like pancakes," Joanna said.

"Practice makes perfect."

She'd almost progressed past having batter dripping all over and no recognizable pancake to declare. Even Isabelle thumbed her doggy nose at them.

But Lou Ann hung in there and now she was the pancake queen.

Everyone, including Isabelle, lined up for their pancakes.

The pancakes turned out perfectly, and Lou Ann hoped the rest of her day would work out half as well, because investigations were never perfectly round.

Joanna sat Joley Kay in her highchair, and then the three adults gathered around the kitchen table.

Lou Ann cut a pancake into baby-sized pieces and set them on the baby's tray.

Most ended up on the newspaper covering the floor around the highchair. It made cleanup quicker and easier and it also got everyone out the door in time.

Joanna stuffed the last of her pancakes in her mouth, chewed quickly, and swallowed and then wiped off the extra maple syrup around her mouth and kissed Lou Ann.

"Goodbye, Aunt Lou Ann. I need to take off to the hospital. See you later, monkey," she said to Joley Kay. Joley Kay hurled a pancake to the floor.

Thank God for that newspaper.

That must have been a baby-style goodbye.

"Awesome breakfast, babe. I'm off to the field office. I take it you're off to the nightclub."

"Yep, among my many stops today."

"I think I'll make it for dinner unless there's a sudden change in my schedule. I'll text you either way."

"I may not make it for dinner either, because there might be a sudden change in mine."

"Understood. I'll take the baby and Isabelle over to Suzy's."

"Thanks."

"Don't mention it. My car's already a mess." Harry winked. "But like my car, I also clean up well." Harry picked the baby out of her highchair and wiped the pancake-crusted syrup off her lips. Joley Kay fidgeted and turned her head one way and then the other to avoid the wet washcloth.

"Gotcha" Harry crowed.

"I packed her bag and Isabelle's too last night," Lou Ann said.

"It eased the pang of having to leave Joley Kay and Isabelle. She needed for both to feel her touch the rest of the day.

"Bye-bye, baby. Bye my Isabelle."

A goo and a bark, and they were gone.

Now she was left to focus on the rest of her day, and on Gloria.

Lou Ann dressed, slipped on her shoes, and grabbed her pad and pen.

Readied, she was reaching for the front door, when her phone buzzed.

She snatched her cell out of her satchel before it could go to voicemail.

It was Barb Kent, the ME.

"Hey, I was almost out the door."

"I need you to come to the office *now*."

"I'm on my way."

THE LAST DEATH

The bartender, Kelseigh, and Jade, and the new cast of characters, Cassie and Tyler, just moved down Lou Ann's list.

16

Joanna adjusted her scrubs and straightened her ponytail in the mirror then bared her teeth to make sure there weren't any leftover remnants of breakfast. Attending morning report with caked syrup would be embarrassing, especially if Ian, aka Dr. Hotty, saw it. Thankfully her mouth and teeth were clean.

She shoved her clothes into her locker and bounded out of the locker room. Being late counted.

Joanna moved up closer to the center of the pack than yesterday. Staying in the back worked for her on her first shift, but on her second one, it was time to assume a stronger position—because the last thing she wanted was to look weak.

Newell, Margo, and Otto had made her weak—vulnerable—broken. They'd developed their tortures in order to force compliance and instill fear. That's the way they worked.

But Claudia would be watching her to make sure she'd made the right choice in placing Joanna in the ED. It was Joanna's first choice and she couldn't imagine being anywhere else in the hospital. Now it was time for her to start showing strength and make everyone believe she belonged in the ED, including herself.

Ian sidled up to Joanna.

"Good morning, Nurse Joanna."

Joanna suppressed a smile. "Good morning,... Dr. Hottman."

She almost called him "Hotty," which he probably would've enjoyed.

"Did you bring money today?"

"Yes, for you and me."

"I guess we'll have to have lunch together, again."

Joanna grinned. "I guess so."

Ian stood next to her without moving forward. But he towered over the crowd, and his ego further boosted his charisma.

After the morning report, Joanna resumed taking care of the patients Dr. Stan Farkas, the other ED attending on shift, was seeing. The nurses, excluding Shelly, could be watching her and Ian, if the rumor mill hadn't already started.

Shelly gestured to Joanna.

"What's with you today?" she asked.

"Nothing. Why?"

Shelly pulled her further aside.

"Why are you avoiding Hotty?"

"Because you and everyone call him Hotty."

"Were you and I not here yesterday?"

"Don't be silly."

"I can say the same about you. Come on, he keeps looking at you, in a subtle way. If you don't see any of his patients, it'll be more obvious. So see some of Stan's patients and some of Hotty's. It's a perfect compromise. Just a suggestion."

Shelly was right. The more she avoided Ian, the more others would notice.

Stan Farkas was a nice enough doctor. Like Claudia, he'd worked the ED for fifteen years. He treated the patients with courtesy, but he had a monotonous voice. After speaking with Kaylee last night, Joanna slept well. But after being around Stan for just a few minutes, she had to suppress more than one yawn.

Hottman buzzed around Joanna while she completed her notes in the computer.

His pacing distracted her, and she worked harder to keep her focus on the words marching across her screen.

"Hey, when you're finished with your notes, I need your assistance."

"I'll be with you after I e-sign my note and log off."

"Okay."

He sat in the chair next to hers and crossed his legs, and then he began to make a clicking sound with the tip of his tongue against his palate.

Joanna turned toward him with a frown.

"You're annoying me."

Ian grinned.

She returned her attention to the computer, logged off, and spun around in her chair

"All right, what do you need?"

"I need you to help me do an LP."

Day two and she'd never assisted on a lumber puncture.

"Umm, I haven't done one," she admitted.

Ian shrugged. "I'll tell you what I need. Look, I'll show you how to set it up. Then you position the patient. I do the tap. Then we're done." Ian stood and cocked his head. "Come on, let's go."

Joanna followed Ian to the central supply room where he grabbed a lumber puncture kit.

Then they approached room 15.

"This is the isolation room," Joanna said.

"Yes. Our patient may have encephalitis. He returned from camping a week ago. He has received the meningitis vaccine, so it's unlikely to be meningitis.. I think this is either tic or mosquito bite-related. It happens and he was unlucky. But he doesn't have an immune disorder. Plus, he's young and healthy, so he has that going for him."

He pointed to the surgical gowns, caps, and face masks with protective eye shields.

They cleansed their hands with the hand sanitizer attached to the wall outside of the room, and put on their personal protective equipment.

Joanna followed Ian into the room.

Her eyes widened. The masked boy lying on the bed couldn't be more than a teen. A man and a woman wearing face masks stood with their eyes reddened, their foreheads creased with worry.

"Doctor," they both said.

Ian pointed to Joanna. "This is Nurse Joanna."

Joanna nodded.

The boy was pale and sweaty, an IV pump pushing fluid into the vein in his bandaged hand.

Joanna's heart pounded and a drop of sweat trickled down her spine.

She lay in that locked room thick with stench, captive, her skin on fire, her brain muddled, her vision blurred. She panted at first to cling to life, but couldn't keep it up. Then everything blessedly blackened. The pain ceased. She was dead, but barely alive in some abyss. The sick boy brought it all to the surface.

"Nurse?"

Joanna blinked to find Ian staring at her.

"Yes, Dr. Hottman."

"I'd like to introduce Mr. and Mrs. Greer, Dylan's parents, since

Dylan is only seventeen."

Seventeen. Seventeen. Echoed in her head. She was seventeen.

Ian continued, "and his parents and Dylan, too, have signed the consent for the lumbar puncture. Lab has drawn a complete panel, including blood cultures. His white count is 32,000, and he's hypokalemic, so potassium has been added to this IV. After the LP, we'll put him on antibiotics. The consent is on the beside stand. Let's pause."

"This is Dylan Greer, medical record 22016578, and he a minor, and his parents, have consented to a lumbar puncture. He has no known drug allergies," Joanna confirmed.

"Do you you understand, Dylan, what procedure we're going to do?" Ian asked

"A lumber puncture, needle in spine," he mumbled.

"Do you have any further concerns, Mr. And Mrs Greer?" Ian asked.

"No doctor."

"Let's proceed."

Joanna went into the room's cupboard and grabbed a packaged size eight sterile gloves and popped them on the sterile field that Ian already set up.

"Normally, it's easier and better to have the patient sitting on the side of the bed. But Dylan has been vomiting and is too weak to sit up, so we're going to perform the LP with him lying on his side.

Joanna helped Dylan to his side. The heat from his skin penetrated her gloves and his wet hair was plastered to his neck.

He squinted so he could see her.

She held him in place with his knees flexed.

"It'll be okay," she soothed. "It'll be over soon."

"Mmmm," he mumbled.

Ian prepped and draped Dylan's spine.

"This first part may sting. I need to inject the lidocaine, an anesthetic," Ian warned Dylan.

Dylan didn't flinch.

Neither did she during those last moments in that cell. Exhaustion does that. And Dylan had reached that point.

"You may feel some pressure."

Ian inserted the needle into Dylan's spine and removed the guide wire. Clear spinal fluid dripped from the needle hub and Ian collected four tubes of the fluid.

"All done," Ian said. You did well."

The boy remained silent.

Ian removed the drape and placed a bandage over the site.

Ian dropped the needles into the red needle-and-sharps disposal unit mounted on the wall, while Joanna cleansed the remains of the surgical field.

"I'll let you know when I get the results," Ian told Mr. And Mrs. Greer then added, "Unfortunately there aren't any beds available in the intensive care units which Dylan will need. However, a bed should become available soon."

"We'll stay with him, if that's okay," Mrs. Greer said.

"Absolutely. Also the cafeteria is one floor up. Once you exit the elevator, turn right and then follow the signs to the cafeteria."

"I can get you coffee, tea, juices, or soda," Joanna offered.

"Two coffees would be wonderful," Mrs. Greer replied.

"Done. I'll be back."

Ian and Joanna removed their PPE and cleansed their hands under the sanitizer.

"Good job, Joanna…Nurse Joanna," he corrected himself.

"Thanks, but I didn't do much."

"What not much? I needed assistance and you gave it. But more important, you soothed Dylan, and you also soothed his parents. I can't imagine the terror of having a very sick child."

"They're distraught, and it may be a while before Dylan gets an ICU bed, so it was the least I could do. And now I'm off to get two coffees from the break room. Do you need anything else? Any more help?"

"You don't want to work with Stan?"

"Dr. Farkas is fine."

But she prayed Ian needed her before Stan did.

Shelly buzzed past Joanna and Ian.

"I got it. I'm working up Stan's next two patients, if you don't mind, Joanna," she said, and grinned.

"All right, since you already started."

Shelly winked at Joanna while Ian spoke with Stan.

"I'll be right with you, Dr. Farkas," Shelly said.

She waved her hand slowly, scooting Joanna toward Ian.

Joanna rolled her eyes.

"Nurse Joanna, can you please work up the patient in room 8 after you get those coffees?"

"Sure."

Joanna delivered the coffee and then looked up the patient in room 8 on the computer—a 21 year-old male whose chief complaint was rectal pressure.

She proceeded to the room to obtain a history and the details of his complaint.

She'd just introduced herself to him, when he sneezed and an eraser torpedoed out of his ass.

The guy blinked. "I had no idea that was there."

"Okay. Are you feeling better?" It was the only thing she could think to ask.

"A little sore, but yeah, better."

Joanna donned a pair of exam gloves and bagged the two-inch, used-to be pink eraser.

She stepped out of the room.

"Oh, Dr. Hottman," she called.

"Yesss," he said with a full grin.

She held up the baggie. "You knew."

"I just reviewed the X-ray."

"Uh-huh."

"Turns out he's been here multiple times with a variety of items."

"You knew that too."

Ian shrugged. "That's the ED for you."

And such was her second orientation day. She'd just have to get smarter.

She narrowed her eyes at him and grumbled. "Looks like lunch isn't very promising for you."

"You can always return to work with Stan. But he isn't as much fun as I am."

She waved the baggy at him. "No, apparently he's not."

"So lunch is still on?"

"Consider yourself lucky today. As soon as I dispose of this item and discharge the patient, I'll walk you to the cafeteria."

He waggled his eyebrows. "I'll be waiting."

17

Lou Ann parked in the medical examiner's lot, reluctantly stepped out of the air-conditioned vehicle and into the stifling heat, and it wasn't even noon. Her slicked-back ponytail was already drooping and her lungs pumped extra hard. She hurried inside the office. The autopsy suites would be blessedly cool and she'd gotten used to the mingled smells of dead tissue and formalin, the clang of instruments against steel, and high pitched zzzz of the bone saw.

Lou Ann waved to the receptionist.

"Hi, Inspector Jasinski. Dr. Kent's in the back."

"Thanks."

Lou Ann entered the suite, the cold, musty death odor enveloping her. Her eyes went straight to Gloria lying on a steel table with her chest and abdomen exposed and emptied via the Y incision, her sternum and ribs cracked. Her wet blonde hair cascaded from the block supporting her neck.

"Good morning, Lou Ann."

"Hey, Barb. I see you're pretty far along on Gloria."

"Yeah, I got an early start."

The diener began to close the Y incision.

"Hey, Chuck."

"Hi, Inspector. Barb's just finishing up with the organs. The cranium is next," he warned.

Ordinarily, Lou Ann could withstand watching a corpse's face peeled away to expose the cranium and then a bone saw cutting through the skull and the brain extraction that followed. But this was Gloria.

Lou Ann sucked in a deep breath, and then almost gagged at the smells which she was normally used to.

"You don't have to stay for this. You can wait for me in my office."

88

"No. I'll stay."

She'd stay with Gloria until the very end of the autopsy, as well as be there for the eventual funeral ahead.

"I managed to get a blood sample from her heart and that's being processed in GCMS."

Lou Ann was well versed in what the gas chromatograph mass spectrometer could reveal.

Lou Ann shook her head. "Barb, I have a hard time believing this is a Fentanyl OD. I saw her body. You saw her body. I saw her on security tapes at both Spark and the apartment. She left the apartment and entered the club with a normal gait. Then at Spark, this guy is guiding her out because she's stumbling, and she continues to sway at her door. The manager let her in and supposedly just put her to bed. If it was a Fentanyl-laced pill in her drink at the club, she would have collapsed way before, or even dropped dead. No way she's a drug user."

"Lou Ann, I know you don't want to think that Gloria experimented with drugs, but CSU and you did find a Percocet pill in her nightstand drawer."

"Yeah, I'll give you that. Could've been planted."

Lou Ann shook her head at herself. She had to stretch for that.

"That pill tested positive for Fentanyl. And there's more. There was semen in her vagina."

Her mind shot straight to David. Lou Ann paused. Could be Tyler's or the unknown guy's, or any other unknown donor.

She'd track them all down, process of elimination.

"What about the other girl, the one who couldn't be revived in the ED? The one with the same yellow Spark admission wristband?"

"She's next. Her mother rushed here from Jacksonville after the roommate called her. The mother is understandably completely distraught. Likewise she's adamant that her daughter was not a drug user. Elizabeth worked as barista for the summer to defray upcoming university tuition. She had Sunday off and decided to go to Spark."

It was a long shot, but maybe Kelseigh and Jade knew Elizabeth too.

Lou Ann knocked on Kelseigh and Jade's door not sure they'd hear it because of the amped-up music behind the door. She knocked harder and waited. The music was muted and the deadbolt clicked. Kelseigh, who was wearing lounge pants and a T-shirt opened the door.

"Oh, hi."

"Hello, Kelseigh. Is Jade home too?"

"Um...she's sleeping."

"May I come in?"

"Sure."

Kelseigh opened the door wider.

Lou Ann stepped inside to find the hot mystery guy on the Spark surveillance tape spread out on the couch.

He looked up at Lou Ann. "Hey."

She glanced at Kelseigh, who took a step back.

Lou Ann returned her attention to the guy on the couch, who was shirtless and wearing jeans at a precarious hip level.

"I haven't met your acquaintance." *The security tape notwithstanding.*

"I'm Mark," he snarked as if she was bothering him.

"Nice to meet you."

"Yeah," he replied with an even deeper and more disinterested voice.

"Mark what?"

"Marky-Mark."

Cute.

Jade emerged from one of the rooms, her eyes crusty.

"Hey, Ms. Jasinski."

Jade scratched her face and walked over to the couch.

"Hey, move over," she said to Mark.

Mark tossed his legs over the couch, sat, and shifted to the opposite side.

"Thanks."

"Don't mention it."

Lou Ann sat in a chair and sank. The springs had seen better days. But these were college kids, and furniture wasn't a priority. It was the same for her back in the day.

At least she now knew Mark's name. Last name was still up for grabs, but she'd get it one way or another.

"Do you know where I can find Cassie?"

"I'm so pissed off at her. She promised to take Gloria home."

"Not her fault," Mark said.

"Did you drive her home?" she asked Mark.

Mark flipped up his palms. "No. Why?"

"Someone took her home."

"Maybe she took an Uber."

"Perhaps."

"Check with that Tyler dude, lady."

Jade slapped Mark's shoulder. "Hey, don't be disrespectful!"

'Sorry." Mark grabbed his shirt and his Air Jordans. "I gotta get going. Pleasure to meet you, Ms. Jaksik."

She didn't bother to correct him.

Mark waved. "See you guys. Thanks for letting me crash."

Mark left.

"How did he find you?"

"I gave him my cell number. Big mistake. He showed up high, and I didn't want him to go out there and hurt someone or kill someone or get in a wreck himself. So we let him crash here. He was actually pretty nice at the club."

"What's his real last name?"

"Jackson. He was such a loser to you. I just wanted him to leave."

"How about Cassie?"

"She lives at the Tradewind apartments, 4D. Cassie Connor."

"What about Tyler, and what's his last name?"

"His last's name is Young, and he lives with his parents."

"And where would that be?"

"Over on Sweet Gum Lane, the big-ass white house with black shutters with, you know, those Grecian style columns and a circular drive. Tyler drives a white Jag."

Lou Ann rocked up and out of the upholstered chair.

"Thanks, ladies."

"I should've dragged GiGi by her feet out of that place. I could've watched over her. Brought her here or slept over. She'd be alive."

"Maybe."

"I hope you find out what happened to her after I left. She was upset about Tyler, but I promise you she wasn't suicidal."

Lou Ann followed her GPS to the Tradewind Apartments, and once inside took the stairwell for the extra, needed cardio bump.

She halted in front of 4D, rapped on the door, and almost immediately felt someone peering at her through the door's spy-hole.

Lou Ann displayed her investigator badge.

A deadbolt clicked and the door opened.

She recognized Cassie from the surveillance tapes.

"Jade let me know you were coming."

Lou Ann waited.

Cassie gestured. "Please, come in."

Her furnishings were two steps up from Kelseigh and Jade's place.

Cassie sat on a plush beige couch, leaving space for Lou Ann to sit there too.

She eyed Lou Ann. "You want to ask me about GiGi…Gloria."

"Yes. Jade told me Gloria refused to go home with her and that you agreed to take her."

"That was the plan."

"So what happened?"

"Tyler and that Mark dude. They were competing for her, and Mark was winning."

"How was he winning?"

"He was suave. He could get away with that because everyone was a bit buzzed."

"Was Gloria buzzed?"

"Buzzed? She was so high she was actually staggering which was really bizarre because she had one glass of wine at Jade and Kelseigh's and one drink at Spark. It didn't make sense."

"Was anyone else as high as Gloria?"

"Mmm, it'a nightclub and people connect. Some were crazy on the dance floor, but when I went to the ladies' room, there was a girl in there who was stumbling around, and she had to hold onto the sink to steady herself. I asked if she was okay, and she just rolled her head and then stumbled out. I lost track of her."

"Do you remember what she looked like or what she was wearing?"

"A really cool deep green dress which looked great with her blonde hair."

"This is hard to look at." Lou Ann took out a photo of Elizabeth's pale face with the rest of her body covered.

"She's dead!"

"Yes."

"That's her! The girl from the bathroom!"

"I'm investigating what happened to her and Gloria. They were both stumbling that night." She looked into Cassie's eyes. "Do you know how Gloria got home that night?"

"Mark or Tyler, I presume."

"Mark denied."

"Yeah, he would. I'd ask Tyler."

Lou Ann stood. "Thanks, Cassie."

"You're welcome. I'm so sorry about that girl."
"So am I."

18

"Are you at a point where you can take a break?" Ian asked.

Joanna looked up from her computer screen. "Yes. Still no ICU bed for Dylan, but there are two transfers out of medical ICU to step down." She crossed her fingers. "Looks like we can get Dylan an ICU bed after lunch."

"That's awesome. Then the sooner we have lunch, the sooner we can transfer Dylan."

"Not that we're not giving him top-notch care, but the ICU is the best place for him and the Greers. They'll be so relieved."

"Those coffees went a long way for them."

"I thought they would."

Ian gestured to Joanna. "After you."

"My treat today."

Ian winked. "My treat too."

Heat percolated to her face at his double entendre.

"I'll be right back. I need to get money out of my locker."

Joanna rushed off before Ian could see her uncontrollable blush.

She ducked into the locker room to find Shelly at her own open locker.

"You need a splash of cold water."

"Is it that bad?"

"You're beyond pink."

"What do I do? I can't keep him waiting."

"No, you shouldn't." Shelly grabbed Joanna's shoulders. "Breathe. In and out."

Joanna inhaled and exhaled three times.

"Better. You're down to a pale pink."

Joanna opened her locker, grabbed her money, and stuffed it in the front pocket of her scrub top. She shut and locked the door, and then

94

leaned her cheek against the door to suck out its coolness. That helped. She took an extra cleansing breath.

"Perfect,," Shelly said.

Joanna hurried out of the locker room before Ian could notice her delay. She bounded toward him saying, "Let's go."

"Let's take the stairwell," Ian said.

It was only one floor up, and it was the lunchtime crush, and they'd wait for an elevator just to go one stop up.

Ian opened the stairwell door.

Joanna passed through and Ian followed. The steel door slammed shut.

She hadn't been in the stairwell before. "We're not locked in or about to set off an alarm?"

Ian laughed. "We're trapped here forever." They exchanged looks. "I used my pass."

Joanna tried to curb her claustrophobia using deep breaths and calming thoughts.

She'd never suffered from the condition until she'd been trapped for weeks in that windowless cell. Joanna suddenly froze. Her heartbeat race to her ears, and she breathed faster to lower the pressure growing in her chest. She inhaled in short gasps, struggling to take in enough air, and her heart pounded out of her chest, each beat echoing in her ears. She placed a trembling hand over her chest, feeling the frantic rhythm beneath her fingertips. Her legs weakened, and her knees trembled. She tried to stand upright, but the trembling spread from her hands to her arms and eventually to her entire body, making even the simplest movements feel challenging. Joanna grabbed the side rail to steady herself.

"Hey, are you okay?"

Ian reached out and cradled her hand.

"Your hands are sweaty."

There was no way out of this. He'd discovered yet one of the consequences of her past.

"I'm sorry. I am a bit claustrophobic, although strangely, in stairwells but not in elevators."

Ian tightened his grip. "No. I'm sorry. I didn't know. It must be the door slamming shut as opposed to the smoother open and close of elevator doors. That's got to be it. We'll go back. It's okay."

He got that right. But she couldn't reveal why.

"No. It's a stupid fear. I want to keep going."

"It's not stupid. We'll take one step at a time and I'll not let go of your hand."

They'd reached the first of two flights.

"Spiders freak me out," Ian admitted. "I hope we don't encounter any."

"You're just saying that to make me feel better."

"Yes and no, because I have this thing about spiders because I was bitten once as a kid and ended up in the emergency room with my equally unglued parents. Turned out it wasn't a poisonous spider, but it left me with a very sore ankle. After that, I was fascinated by the workings of the ED, and the attending physician was awesome. I was sold, and here I am. And I've treated countless insect bites."

"And see? Here we are," he continued. "You made it and no spiders!"

Joanna grinned. "No spiders."

Ian opened the exit door. She slid her hand out of his. They couldn't be seen holding hands,. That PDA would surely shoot straight to the rumor mill. But it was true—a truth neither was ready to announce.

They walked toward the cafeteria, chatting but not holding hands.

The line of hungry staffers was even longer than yesterday.

"Choose whatever you want," Joanna said.

He nudged closer to her in the line.

"I will."

They reached for the pizza slices at the same time.

"Wise choice, Nurse Joanna."

"Ditto, Dr. Hottman."

They proceeded through the line.

"Brownie?" Joanna asked.

"Sure. I'll pay for dessert."

"Nope. A deal's a deal. I came prepared."

"Yes, you did."

Ian led Joanna to the elevator bank, each carrying their to-go lunch.

"Walking down the stairwell might be awkward," Ian said.

"Yeah, I agree that the elevator would best. But I think we can take the stairwell to the parking garage later…if that's okay?"

"Absolutely. We'll do that at the end of the shift, since we'll end together."

*End together. End together…*echoed happily in her head.

Joanna and Ian entered the buzz of the break room. There were two empty seats together and one available on the other side of the table and Joanna headed for the latter.

She sat quickly, as if she was playing musical chairs and then the music had just stopped.

Another nurse grabbed the seat across from Joanna, leaving the one kitty-corner to hers, and Ian took that last seat.

Joanna and Ian opened up their identical lunches. No one seemed to notice except them.

Ian picked up his pizza slice, surreptitiously winked at Joanna, and lifted it as if to toast their success, and Joanna covertly did the same. Then they both took a secret, celebratory bite at the same time.

It was the best-tasting pizza she ever had. It wasn't the gourmet kind, or the kind she'd shared with her family, but it was how it ended up on her cafeteria paper carrier that made it mouthwatering.

She'd polished off the slice one bite before his and dabbed a napkin to her mouth. She took a swig of her water to wash it down and waited to challenge Ian to win the brownie. He beat her there and grinned in victory.

She half-smiled because a full one would attract attention to their shenanigans.

Today's lunch had been worth every cent.

<h1 style="text-align:center">19</h1>

Lou Ann's stomach growled, demanding her attention. She pulled up into a sub shop and ordered her favorite turkey sub and a bottle of cold water.

She decided to sit alone in her air-conditioned vehicle letting the engine idle while she ate her sub and planned the rest of her day.

So far, Cassie was the most helpful interview. Hopefully Tyler would be equally forthcoming, but somehow she doubted it.

She finished her sub and drank most of the cold water, reserving some to splash on to her face to help her combat the summer heat wave.

Lou Ann punched in Sweet Gum Lane in her vehicle's map app and followed it.

She passed scores of affluent houses and approached Sweet Gum Lane's cul-de-sac and there at the very end stood a white house with black shudders, Grecian columns, and a white Jaguar parked in the circular driveway, exactly how Cassie described it.

This had to be the place.

Lou Ann parked her vehicle on the side of the road.

Damn, that's one fine house.

She got out and walked to the house, stopping to admire the sparkling white Jag that drank up every piece of heat. Strange that it wasn't parked in the three-car garage, but perhaps the garage was full up with Mommy's and Daddy's vehicles, whatever they drove.

She passed the Grecian columns. Kaylee would get a giggle out of those.

The whole house could fit on the front lawn of Kaylee's inherited Greek mansion Demetrios willed to her.

Kaylee was a young woman who should move on. Lou Ann was convinced Demetrios would've wanted her to. The key was to convince Kaylee of that.

Lou Ann walked up to the door and rang the bell.

Footsteps click-clacked behind the door. It opened to reveal a woman with golden highlights in her perfect shoulder-length haircut, fresh-faced makeup, and wearing teal pencil pants and a white sleeveless cotton shirt. Lou Ann would never dress like that, even if she owned the exact same outfit. The first thing she did when she got home on a hot day was to snap her bra off and scoot into a tee, shorts, and flip-flops.

Lou Ann looked down at the woman's bejeweled high-heeled sandals, probably responsible for the click-clack against the polished terrazzo floor.

"May I help you?"

"Mrs. Young? I'm Lou Ann Jasinski, Homicide and Death Investigator with the Sheriff's Department."

The woman's eyes went huge. "Yes, I'm Mrs. Young. And what is this all about?"

"I'm investigating the death of Gloria Perez, and I understand she and Tyler used to dated and he was one of the last people to see her alive. May I speak with him?"

"Oh, my God. I just got home, and I haven't watched the news. Tyler and Gloria, or GiGi as she liked to be called, were together. But they recently broke up. My family and I really liked her and I believe Tyler still loved her despite the breakup. I'm shocked. Oh, I'm sorry. Please come out of that smothering heat."

Lou Ann entered the elaborately designed foyer and noticed a crystal chandelier above her. Her mouth soured. This chandelier was a tenth the size of what once hung in Demetrios's expansive, marble foyer. That chandler came crashing down on that fateful day when she and Harry arrived to Greece to rescue Kaylee, and during that attempt, the head and greedy and enraged sex trafficker, Gerald Newell, like the coward that he was, shot Demetrios, and in the aftermath, the spray of bullets to cover Kaylee's kill shot, annihilated that foyer. Kaylee, who inherited the mansion, had replaced both the chandelier and the bloodstained marble.

Mrs.Young led Lou Ann into a colonial style living room, and invited Lou Ann to sit in a red-velvet upholstered and mahogany-framed high-back chair while Mrs. Young sat on a matching sofa.

They stared at each other.

Lou Ann broke the tense silence.

"I spoke to a young lady, who was Gloria's friend, and she gave me an address where I could find Tyler, so I apologize for this impromptu, but very important visit."

"I understand. I'll do anything to help you find out what happened to Gloria, God rest her soul."

"You can summon Tyler."

Lou Ann knew he was here because his Jaguar was parked in the driveway.

"Certainly. He's probably in his bedroom. I'll get him for you."

Lou Ann waited. Maybe Mom would tip him off that she, death and homicide investigator, is looking for him, and he'd make a quick exit.

Three minutes passed, and Lou Ann was about ready to chase Tyler down when Mrs. Young screamed.

Lou Ann bolted out of her chair and raced toward Mrs. Young's screams.

She ran down the hallway and into the open door to discover Tyler's mom shaking him and crying, "Wake up! Please wake up! Oh, my God! Sweet Jesus! Wake up!"

Lou Ann quickly grasped the situation and rushed to Mrs. Young. She didn't know the woman's first name.

But first Lou Ann dialed 911.

"This is Investigator Lou Ann Jasinski from the Sheriff's Department and I have an unresponsive male at 1612 Sweet Gum Lane."

"Rescue is on the way."

Her immediate next step was to pull Tyler's mom off him.

"Please, let me get to Tyler."

She dragged Mrs. Young away from her son, until the woman sat on the floor shaking, and rocking back and forth, and moaning.

A dried foam had apparently oozed out of Tyler's mouth. Lou Ann leaned closer to listen for his breathing. Nothing. She palpated his carotid artery. No pulse. Lividity was set, but the rigor had passed. He'd been there at least 24 hours but the AC on full blast spared decomposition. He was dead. Lou Ann widened her eyes. Tyler was wearing the same yellow Spark wristband that was around both Gloria's and Elizabeth's wrists! Another Spark nightclub casualty! His body would now belong to the ME, and she now owned another crime scene.

The wail of Fire Rescue's truck blared louder and louder as it approached 1612 Sweet Gum Lane.

The Fire Rescue's truck squeaked to a halt.

Lou Ann squatted next to Mrs. Young.

"The paramedics are here. While you stay here with Tyler, may I let the paramedics into your house?" Lou Ann softly asked.

Mrs.Young continued to sob, but nodded.

Lou Ann got up and returned to the foyer and opened the door.

Two paramedics approached.

"I'm Lou Ann Jasinski, Homicide and Death Investigator with the Sheriff's Department, and the one who who called 911," she said to the paramedics at the doorway. I'll lead you to the victim's bedroom."

Both paramedics nodded

The paramedics, who carried a gurney, followed Lou Ann and entered Tyler's bedroom.

Lou Ann backed off, letting the squad declare him dead. She wrapped her arms around Mrs. Young and escorted her from the room.

"I'm so sorry."

"I have to call my husband," she said in a robotic voice.

"Do you want me to call him, or anyone for you?" Lou Ann asked.

"No."

"Can you stay with a neighbor or a friend? There will be a lot of activity going on in your house. I can walk you next door."

"I can't leave him."

"I can imagine how heartbroken and shocked you are. But we need to find out what happened to Tyler. Please. It's for Tyler."

Mrs. Young wrung her hands. "I need to know why. Why my baby? I thought he was sleeping. God forgive me."

"You didn't know. I didn't know. Trying to piece together what happened to Tyler is going to take time."

"Trying? *Trying*?"

"Yes, we always do what we can. But we have two other young people who were at the same place Sunday evening, including Gloria. That's going to help us."

But Lou Ann couldn't guarantee that those shared connections would be helpful. But this wasn't the right time to discuss this potential dead end with a distraught parent. That would have to be approached with care.

Lou Ann took Mrs. Young's hand and led her outside the house and to discover that several neighbors had already gathered.

"Jennifer!" a woman called.

Jennifer Young ran straight to the woman's outstretched arms.

The woman hugged her tight and looked at Lou Ann, who nodded.

The neighbor woman escorted Jennifer Young to the home across the street.

Lou Ann knew it was the hardest and most compassionate thing to do. Mr. Young would be next to arrive, and as parent herself, who'd just delivered the worst news possible, it would be hard for her to shepherd him away, too.

Tim Farmer, her own former trainee, arrived along with other sheriff deputies to control and guard the scene.

"Hey, Tim."

"Got another one, huh?"

"Unfortunately so."

"Okay, folks, I need you to back up. We have to get one vehicle out and make way for others. I appreciate your cooperation," Tim announced to the crowd.

Lou Ann took pride in having managed to train Tim well despite her former nemesis, Lieutenant Dan Mathews, who sat in his office feeling important.

"I may need to keep you here past 4:30," Lou Ann said, and then grinned.

Tim remained under Dan's thumb, and Dan never would change his edict that every report must be delivered to him by 4:30 p.m. so he could make haste out of the building. She had left Dan inhaling her fumes after she rose and bolted free of him as the newly-minted Sheriff Department's Death and Homicide Investigator.

"Whatever you need, Investigator Jasinski."

"Oh, I need."

The growing neighborhood crowd backed away as Tim instructed.

The media crush would be next to push back, but Tim could handle it.

Tim directed Fire Rescue out the circular drive and guided in the CSU vehicle, and the ME van.

Lou Ann already had a chance to quickly study the scene, and she was already fairly sure that Tyler's death, like Gloria's and Elizabeth's, couldn't be suicides. Something bad was happening that Sunday night at Spark.

But why these three and not Jade, Cassie, or "Marky-Mark"?

She was aware that Elizabeth was also there, not from the

surveillance video, but because Cassie had mentioned encountering her in the ladies' room.

Based on Cassie's description, Elizabeth, like Gloria, was stumbling around that night. But Tyler didn't appear unbalanced, and neither did Mark, or Cassie, or Jade. Mark denied that he took Gloria home. But she got there somehow. Tyler? If it was him, he couldn't help her out now. Perhaps someone remembered them, but there was no way to find the 200 people who'd been there that night. She'd have to get help from the media for that. But she could start by checking every UBER. Lyft, or taxi pick-up that night.

Because it was it a suspicious death—one that was 24-plus hours old—CSU would make sense of the scene.

Lou Ann waited in the living room trying to fathom how this situation spun out to include yet another death. She must be under a dark cloud.

Barb walked in while CSU finished photographing and processing the scene.

"Not much here, Lou Ann," one team member said. "Looks like another OD. We'll send you a copy of the photos."

"Thanks."

"That leaves us, Barb."

Barb examined Tyler.

"Same foam at the mouth. Dried now. So his mom thought he was sleeping for like a day plus?"

"I believe her. What I witnessed was genuine shock. It wasn't dramatics, and I've seen plenty. When Joanna and Kaylee were seventeen, they slept a lot. Maybe she thought he was hanging out in his room. He's 21. Maybe she let him have his privacy."

"What? He wasn't eating?"

"Yeah, I get where you're going. But kids stash all sorts of things in their room. He was independently dependent. A 21-year-old kid. Which is one reason I don't get the attraction between him and Gloria, because she had her own place, and a burgeoning career. I'll find out what kind of job Tyler had. They sure didn't have much in common, but then love is strange."

Like Kaylee and Demetrios.

"What's not similar to Gloria and Elizabeth based on what I viewed on the surveillance video, he was walking around normally, which makes me think he left the club the same way. The question is what happened between the time he got home Sunday night to approximately 24 hours ago. Plus, we know Gloria was found wearing the same dress. Tyler is wearing boxers and a tee. So he was coordinated enough that he was able to undress before presumably plopping onto his bed."

"Gloria and Elizabeth were petite, just under BMI. But Tyler's body mass is greater. It would have taken longer for him to become inebriated or have a drug percolate through him," Barb said.

"Point taken."

"I'll transport him to the morgue, where I've recently taken up residence."

"Hopefully we won't see any more yellow wristbands."

"'Hopefully' is not a guarantee."

"No, it isn't."

A man burst into the bedroom with Tim right behind him.

He gripped and pulled his hair. "My son! My son! What happened to my son!"

Tim caught his breath. "I tried, Lou Ann, but…"

Mr. Young broke through the guarded line of deputies. But with his linebacker size along with his being in crisis mode, he proved to be unstoppable and understandably so.

"It's all right, Deputy. I'll handle it."

Tim left.

"Please, I…I…need to see him. I don't understand."

Barb nodded.

"Tyler. Tyler." He muttered with tears streaming down his face.

"When? When? His car's there."

"Mr. Young. I'm Dr. Barbara Kent with the medical examiner's office. I'll be caring for your son. My deepest sympathies to you and your wife."

"And I'm Lou Ann Jasinki, Homicide and Death Investigator with the sheriff's department."

"Homicide!"

"And Death Investigator," she added.

"Who's responsible for this? I want to know! I have a right to know!"

"Yes, you do," Lou Ann said, to help him slow down long enough to pause and take a deep breath.

It was true, but sometimes there wasn't a clear answer or no answer. She prayed there was an answer for Daisy's and Glenda's, Elizabeth's parents', and now the Youngs' sakes. Families lives forever changed. She knew about forever family changes. *Harry and I lived it and still do.*

Mr. Young kissed his son's forehead and pulled away, taking out a handkerchief and wiping the tears and snot off his nose.

He snorted. "Where's my wife, Jenny? She called me."

"She's across the street with a neighbor," Lou Ann said. "I can walk over with you," she offered.

"No, that's okay. She's with the Jessups. They're our good friends."

"That's important. I'm going to give you my card, and I'll also be in touch. Again, I'm so sorry."

"And here's my card," Barb said.

Mr. Young tucked both in the breast pocket of his jacket. He'd left earlier for work not knowing he'd return home to find that something terrible happened to his son. She winced thinking how his brain must have circled and circled while his heart was cracking the whole way. He'd never forget that drive.

Lou Ann watched the desolate father cross the street and enter his neighbor's house.

She approached Tim.

"Gather all the deputies. I need them to form a ringed barrier with their vehicles outside the home. I don't want anyone to see the young man leaving in a body bag, and most important, not his parents, who are probably looking out the window right now."

"Got it."

A convoy of sheriff vehicles blocked the view.

Tyler left the home secured in a zipped cocoon for the dead.

"I'll see you later," Barb said.

'You're up there on my agenda."

"I wish I wasn't."

"So do I."

20

Harry was the third FBI Agent who rode in the second Coast Guard vessel deployed to investigate an unregistered boat in Tampa Bay waters.

Another damn boat! Another bust! Another day!

Their vessel approached the strobing lights of the initial responding Coast Guard vessel.

The boat in question had originally been pulled over for speeding. But further inspection revealed that the boat not only failed to have a Florida registration, but the occupants appeared overly nervous. Also the initial responding Coast Guard noted multiple splashes surrounding the boat. Hence Harry and the two other special agents were summoned to investigate a suspected panicked drug dump.

Harry and the two other agents boarded the suspected boat, armed, along with the Coast Guard, who likewise came prepared for a takedown.

One guy on the motor boat reached for his side, but he was met with multiple high-capacity firearms staring at him.

"Consider well your choices." Harry called to the guy. "That goes for the rest of you. We can always do this the hard way."

"Uh, I was just reaching for my ID."

"Okay, hand it to me."

Firearms lurched forward.

The guy and Harry locked eyes.

The guy reached further into his bulging pocket.

No ID came, but a pistol did.

And then another one and another one from the men on the boat.

And in a hail of bullets, the suspects on the boat who'd drawn their weapons and threatened Harry, the other agents, and the Coast Guard, fell in a mowed-down domino fashion.

"Choices," Harry repeated after the gunfire ceased.

The guy who pulled out his pistol writhed on the floor, and another groaned. The other two were lifeless.

"Get them out of here!" Harry yelled.

One agent and the Coast Guard loaded the injured but alive for now, and the two dead ones, onto the first vessel. The vessel sped off while providing assistance to the injured ones and transporting them to the nearest trauma center, while the other two would meet the medical examiner's office in Hillsborough County.

Harry and the other agent and the Coast Guard from the second vessel stayed aboard the drug dealers' boat.

"What's wrong with these barrels of fish?" Harry asked.

"Hmm? Let's find out," the other agent said.

They pushed the barrels over, and along with the fish, plastic bags of powder spilled out of two barrels, and two bags of blue-marked tablets came out of the fish-topped barrels, and yellow ones spilled from three others.

"Not seen these before," Harry said.

"You got me," one Coast Guard said.

"Beats me. Fentanyl comes in a rainbow of colors designed to attract kids, but these are shaped different," the other agent said.

"The lab will tell us. No sense guessing,"

"Bales of cocaine must have went overboard," Harry said. "Less for us and more for the sharks."

Large bales had been dumped into the ocean for years by drug smugglers evading authorities. Some washed up on Florida's beaches and some were consumed by sharks and other creatures, as evidenced by their erratic behavior and deaths with ocean biologists documenting the levels of drugs in the creatures.

"Let's haul the boat in. Quite a catch today, right?"

"Yeah, Boxer. Another commendation for us, and two take-outs."

Harry frowned. "I warned the guy about choices, but he didn't listen. That's what happens."

Harry and the other agent got off the Coast Guard vessel and headed back to the field office.

Harry got a cold bottle of water to hydrate from his time with the brutal sun beating down on him while on the Coast Guard vessel. The heat of the gun battle made it much worse.

He drank half of the bottle, took out his personal cell, which he could have because he was no longer on an assignment.

Lou Ann answered on the second ring.

"What's the matter? Is something wrong with the baby?"

"No. And I'm at the field office getting ready to finish a report."

He heard sigh of relief. Lou Ann wasn't accustomed to hearing from him during his days and/or nights on assignment—unless there was a grave crisis at home. But given her cases with the suspicious deaths of two young women, and his part of a drug bust, he had to let her know.

"The Coast Guard and I and two other agents went aboard an unregistered, foreign boat loaded with drugs of all sorts in Tampa Bay waters. There was a shootout. Two suspects died and two are on their way to Tampa Regional's Trauma Center."

"You could've been shot, killed!"

"Yeah, that's always a risk. You know that. You take that risk every day."

Silent pause.

Harry continued, "I would've preferred to take them all in and get intel, but two are dead, and the other two may not make it, which leaves me with a mega drug bust, but I may not be able to track their connections. But when one drew first, we had to react. It was four on four."

"I'm relieved to talk to you."

"Same here. But I need to tell you about the drugs. Among the cocaine and meth, there were two bags containing a different shape, and not the typical markings of Fentanyl. So as we discussed before, your victims' deaths were not the typical Fentanyl kind. Joanna also said that nothing worked on that young woman who coded and died in the ED."

"Elizabeth Canto."

"The drugs are being analyzed. I'll be late for dinner."

"Me too. I'll let Suzy know."

"Later, babe."

"Later."

Harry leaned forward in his desk chair and dialed the lab.

"Hey, Freddie. It's Harry. Can you contact me as soon as you've ID'd the drugs, especially the yellow triangular ones."

"Yeah, I received the bags and yeah, haven't seen them before. But I'll find out if they've showed up in other busts. I'm on it."

"Thanks, man."

"Glad to help. Curious myself."

Harry ended the call and tapped his pen on his desk.

THE LAST DEATH

Perhaps he'd stumbled on a deadly new drug.

21

Lou Ann parked in Spark's parking lot. The three vehicles were the same ones she'd noted during her last visit. But Moreno, the owner, wasn't outside this time.

She relished the idea of surprise visit.

Lou Ann entered the club through the unlocked door.

Beams of late afternoon sun pushed through the windows like a spotlight in the dim and musty, empty club.

Moreno came out of his office door.

Surely she was on the CCTV surveillance.

"Ah, Investigator Jasinski. How may I help you today?"

'First, I want to thank you for the encrypted video surveillance you sent me."

"Happy to help." Moreno shrugged. "So…uh…what is your pleasure?"

"Is your bartender here?"

"Which bartender do you want to talk to? I have four of them."

"The one or ones working Sunday night?"

Bottles clanked.

Lou Ann whipped around. She recognized the guy behind the bar from the video surveillance.

She pointed to the guy behind the bar.

"That one."

What did Moreno expect, since he gave her the encrypted video? Did he not think the bartender wasn't clearly shown on that video? But as Harry said, the video appeared to be trained on certain customers, and that was exactly what Moreno counted on—that none of his employees were involved in any tainted drinks. Which was possible, and was part of what she was obligated to consider.

"Hi," she called to the bartender, as she approached the bar.

She scooted onto a barstool.

"I'm Inspector Lou Ann Jasinski with the Sheriff's Department."

The bartender did the fast-blinking thing again, unconsciously signaling his anxiety.

Why? Or maybe she'd overreacted, but she doubted that.

Moreno lurked in the background in her peripheral vision.

The bartender tossed his polishing towel on the counter.

"Miles Bates," he identified himself.

"Pleasure to meet you," Lou Ann said.

"Mmm."

"Were you working alone on Sunday night?"

"Yeah. The other bartender called in sick, so I had to deal with the crowd by myself."

"I understand that the club was busy Sunday night."

"You understand correctly. I was working my ass off."

"I told you Miles, that I couldn't get any of the other two because they're part time and I'm not paying overtime," Moreno called.

"Mr. Moreno, I need to speak with Miles uninterrupted and in private. Please."

Moreno shot Miles a narrowed "be careful of what you say" glare and went back into his office.

Lou Ann leaned forward with her elbows on the bar.

"I just want to speak with you. I'm not looking to get you in trouble with your boss."

She needed to gain his trust. She could care less about the fallout from Moreno, who was next on her list. Her goal was to extract info from Miles.

"I was here, yesterday, and I noticed a new shipment was being unloaded, including liquor." Lou Ann pointed at the rows of liquor bottles in front of the mirrored bar wall. A handful of bottles were half empty. "Are all those new stock?"

"Some. Most," he qualified. "But I wasn't here yesterday. It was my day off. I just get the bar ready for tonight. That's my job."

"Do you know which bartender was here?"

She could and would ask Moreno, but she also wanted to ask Miles.

"I believe John was here. He never leaves everything in order, but he's a newbie—a recent mixologist—so I'd give him some slack. Plus, he was the one who called in Sunday night. Guess he got better. But I still was stuck fixing his inexperience."

"How long has John worked here?"

"About a month, part-time."

"How about you?"

"I've been here before Moreno. I started three years ago with a former owner. Moreno bought the bar from Maxwell Star. Nice guy, but he cut a deal he couldn't walk away from with Moreno."

"Was the bar not in the black?"

"Yeah, but barely. But Maxwell loved the place. He began the place. It was named Carousel, but Moreno renamed it Spark and added Sunday nights."

"Do you know what happened to Maxwell?"

"Nope. We lost touch. I texted him and called him and he readily returned both, but his replies stopped like six months ago. I don't why. Maybe he felt uncomfortable given the new ownership and he probably felt my loyalty should be with Moreno. He probably moved on."

"I'm investigating the deaths of three young people who all were here Sunday night."

"Yeah, I heard about it on the news, and I saw you. So I expected you'd come by eventually."

"Did you notice anyone not feeling well, or did you deny alcohol to anyone Sunday night."

"Yes, and yes."

Lou Ann's ears pricked up.

"Yes, as usual, I had to cut off some club-goers because they were already unsteady."

"How many on Sunday night?"

"About five. I ended up calling an UBER for two. The other three said they had a ride home."

"Do remember who the two were?"

"A young woman and a guy, both like in their twenties, clearly above twenty-one because I ID everyone since the bouncer sometimes waves some through without looking carefully enough at their IDs. I talked to him about it, and even went to Moreno about my concerns. He told me he'd take care of it, but it still happens."

"Who is the bouncer, and is that still an issue?"

"George Mason, aka Gorilla George. He still wrestles. Everyone's afraid to cross him, the rest of us, customers, and even Moreno, who hired him specifically for his massive build."

"How long has Gorilla George been a bouncer at Spark?"

"He was here before, with the previous owner. Moreno kept him on."

"Thanks for your time, Miles."

'You're welcome. I feel really bad for those young people. I've kept my eyes on all the liquor. Whoever left my bar, they left with a drink free of anything. I swear to you. Whatever left my bar, was altered later. Honest."

Lou Ann nodded.

"Can I get you a drink, Investigator?"

"I appreciate the offer, but I'm on duty."

"Of course. Sorry."

"No problem."

Miles reached into the mini fridge.

"Cold water? It's sealed."

Lou Ann smiled. "Sure."

Miles handed her the cold bottle.

"I'll trade you. Here's my card. If you think of anything else, give me a call."

Lou Ann cracked open the water bottle, took a long swig, and headed to Moreno's office.

Lou Ann rapped on Moreno's office door.

"Enter," he droned.

She opened the door to find Joe Moreno man-sprawled in his office chair.

'Shut the door."

She raised her eyebrows. She didn't take orders. She gave them. So she left the door open. If he wanted it shut, he'd have to get out of that chair and do it himself.

"All right. Have a seat," he said.

She sat in the same creaky chair.

"Look…Investigator…I already gave you the encrypted copy of Spark's video surveillance. Yet you're back here again. The press follows you, and hence is digging into me and my business. My business is taking a hit."

"I can understand that. But three young people who spent time in your club are dead. My job is to investigate their deaths. You can inform the press that you're doing everything possible to find out what happened. That will go a long way, for you, for me, and for your business."

Moreno leaned forward. "Look, I can't, nor can my bartenders, or my bouncer, have any control about shit that comes into my door. I can't have staff frisking anyone who comes into the club." He massaged his temples.

"I'm not recommending that you frisk anyone. I'm asking you to ramp up your awareness."

Moreno sucked in a breath. "All right. But what I need from you is to put it out there that we're taking these tragedies seriously, and that we're cooperating with the investigation, and yes, that we've increased our surveillance. I want people to feel secure here and to continue to have a good time at the club."

How disingenuous!

"I'll see what I can do to arrange a press conference with you and me."

Actually it was a pretty good idea. She could prime the media with just the right amount of information to cast a wider net.

"Yeah, that'll work. And I'll speak with my employees about sharpening their eyes."

"I'm glad we've made progress."

Except for the open door.

22

"Are you free for about fifteen minutes?" Ian asked Joanna.

Her heartbeat ramped up.

"Um…yes."

"Great. Come with me."

Joanna looked around. Everyone was busy.

Should she go? She already said yes. She couldn't back out now.

Ian cocked his head, and Joanna approached him.

Ian grinned. "Did you think…?"

Joanna shook her head. "No. No."

But yes, she wanted it to be yes to a clandestine meeting.

"I want you to come with me to check how Dylan is doing in the ICU."

"Oh, okay. I'd like to do that…with you. I mean you and I did take care of him."

Great! Just stumble around, babbling incoherently!

They exited the ED and walked to the elevator bank. It was only two floors up, but given her panic in the stairwell, Ian chose the elevator.

Ian punched the elevator button and the doors slid open seconds later without any passengers. They were all alone.

He gestured, "After you."

Joanna stepped in and moved to the back of the elevator.

Ian pressed the third floor, and also stood at the back of the elevator next to Joanna.

She had walked to the back out of reflex to press against the wall. He'd noticed.

Joanna quickly laughed to cover her odd behavior. "I'm used to a crowded elevator."

Ian grinned. "Me too."

The heat from his body crawled to her fingertips and up to her hand, and then to the back of her neck, and before it could expand further, the elevator doors opened.

People entered, surely thinking they weren't going to get off.

"Excuse us, please," Ian said.

He grasped her hand as if she would get lost in the crowd, and they stepped out.

The whoosh of the closing doors fanned her sweaty neck.

She couldn't do anything about her moist hands because it was too late. He'd surprised her.

They mutually slid their hands apart before anyone noticed.

"The ICU is down the hall and to the right."

Claudia had given her a whirlwind hospital tour during her interview, but she'd been so nervous that she hadn't been able to recollect where the ICUs were. The hospital had three of them, and they all looked alike to her.

Ian ran his hospital ID through the scanner allowing them to enter the ICU.

The beeping monitors and nurses weaving in and out of the sliding unit's rooms smacked Joanna in the chest.

She'd been in an ICU room, hiding behind sliding glass doors, waiting for Newell to find her remarkably alive and drag her way, and he could do that being a doctor—a doctor who hid in plain sight.

But that didn't happen. What did happen was that she masqueraded as Kaylee, without having any idea of who or where this Kaylee was. All Joanna recognized was that her pretend identity got her the ultimate ticket far away from her captor.

Ian glanced back at her.

"Dylan's in ICU 4. This way," he pointed.

He pushed the room's glass doors open and he and Joanna entered.

Dylan lay on the bed, a mask strapped over his mouth and nose with the rhythmic hiss of oxygen pumping into his lungs. IVs snaked around his arms and ended in IV pumps dispensing an array of bags of different sizes, while neon green waveforms blipped a loud staccato on the monitors affixed over his head. A clip squeezing his index finger displayed his blood oxygen saturation, and from what Joanna observed, Dylan's oxygen level was thankfully holding steady and acceptable. A Foley catheter tube dumped amber urine into the attached bedside container with its blue-striped hashmarks measuring every drop.

From Joann's quick assessment, Dylan was holding his own.

Mr. And Mrs. Greer, who'd remained at their son's side from the moment he arrived in the ED, got up from their chairs.

They glommed onto Joanna first.

Mrs. Greer hugged her. "You were so kind to us bringing us coffee, but most important, you sat with us. You could've just delivered the coffee and walked out, but you didn't. Thank God for you. We're going to write a letter to Administration."

"Thank you so much, but that's not necessary."

"We know," Mr. Greer said.

'Oh, and Dr. Hottman, we want to thank you for taking care of Dylan, and thank both of you for coming to check on him," Mrs. Greer said. "You diagnosed him right away, he's already improving, and we are grateful to you."

"I'm glad Dylan is improving," Ian said.

Ian was especially gracious since he came in second in recognition. But she didn't save Dylan. That was on Ian, and she'd emphasize that to him later. He'd been here years, whereas this was only her second day. Mini-ouch! But her job, as she saw it, was to not only care for the patient, but for the whole family. She didn't expect plaudits, but they nevertheless brightened her day.

Holistic care was a nursing tenet, but it was her family—Lou Ann, Harry, and Kaylee, not to mention Isabelle, and Joley Kay—who taught her about a kind of unconditional family love that she'd never experienced before.

Dylan looked up past his CPAP mask and gave Joanna and Ian a thumbs-up.

Ian mirrored Dylan's gesture. "Back at you!"

Joanna smiled and tapped the foot of Dylan's bed. "Keep up the good work!"

"We're going to keep an eye on you!" Ian teased.

Dylan's face creased into a half-smile underneath the oxygen mask.

Dylan's parents sighed with relief.

Joanna caught Dylan's gaze "We're going to leave and let you rest." She then looked at Mr. and Mrs. Greer. "And that goes for you too. You need rest."

"Will do," Mr. Greer said.

Joanna and Ian waved to Dylan and to his parents, pushed open the glass doors to Dylan's ICU cubicle, and Ian then closed the doors behind them revealing a woman in scrubs standing there.

"Hi, Janet," Ian said. He looked at Joanna. "This is Dr. Janet McCall, the ICU specialist. She's one of the best of those who are in charge of the medical care in the ICU."

"It's nice to meet you, Joanna. How do you like the ED?"

"I'm liking it a lot so far. But I'm still on orientation, day two."

"Wow, I wouldn't have guessed you're a newbie from your notes."

"You read them?"

"Of course. I read everyone's contemporaneous notes, and yours were not only thorough, but helpful." Janet smiled at Ian. "And I read yours too."

"Gee, thanks."

"As you see, Dylan is improving. I haven't needed to intubate him because he's holding his own. His blood gases are good, and his pulse ox has remained stable. Urine output is adequate, vitals have been rock solid, and he's been afebrile. The LP you did has returned consistent with a viral meningitis with 7K WBCs, with predominantly lymphocytes and neutrophils, and the bacterial cultures so far show no growth. Protein and glucose returned normal. Thanks for doing the LP early on and before antibiotics were started. I've since switched him to Acyclovir. His white count is down to seventeen thousand."

"I'm glad," Ian said.

"You should be," Janet replied.

Ian nodded to Joanna. "I had some help." Then added, "We'll be off. Back to home base."

"It's nice to meet you, Janet."

"Same here, and if you ever consider leaving the ED…"

"Thanks, but I'll stick with the ED."

Ian and Joanna waved to Janet and exited the ICU.

"Good choice."

"I think so too. And like you said, back to home base."

23

Lou Ann parked in front of the out-of-place seventies-styled row of one-story apartments.

They still existed?

Seminole had never been in her assigned sector.

But for an older—much older—building, it was well maintained and appeared to be recently painted, plus the added landscaping gave it an upgraded look. It was the boxy, "Mike Brady" architecture that gave it away. Then again, it was probably more solidly built.

Lou Ann retrieved the piece of paper Moreno gave her with the bouncer's address, knowing she would've eventually tracked it down. But It was faster this way.

Yes, she'd arrived at the correct address.

She exited her vehicle and approached apartment six.

A yellow ceramic flowerpot with a kaleidoscope of zinnias abutted the navy-blue painted door.

Strange for a bouncer and wrestler.

A Ford F150 truck hogged the white-painted parking space outside the apartment, and it screamed "Gorilla George lives" here. A Toyota Camry was parked next to the truck. Even with the driver's seat pushed as far back as it could go, Gorilla George would not fit in that one.

Lou Ann knocked on the apartment door.

The door opened, revealing a young woman with her brown hair piled on her head in a loose bun and wearing what looked like red-heart-printed pajama bottoms and a red cotton camisole.

She eyed Lou Ann.

"May I help you?"

"I'm sorry. I must have the wrong apartment."

The woman put her hand against the door frame and leaned

against it. "Who are you looking for?"

She was about to say Gorilla George but thought better of it. "I'm with the Sheriff's Department and I'm looking for George."

"He's not here."

The woman pushed off the doorframe and began to shut the door when a deep voice called, "Who's at the door?"

The woman winced.

"Some woman who says she's from the Sheriffs Department."

"Oh, yeah?" The voice got closer.

"You got like a warrant or something?" the woman asked through the partially open door.

"Oh, no. I'm sorry. I'm not here for anyone." She forgot to introduce herself. "I'm Lou Ann Jasinski, Homicide and Death Investigator."

"Well, there ain't nobody dead here either way."

A hulk of a man with his wavy blonde hair teasing his shoulders loomed behind the woman, making her look childlike.

"Chas, you can back away now. It's okay. Ah…Ms. Jasinski…if that's okay?"

"Yes, that's fine."

"Joe texted me that you'd be by." He beckoned to Lou Ann. "Come in."

Lou Ann stepped into a sparsely furnished but clean living room. Less was more.

A brown leather couch, and a matching leather recliner flanked a glass-topped coffee table. A 52-inch flatscreen TV was mounted on the opposite wall.

On the wall behind the couch, built-in shelving spanned beyond the length of the couch, and gleaming trophies lined the bottom shelves, while three big fat bejeweled belts showcased the top shelf. A giant could wear those belts, but then she eyed George, and those could only fit him. Giant George was a better name for him.

"Wow! Those are awesome," Lou Ann said.

"The trophies are from high school wrestling, and the belts are from my heavyweight championships."

"Another one is on the way," Chas announced proudly.

George shrugged. "Yeah, well."

Chas squeezed George's massive bicep with both hands. 'My champ!"

"Please, have a seat," George said.

Lou Ann sat on the couch while George squeezed into the recliner as if it was an airline seat.

"Can I get you a drink?"

Lou Ann paused. She was on an interview mission, not on a social one.

"No thank you."

"It's about to be a scorcher again. We've got bottles of cold water. Hey Chas, get the investigator a bottle." George looked at Lou Ann. "You can take it to go."

"Okay."

The heat actually was oppressive.

"Sure. Thank you, Chas."

"It's Chastity. He's the only one who calls me, Chas."

"I apologize, Chastity."

"I'll be back with the water."

"You'll have to excuse her. She does have a sweet side once she lowers her barrier."

Chastity reminded her of Kaylee and her long-ago walls.

"I met her when she was a waitress at Carousel before it became Spark. I stayed on to help front my wrestling. Wrestling is my true love. Bouncing is just a job. Chas...Chastity...felt uncomfortable around Joe, so she quit."

"How did he make her uncomfortable?"

Chastity was the one to ask, but for the moment, she wanted to continue building a good rapport with George. Plus, she unexpectedly liked him.

"He was too touchy-feely. I told him to knock it off. Never happened again, per Chas, but she walked out of there. She's happier working at the ring as an announcer. Not the girly ones walking around. They refused to hire her until they got exposed to her loud and commanding voice. These days no one says a thing about her being a woman. Now, full disclosure, she got one speeding ticket, and a parking one. So she's a bit sensitive."

"I'm not here for that."

"She knows that now. And don't worry. She'll warm up to you. We both obviously heard about the young people who were at the club and died later. I wish I could help, but I can't explain it. I'm dumbfounded too."

"Did you notice two young women stumbling around?"

George sighed. "I've seen that a lot. The bartenders are pretty good at cutting people off. But alcohol affects people differently. Two drinks for some are nothing, but for others, and pardon me, especially like women, two drinks are too much."

"Have you noticed whether a lot more customers were stumbling around so to speak?"

"It's summer. It's college kids."

"So, yes?"

"Yes."

"Have you noticed anyone strange coming into the club? Perhaps someone who's not a regular?"

"Hmmm, I recognize the frequent flyers. And I never let anyone in who was already overtly high or inebriated because that's asking for more trouble. But there was a guy on Sunday night who was older than the usual. Late twenties I would guess. I remember him because of his attitude. You know I card everyone." George laughed. "I'd even card you. But I grabbed him by his shirt because he didn't stop when I told him to. That's another thing…come to think of it…he was wearing a blue button-down shirt and dress pants—not typical club stuff, but each to his own. I do remember grabbing him. But he flashed his ID and I was satisfied that he was well past 21."

"Did you see him leave?"

"Yeah."

"Do you recall approximately what time? Club closing? Mid-closing?"

"Not at the end of the night. In fact, he didn't seem to stay long."

"Did he leave alone?"

"Yeah. Same way he came in."

"He wasn't with a bunch of guys or a date?"

"Not that I recall."

Chastity arrived with two cold bottles of water.

"Here you go."

"Thanks."

Chastity sat on the far end of the couch.

"Sorry I was cranky earlier. No disrespect intended. It's just that you're with the Sheriff's Department. I thought maybe he or I done something wrong."

"No."

"Yeah, I know you're here because of those kids dying. Tragic."

"It is. I understand you no longer work at Spark."

"Nope. Not since Moreno took over. Just became a different place. He was too touchy-feely. Didn't grab any private areas, but would touch my shoulder. Invade my personal space. Plus, he paid crap and would ask about tips, which in my book was none of his business He did that with Melissa, and she quit too. Now I'm more than happy working at wrestling nights."

"I hear you're really good with that."

"It makes a big difference when you do something you enjoy Waitressing wasn't for me. It is for some. But now I can pay my bills, plus I just bought a new car. And I was excited and had no idea I was speeding—not bad, but over the speed limit. I'm going to pay the ticket."

"That's fair. So, Chastity, when you were at Spark, did you notice any customers who seemed strange?"

"I used to deal with the occasional strange guy, but overall the club-goers were there for a good time and they were pretty decent with tips. But now that I really think about my time there, I remember the time I walked into Moreno's office and he yelled at me to get out. There was some guy in his office and they were arguing. I backed out. After that Moreno was constantly in my face. It wasn't worth it anymore."

"Do you recall what the argument was about and who was in the office?"

"Something about the guy demanding that Moreno pay some bill. It was early on, when Moreno bought the place and apparently owed some money. He did a lot of changes. That all costs."

"Hmmm. Had you seen that guy in the office or at the club before?"

"Nope. I didn't get a good look at him since I left quickly. He looked maybe younger than Moreno, but not too young."

"Did you see him leave?"

"No, because I got busy waiting tables. But Moreno did come out of his office later and was sugar-sweet to me even apologizing for yelling at me. He did say the guy was a real ass and that he got the better of him. I said okay and finished the night. I quit the following week. Never looked back."

Lou Ann had come to interview George, but it was Chastity who gave her a treasure trove of information.

"Thank you both for talking with me."

"I hope you can find out what happened to those young people. Maybe it was a fluke, but maybe not," George said.

"Ditto," Chastity added.

George pushed out of the recliner. "I'll be right back."

He returned and handed Lou Ann two tickets. "These are tickets to my wrestling match Wednesday night. Bring a guest."

"Thanks."

And Lou Ann knew the perfect plus-one, Harry.

"I hope to see you there."

"And I'll be announcing," Chastity said.

"A double entertaining night."

Lou Ann stood. "Thanks again for your time, and for the tickets. And the water."

Lou Ann handed George and Chastity her cards. "Feel free to call me if you think of anything else."

George and Chastity walked her to the door.

Lou Ann got into her vehicle, took a refreshing sip of water, and fanned her two tickets.

Harry's going to love this.

24

Joanna caught up on her nursing notes in time for the next shift.

"All right, let's huddle for the change of shift report," Claudia announced.

The outgoing team gathered with the incoming one.

Ian moved next to Joanna, and his hand whisked against hers.

The buzzing among the groups kept them from noticing his gesture, nevertheless he took a step sideways, but not a big one.

"People! Let's quiet down, please," Claudia called above the chattering staff.

The ED went silent for a moment.

The care plans for the remaining patients were solidified.

Then Dylan's journey from the ED to the ICU came up.

"Joanna," Claudia said.

It was only her second day—second-day orientation. No one noticed her at report yesterday, but today all eyes were on her. One-on-one conversations she could handle. But the last time she had to speak in front of a crowd was when she sat on that courtroom witness seat in front of all those people and the media. It sapped all her strength. She never wanted to speak in front of another crowd again, and now this. She suddenly longed for yesterday's anonymity.

Joanna ran her tongue around the inside of her mouth hoping for a modicum of moisture so she could speak, and hopefully using intelligent words—actually any comprehensible words would suffice. Heat spread to her earlobes.

She cleared her throat and glanced at Ian with an SOS plea. He nodded a "you can do it" response. She couldn't back out now, because everyone was waiting especially and most important, Claudia.

After a final deep breath, she began her summary of Dylan's care.

Her first words were shaky, but then they smoothed out to a concise, professional account. The team members clung onto every word, nodding. She'd finished!

Ian smiled and nodded.

His recap came next.

His experience carried him without a hitch.

"All right. That's it. See you all in the morning," Claudia said.

Joanna headed to the locker room.

Ian caught up with her. "Hey, wait a minute. We're going to take the stairwell. Are we still on?"

"Umm. Yes. I'll meet you at the ED exit door."

"Sounds like a plan."

"Dr. Hottman. Joanna. I need to speak with you," Claudia said behind them.

Oh, no. She's going to warn us to stop any show of romantic interest.

Ian and Joanna turned to face her.

"Administration just called me. I need to see both of you in private. Let's go to the conference room down the hall."

It's only my second day and already I've broken rules. Here goes the first black mark next to my name.

"Sure," Ian said.

Joanna's heart rate took flight. She simply nodded. And she was relieved to know her presentation was well received.

Ian and Joanna stepped into the conference room and Claudia followed and then closed the door.

Sit? Stand? Walk the virtual plank? What to do next? She chose to stand since no one else sat down.

"I'll keep this brief. You'll be receiving a letter from Administration."

God! I'm being fired before I even started.

Claudia continued, "Mr. and Mrs. Greer have written a lovely letter to Administration commending both of you for Dylan's care, and, Joanna in particular for your kindness to them at a particularly difficult time for them. I wanted to relay that to you both in person first."

This didn't have to do with her and Ian after all.

"And Joanna, you did an excellent job for being in the spotlight." Claudia smiled. "I'll see you both tomorrow."

Claudia left the room.

"*Whew!* I thought she was going to say something else."

Ian chuckled. "Me too."

"That's certainly a great way to end the shift," Joanna said.

"It's not over yet. You told me you would meet me at the exit door."

"I did."

Joanna sprang to her locker. The day shift staff, including Shelly, were gone, and she had the locker room to herself.

She did a victory dance before changing out of her scrubs and into jeans and a summery floral blouse. She traded her work clogs for sandals and gave the locker door a happy swing shut, and then stopped in the locker room bathroom, looked in the mirror, and removed the band around her ponytail.

No! That's too much.

Joanna swept her hair back into the ponytail.

She looked in the mirror again.

Okay go.

She rushed to the women's locker room door and screeched to a halt before walking out and headed for the exit door where Ian waited, wearing jeans, a pullover shirt, and sport shoes.

They eyed each other and grinned.

"You ready to go?"

"Yes."

His cheeks pinked at the obvious answer.

Ian swiped his hospital ID at the stairwell door, and it flashed green.

He opened the door, waited for Joanna to pass through, and then he entered the stairwell taking care to ease the door until it clicked shut.

"Didn't want it to slam like last time."

"Thank you."

She stopped avoiding him because of his reputation, but it was her past "reputation" that she'd make sure didn't surface.

Joanna held onto the railing while Ian walked next to her, matching every step down to the ground garage level.

"I'll walk you to your car. Where are you parked?"

"Three rows down on this level."

The parking garage was well lit, and the employees had the first two levels. But Joanna always carried a flashlight in her purse and had her cell handy in case she had to call 911 and her car keys always ready. Lou Ann and Harry taught her that. Harry had even schooled her in defensive techniques. But having Ian with her calmed her mind.

"It's the blue Honda Civic right there."

"Okay."

Joanna clicked the car's remote, and the car beeped and the headlights flashed.

"Thank you, Ian."

"You're welcome."

He opened her car door.

"Ummm…"

The glib Dr. Hottman was suddenly reaching for words.

Joanna got into her car and sat.

But before she could close the door, Ian leaned closer.

"Do you maybe want to go to dinner sometime…when we're both off?"

"My orientation ends Friday, so I have the weekend."

"That works. I have Saturday off—a rarity."

"Saturday would be fine."

"Want to trade cells?" he asked.

"Ummm, sure."

They tapped their phones and exchanged them.

At least they both spoke iPhone.

Joanna entered her contact info in his while he put his in hers.

"Trade you," he joked.

They fumbled cells like an odd kiss.

Ian closed her door and Joanna lowered her window.

"See you tomorrow."

"I'm counting on it."

Joanna drove away with Ian in her rearview mirror.

She couldn't wait to tell Kaylee!

25

Lou Ann drank the last of the bottled water George and Chastity gave her and plunked the empty bottle into her vehicle's holder. Her car's phone screen rang. It was Harry.

"Hey, Harry."

"I'll be real late tonight because I'm still writing up the shootout report."

"Are you okay?"

"Yeah, as much as I can be. A kill is a kill."

"I'm sorry."

"So am I."

Lou Ann decided to not mention the wrestling tickets yet. They both needed a night out.

"I'm on my way home. I'll pick up Joley Kay."

"Give her a goodnight kiss for me."

"I'm sure you'll sneak in and kiss her while she sleeps. But I'll be awake to tuck you in."

"I'll need that."

"I've got Suzy on the other line. Bye for now."

"Later."

Lou Ann answered her car phone.

"Hi, Suzy. I'm so sorry I'm late."

"No worries. Joanna came over and picked up Joley Kay and Isabelle. They were, as always, a pleasure."

"Thank you."

"I'll see them both in the morning. You and Harry rest. I saw both of you on those press conferences. I'm beyond relieved that Harry's all right. Both of you risk your lives."

"I appreciate that, and I appreciate you."

"Go rest. You both need it."

Lou Ann ended the call.

For once, she wanted to pick up Joley Kay and Isabelle. She'd give Isabelle a hug and a biscuit. Isabelle understood her schedule and her love for Lou Ann stood unconditional, but in time her daughter might not understand.

Guilt. Guilt. Guilt.

Joley Kay was unplanned, but nonetheless fully embraced and loved.

She'd rock her sweet daughter tonight, grateful to do that.

Joanna bounced Joley Kay in her arms, the baby's giggles encouraging Joanna to bounce her some more.

"Who's such a big girl!" Joanna cooed.

Isabelle barked.

"You too!"

Joanna reached into Isabelle's doggy canister, plucked out a biscuit, and tossed it toward Isabelle's wide-open mouth. The dog caught the heavenly treat.

"I'll fill your water bowl since Suzy already fed you dinner."

Isabelle sighed with her eyes.

"You just ate."

The dog lay down and rested her snout on her front paws.

"Oooo-kay."

Joanna tossed Isabelle another biscuit.

"Suzy fed you too. Time for your bath and then night-night."

The baby frowned.

"Oh, come on. It'll be fun. I'll get Ducky and Squeaky Bear."

Joley Kay smiled.

"You melt my heart when you do that."

The baby's grin got even bigger.

With the baby snug in her arms, Joanna grabbed one of the pink fluffy towels from the linen closet and proceeded into the bathroom.

After making sure the bath water was just-right warm, she tossed in Ducky and Squeaky into the water and lowered Joley Kay into the bath ring.

"You love your bath buddies, don't you?"

Joley Kay happily splashed while splattering Joanna.

"I need a shower tonight, anyway."

Joley Kay splashed some more.

Joanna laughed. "You go, baby girl!"

Isabelle toddled into the bathroom.

"Oh, you want a bath too? Come closer," she teased.

Isabelle toddled closer.

The baby slapped the water and the spray hit Isabelle's head.

"Doggy! Joley Kay called.

Isabelle barked and the baby laughed.

"She's a handful, huh?"

Isabelle barked again.

Joley Kay dunked Ducky, who popped right back up, causing Joley Kay to giggle. She then hugged both bath toys.

Joanna got the baby shampoo off the edge of the tub, placed a washcloth over the baby's eyes, and sudsed the baby's fine hair, and then rinsed the suds away.

She removed the cloth.

"All done!"

She lifted Joley Kay out of the bathtub ring and wrapped her in the pink towel.

Isabelle gave her a big doggy grin.

"We did a good job."

Isabelle led them to the nursery, where Joanna dried and diapered the baby. She kissed Joley Kay's belly, which made the baby giggle harder, and dressed her in her so-soft baby jammies.

"Jo-Jo," the baby cooed.

Joanna picked the baby up and hugged her to her chest, her eyes misting.

Would she ever be a mother? Was she mother material? Her mother was a failure. And she'd been infected countless times. And even though Dr. Turner, the gynecologist she'd trusted, assured her she was rid of all the sexually transmitted infections that she'd suffered after the multitude of scummy men who invaded her while she was in captivity, Joanna feared that the damage left her too scarred to conceive in the future.

Joley Kay wrapped her tiny arms around Joanna's neck.

Joanna sucked in a sniffle. "I love you too."

Lou Ann walked into the house.

"Hey, I'm home!"

Joanna bounded into the living room while holding Joley Kay, with Isabelle hot on their heels.

"You're right on time! Suzy fed Joley Kay and we just finished our bath!"

Lou Ann fought to freeze her smile.

Joanna not only picked up Joley Kay, but Joanna bathed her and put her in her jammies. There wasn't anything left for Lou Ann to do.

"That's great," she forced out.

Joley Kay squirmed in Joanna's arms and waved her hands toward Lou Ann.

"Mama! Mama!"

"Oh, my!"

And she was jealous!

Joanna released the baby to Lou Ann, who rained kisses on her daughter's freshly shampooed head.

"Should I wait for Harry to heat up leftovers?" Joana asked

"No. Harry told me he was going be very late because he has a lengthy and complicated report to file. He was involved in a drug takedown where two of the international drug traffickers were shot and killed, and two, who were injured, are in custody."

"Oh, my God. I had no idea. I haven't turned on the TV or listened to the radio. And I was at the hospital all day. No TV. I...I...am shocked."

"So am I. But he was with other feds and Coast Guard. One suspect drew a weapon and it happened quickly. He's okay. It was a massive drug bust."

"I get so scared for both of you. You're my everything."

"Hey. It's all right. We both fight bad actors, but we're alert and intuitive. Harry's been involved in assignments that he couldn't divulge, but at least the media reported what went on today instead of us being the dark."

Joanna hugged Lou Ann over Joley Kay.

"I'm so glad you're home, and I'm relieved Harry will come home tonight."

Lou Ann stroked Joanna's head.

"Me too."

Harry leaned back in his chair and stared at his computer screen. He and his fellow agent were the last two in the field office, except for the cleaning crew who rustled while emptying trash cans full of candy bar wrappers, cardboard take-out food trays, and paper bags."

He winced at the booming back and forth zzzz of vacuum cleaners.

Harry ran his palm over his forehead and combed his fingers through his hair.

"I can't take any more of this," Ranger, Harry's fellow agent who'd been on the boat bust with him, yelled above the vacuum's growling. "I'm out of here," he announced.

Harry raised his hand while still staring at his screen. "See you tomorrow."

"Yeah, later."

It was down to Harry and the cleaning crew.

Just do it!

Harry hovered his fingers over the keyboard and then started tapping as if he was composing a concerto.

Faster and faster. Words became summaries.

The vacuum cleaner sucked in its last piece of carpet just in time for Harry to finish his report.

Harry raised his hands in a bizarre victory. There were no victors today. But he was done.

He waved to the cleaning crew and headed to the exit, scanned his ID, and walked into the summer evening.

He'd take the sound of crickets over the vacuum cleaner.

Harry sucked in a deep breath and blew out the air from his lungs. The day's bust had gone bizarrely sideways and was still stuck in his head.

He needed to get home, kiss Lou Ann and hug Joanna. And then he'd stare at his sleeping daughter and thank God that he could do all of them.

Harry pulled into the driveway. The lights were on, and Lou Ann peeked through open curtains.

He cut the engine and waved to Lou Ann, who disappeared from her perch and reappeared at the opened front door.

"I told you I'd be up," Lou Ann said.

"That you did."

Harry kissed Lou Ann, and she pulled him into the house.

He wrapped his arms around her and rested his head on her shoulder.

They remained embraced as one—his heart chugging against hers.

"Joanna asleep?" he whispered in her ear.

"Don't think so. She's in her room. Let me warm up dinner for you."

Harry lifted his head and slowly disengaged from Lou Ann.

"I hope you didn't wait for me to eat dinner."

"We didn't, but I planned to sit with you, and I could go for a snack."

"I'd like that."

That way he wouldn't be alone with his thoughts.

Harry headed into kitchen and plopped into his wooden chair, and that wooden chair was a thousand times more comfortable than his ergonomic office one, because this one came with the woman he adored. She beat Ranger hands down.

Lou Ann set a plate of warmed grilled chicken, mashed potatoes, and green beans in front of him.

"Hurray for microwaves," Harry said.

"Sorry that it might be a bit dry."

Harry loaded a forkful and shoveled it into his mouth.

He nodded. "Mmmm."

It was dry, but it didn't matter.

Lou Ann opened the fridge and took out a cheesecake.

"Ooooh. You're killing me!"

They hesitated.

Lou Ann set the dessert on the table.

"You don't need to finish that."

"Yes I do, and then we can end on a sweet note...because I could use a sweet ending."

Harry finished his dinner, and then they shared a fat slice of cheesecake.

Joanna entered the kitchen, went straight to Harry, and hugged him.

"Thank you."

"I didn't know."

"At least I didn't ruin your day."

"I'm beyond grateful that you didn't."

"Have a seat and have cheesecake with us," Harry said.

Joanna slid into a kitchen chair. "Don't mind if I do."

"How was your second day?" Harry asked.

Joanna looked at Harry and then at Lou Ann. Given that both had a beyond hard day, especially Harry, should she even broach the subject of her and Ian?

Harry set his fork next to his slice of cheesecake while the twinkle in his eyes invited Joanna to elaborate.

Lou Ann cocked her head toward Joanna, her eyebrows raised to further prompt her.

Neither Lou Ann nor Harry took another bite of cheesecake.

Joanna stabbed her fork into her dessert, loaded it with a forkful of sweet, creamy cheese, and shoved it into her mouth, giving herself time to think about her response.

But Lou Ann and Harry continued to stare at her.

How much should she share? Perhaps the best course was to simply say that she was gradually becoming more efficient, which was true. But the increasing spark between her and Ian wasn't something she was ready to share.

She swallowed and then balanced her empty fork on the side of her plate.

"My second shift went much better than my first."

She was about to reveal that no one died, but she quickly quashed that because of Harry's tragic day. It didn't seem right.

Harry winked. "We're waiting."

He wasn't going to give her a pass, and Lou Ann clearly backed him in this contest.

"I'm…uh…making a lot of friends, and everyone's been very helpful."

"Mmm, " Harry responded, but obviously not convinced that it was a complete recount of her day.

And he'd be right.

She could never hide from Harry.

Joanna toyed with her cheesecake.

"The doctor that I've been working with—Dr. Hottman—we took care of a critically ill teen—who has since significantly improved—and we each were given a letter that his parents sent to Administration, who then congratulated both of us!"

She stumbled through the true facts but left out her and Ian's lunches and their upcoming date. She'd tell Kaylee first and ask how to divulge that to Harry and Lou Ann, and she needed to get that done before Saturday night's dinner date with Ian.

"Wow! That's great!" Lou Ann gushed. "We're so proud of you!"

"Ditto. And I'm thrilled for you and this, um, Dr. Hottman," Harry added.

"Yes, we were both pleasantly surprised."

Joanna almost choked on her cheesecake because "pleasantly surprised" perfectly described her and Ian's romance.

Joanna got up and loaded her plate into the dishwasher.

She kissed both Lou Ann's and Harry's cheeks.

"Good night. I'm off to bed. I want to rest up for tomorrow."

Joanna walked out of the kitchen and out of Lou Ann's and

Harry's sight, and then skipped into her bedroom and closed the door.

She grabbed her cell, bounced on the bed, and called Kaylee.

Sleep would have to wait.

26

Harry gently lowered the crib's side rail, leaned over, and kissed sleeping Joley Kay on the top of her freshly shampooed head.

"Sleep tight my little one," he whispered.

Joley Kay stirred beneath her pink blanket. Her long baby lashes flickered and her tiny lips crooked into a smile. She let out a half sigh and wiggled back into a deep sleep.

He eased the side rail up till it clicked into position, and then gazed at his slumbering daughter.

Harry sniffled quietly, while he blinked away the tears welling in his eyes.

What if he didn't come home? Would his baby daughter remember him? He sucked in his bottom lip. No. She would only know him through photos or stories about him.

But he couldn't or didn't want to change who he was—what he did. He'd rescued trafficked children—some who were barely older than his own precious daughter. Now they were safe. But the drugs that were pouring in killed scores of young people whose parents would no longer be able to kiss or hug their child—their child forever no matter the age. They'd have to bury them.

He and his team had taken out two and seized the other two on that drug-filled boat. But that was only four out of an army of many.

Harry adjusted Joley Kay's blanket then turned to tiptoe out of the nursery when he saw Lou Ann watching them from the open doorway. They'd always kept the nursery door open so they could hear their daughter with their own ears instead of relying solely on a baby monitor. He trusted his hearing more than the swish and crackle of a mini-loudspeaker.

"Are you okay?" she asked.

"Yeah. You?"

"I'm okay."

"Now that we're all okay, let's call it the end of the day."

"I'm with you."

Lou Ann spooned with Harry, covering him with her arms. His chest slowly expanded and retracted.

She remained silent because there wasn't anything left to say.

What mattered was he was alive within her embrace.

"I visited George today, aka Gorilla George, the bouncer at Spark, thinking I'd get a decent interview, but it was his girlfriend who gave me meaty tidbits about the present owner."

"You don't say. That's good."

"I thought so too. And while I was there I noticed a championship wrestling belt displayed on a shelf along with multiple trophies. He wrestles in between his bouncer gig. And his girlfriend is actually an announcer."

"That's unusual, but if she's got it, then she's got it. I don't mean to be sexist, but I've only seen   ring girls."

"I've got a surprise for you!"

"I'm really tired tonight, but I'll give you a rain check."

"I'll take the rain check, but that's not the surprise."

Lou Ann disengaged from Harry, sat up, opened her nightstand drawer, and retrieved the tickets.

She nudged Harry, and he rolled over.

She waved the tickets.

"How would you like to go to a wrestling match tomorrow night, courtesy of Gorilla George, who'll be wrestling to maintain his title?"

Harry popped back to life, his eyes huge.

"Would I? Hell, yeah!"

"Then it's a date?"

"Yes! It couldn't come at a better time since the shootout is under investigation."

Lou Ann tossed the tickets back into the nightstand drawer and jumped back into bed.

"We both need a night out."

Harry tucked Lou Ann against his chest.

"Thank you," he said.

"Don't mention it. But I'm still going to claim that rain check."

"I'm good for it, babe."

Joanna FaceTimed Kaylee. Kaylee answered almost immediately, and her face popped up on the Joanna's cell.

"Hey, you! Looking good," Kaylee cheered.

"Nah. My makeup is melting as we speak. But you look bright-eyed."

"I have the advantage of the day just beginning here."

"Ian asked me out," Joanna blurted.

"Fantastic! I knew that was going to happen! Woo-hoo!"

"I get excited. Then I get scared. Then I go back to excitement. It's such a seesaw."

"I'll be excited for you. So how did it happen?"

"He bought me lunch yesterday because I didn't bring any money. So tody, I bought him lunch. But something happened on the way to the cafeteria. Ian led me into the stairwell, and when the door slammed, I had a full-blown panic attack. I was back in that cell as the door slammed shut and then the locks clicked into place."

Kaylee's face went pale.

"I'm sorry to have brought it up."

Kaylee shook her head. "No. We need to talk about it. I don't have to cope with door-slamming here because our stairs are long and winding. But I still go there in my mind and then I flick away the fetid memory."

"I was doing the same until the hospital stairwell. He grabbed my sweaty hand, and he offered to go back and take the elevator. But I really didn't want to back away from him. So I claimed I was claustrophobic, which is true in tight spaces. Ian held my hand step by step, and even told me he was afraid of spiders."

"Sounds like a keeper to me. So then what happened?"

"We had a nice lunch together, and then we both received a commendation from Administration regarding a letter from a patient's parents about Ian's and my care of an ill teen."

"That's awesome!"

"We were both ecstatic. Then after the shift was over, we took the stairwell to the parking garage, and this time he made sure the door didn't slam. He walked to my car, and then he asked me out for Saturday, when we're both off. Umm…I didn't talk to Harry about it, but you know Harry, he can always read us."

"How true."

"So, I can hide my upcoming date from Lou Ann and maybe Harry, but the most difficult part is hiding my past from Ian, especially on our first date."

"Not necessary on a first date. You don't have to divulge that until you're ready. Keep the conversation light. You're just getting to know each other. Just take a deep breath. Wear something attention-getting but not too sexy. You'll do fine. He sounds wonderful, and I can't wait to meet him."

"I never trusted men until I met Ian."

"I was afraid that might happen to me in Greece with Demetrios, but I knew from the moment I left the airport with him, that he was a different kind of man. And I was right, just like you know Ian is right for you, and although the invitation to meet him is there, I can tell from your voice and your face that I don't need to meet him to know he's a good man. And there are good men. Take Harry for example. Lou Ann tried, but couldn't quit him."

"Thank you. I can always count on you."

Kaylee laughed. "You'll never get rid of me."

"Oops! I gotta go. Ian's texting me."

"Answer it!"

Kaylee ended her side of FaceTime and then Joanna did.

Her heart pounded and her mouth went dry.

She widened her eyes and read his text.

"Hey, are you up? Sorry so late, but thinking about Sat night."

She swirled her finger over her cell's keys. Did he want to cancel?

She took three deep breaths. She could always claim she'd not seen the text till morning. But she'd be up all night stringing a lie. What to do? What to do?

Then she typed, "Yes," and then held her breath.

He responded, "Great."

She blew out the pent-up air in her lungs and stared at his green-background texts and her one light gray response.

"6 p pick up k?"

"K."

No! No! No! He can't come here.

"Talk tomorrow."

She had to think of something before then. She needed to have Ian to herself before exposing the circumstances of her living arrangement, for which she was immensely grateful. But still…

"Need Zs"

"Gotchya. Night."

"Night."

But Zs wouldn't come easy tonight.

27

Harry bounded into the nursery with the biggest smile he could muster, which wasn't difficult when he went over to Joley Kay, who grasped the side rail of her crib while bouncing up down on the squeaking pint-sized mattress.

"Look who's up!"

The baby giggled. "DaDa! DaDa!"

He lifted her over the side rail.

"Come here, my sunshine!"

She wrapped her arms around his neck, grazing the tips of his earlobes.

He bounced himself and her while she squealed happily in his ears.

"You need a diaper change, young lady."

He laid her on the changing table, whipped off her nighttime diaper, grabbed a baby wipe and cleaned her, and then put on a clean diaper. He'd become speedy at diaper changes because as Joley Kay grew, she learned to squirm more, but he was still too fast for her.

He waggled his brows. "I won!"

Harry blew raspberries on her belly.

She kicked her chubby legs and giggled.

"More? You got it."

Another round of belly raspberries.

She kicked some more, clearly hoping for an encore.

"Later. We need to get you dressed now, you and me. But you first."

With his freshly-diapered daughter in his arms, he walked over the closet, where Lou Ann hung Joley Kay's dresses on tiny padded hangers and arranged them by styles and weather changes.

"Your mommy is a super-duper organizer. How about I let you choose? Point away."

The baby flopped her hand.

"Good choice." He slid a sunflower print sundress off its hanger, sat her back in the crib, and managed to wrangle the little moving target. He pulled the sleep shirt up and off over her head and then slipped on the dress.

"Done!"

"I'll say," Lou Ann said from the doorway.

"I got up early so you could sleep in, and Joley Kay was already awake. So it worked out. I was happy to do it."

It did work out, because he'd slept fitfully. Besides, he craved spending time with his baby daughter. His meeting to review the firing of his weapon while on that drug boat was scheduled for this afternoon. On the upside, he had the morning off.

"Can you watch her while I quickly get dressed?"

"Sure."

Lou Ann picked up Joley Kay.

"Your daddy did a good job."

The baby smiled. "DaDa!"

Harry stuck his head back in. "I'm going to get dressed and then meet you both in the kitchen where I'll cook breakfast."

"Aren't you going to be late?"

"Nope."

Lou Ann cocked her brows.

"Have a review at one."

"Okay. Didn't know."

"That's because I didn't tell you last night."

"I can make breakfast."

"No. I said I would do it."

Joely Kay's eyes bobbed from Lou Ann to Harry, and then back to Lou Ann.

"I'm going to get dressed." He tapped the baby's nose. "Be right back."

He'd provided all the details in his file so Ranger and the two Coast Guard officers would have consistent information. They had no choice but to fire. Otherwise, they'd all be dead on that boat.

He nodded to himself. It was a mega drug bust. Two of the four perpetrators were dead, but he'd put the screws to the other two while they were cuffed and captive in the hospital and manage to obtain intel on other cartel smugglers. He had his methods. They'd given him tidbits. Mostly lies. But their loyalty would seal them behind bars.

Meanwhile, he'd take the too-rare opportunity to send Lou Ann and Joanna off with full bellies, and not let go of Joley Kay until he had to drop her off at Suzy's, and then spend the rest of his afternoon defending his actions.

On the upside, he'd surely be exonerated, and what's more, he and Lou Ann have ring-side seats at tonight's wrestling championship, courtesy of her sharp interview skills. Yeah, but she'd never jump the sheriff ship to the FBI one. Plus, they'd labored too hard to mend their relationship and weren't about to toss it away by working together—their collaborative effort in Greece notwithstanding—although ironically that was what brought them back together.

Harry dodged in and out of the shower and then dressed in shorts and a T-shirt like any other lucky man.

Lou Ann twirled while gently squeezing Joley Kay in her arms.

The baby giggled.

"Aren't you having the best morning! Daddy got you all ready for your day!"

"Da-Da," the baby cheered. And then she add, "Ma-Ma!"

"Yes, Da-Da and Ma-Ma love you very, very, very, much!"

Harry would do fine. He always did. She was proud of him, and she needed to tell him that before she left for the day.

Harry whistled. "Hey, kids! Breakfast is ready!"

"Woo! Let's go."

Joley Kay kicked.

"I'm hungry too."

Joanna came out of the bedroom and squinted. "Did I hear that right?"

"Yes, you did."

"Great, because I'm starved, and I have another big day ahead of me."

"That makes three of us."

Joley Kay squealed.

"Oh, I'm sorry. That makes four of us."

Isabelle bounded past them.

"I stand corrected. Five."

* * *

Lou Ann lowered Joley Kay into the highchair. Joanna kissed Joley Kay and then took her spot at the kitchen table.

"Gee, Harry. No mac and cheese for breakfast?" Joanna teased.

"Although that is my specialty, I've whipped up something breakfast-similar, Southwestern omelets with lots of cheese."

Lou Ann sneaked up behind Harry while he was cooking breakfast and nuzzled his neck.

"I'm so proud of you."

Harry laughed. "You haven't tasted my Southwestern omelets yet."

"Omelets aside, I can't wait until tonight."

"Not in front of the kids!"

Joanna snickered.

"I meant the wrestling championship tonight," Lou Ann said. "But the remainder of the night is negotiable."

Harry winked. "I'll put extra cheese on your omelet."

Plate after plate, Harry loaded each one with his omelets.

"Hey, these actually look and smell delicious," Joanna said.

"I second that," Lou Ann added between mouthfuls.

He cut up bite-sized pieces of a plain omelet with a smattering of cheese and set them on Joley Kay's favorite smiley-face baby plate. Then he sat next to her while Lou Ann flanked their daughter on the other side.

"Go ahead and eat your breakfast since you have to leave way before me today. I'll feed Joley Kay," Harry said.

The baby slapped her highchair tray.

Lou Ann grinned. "Looks like you're wanted."

Joley Kay opened her mouth wide like a baby bird.

Harry spooned the mashed-up omelet into the baby's mouth.

Half went down her throat while half squished out the corners of her puckered lips.

"That was pretty good," Lou Ann said.

"Yep. We're a work in progress, aren't we Joley Kay?"

"Mmmmm," she agreed.

"My review starts at one, but I should be done by five. Formalities take time and the top guys always want out by five. What time are we leaving tonight?"

"Eight."

"That works for me," Joanna said. "I should be home before then so I can stay with Joley Kay."

"Perfect," Lou Ann said.

Harry swallowed his forkful of omelet. "Works for everyone."

Joanna rubbed her belly. "Harry, the omelet was fabulous. It should even hold me over in case I don't get lunch."

Harry stood and retrieved a thermal lunch bag. "Just in case, there's a protein bar, an apple with cheese slices, and a bottle of water."

Joanna stood and kissed Harry on the cheek. "Thanks. It's a real treat having you around. I know everything will go well for you, and I'll be home in time for your and Lou Ann's night out. Wrestling, huh? Sounds awesome. I'm off." She hugged and kissed Lou Ann. "I know you have a packed day."

"I do, sweetheart."

Joanna grinned wide. "I still love when you call me that."

"And I'll never stop."

"Love you both and see you later."

Joanna bounded out the door with her backpack and lunch tote.

Her car engine vroomed into life, and the sound of her spinning tires faded.

Harry winked. "Paging Dr. Hottman?"

"She's come a long way. But I don't want to see her hurt. I saw that sparkle in her eyes before she bolted out the door."

"Neither do I. But we can't hold her back forever."

"I know."

"I don't want to hold you back today either."

"After this breakfast, I'm ready to go."

"I know," he parroted her.

<h1 style="text-align:center">28</h1>

Lou Ann sat in her vehicle, pulled out her notebook, and reviewed today's agenda. Organization was her strength professionally, but also her weakness at home. Joanna and Kaylee noted her "inflexibility" and her need for control—perfect traits for a sheriff's deputy and now a homicide and death investigator, but not so much at home.

Even Harry was freewheeling. Yet she struggled to be spontaneous. But she did have her moments like the wrestling match tonight. She'd never been to a wrestling contest. Never even seen one on TV. Initially she hesitated, but then accepted George's complimentary tickets. Yes, she was a work in progress.

Lou Ann revved the vehicle's engine. After learning about the details of Chastity quitting her waitressing job under Spark's new ownership, and the strange guy she witnessed who apparently was shaking down Joe Moreno surfaced, she decided to pay Moreno another visit. Surely he'd be thrilled to see her again.

She hadn't even made it to the first traffic light when her cell rang.

Since her cell was paired with her vehicle, all Lou Ann had to do was tap the incoming call on her vehicle's screen. Caller ID revealed it was from Barb, the medical examiner.

"Good morning, Barb. Do you have an update for me?"

"Toxicology for Gloria, Elizabeth, and now Tyler are pending at the lab. I realize that Gloria's untimely death is most time-sensitive for you and Assistant Chief Martinez, and especially for Gloria's mother, but I'm waiting on Gloria's vaginal semen analysis. I didn't detect any overt signs of rape. No abrasions. No bruising. No scratches. Her fingernails aren't broken, and I doubt any foreign DNA will be recovered from there. And she was fully dressed, including underclothing. No rips in her clothing either. So any activity as would be evidenced by still active sperm, would've been recent. What I'm getting at is, who was she intimate with before her death? I leave it to you to perhaps to narrow that field. By the way, Elizabeth had no evidence of recent sexual activity."

"I understand and thanks for the update. Gloria was seen stumbling alone on surveillance cameras, and the apartment manager confirmed that, plus then weirdly in person. I'll speak with Gloria's mother and with her friends again regarding who she was seeing. Her friends said that she had a recent breakup with Tyler, and he was at the club that night. Now they're both dead, and Elizabeth too. Neither Gloria nor Tyler—or anyone in their social circle—knew Elizabeth. She's an outlier, but their deaths are connected, and I need to find out how and why. Let me know when you get the results."

"Absolutely."

"And I'll keep you in the loop on my end. Together we'll get our answers."

"As always."

"I'm counting on that."

Lou Ann clutched the steering wheel. She'd forgo rehashing Gloria's fresh, tragic death with Daisy. Mothers were often kept in the dark about their grown daughter's life, and Glenda, understandably, would soon be on her heels about her niece's case. There were too many tentacles connecting all three deaths, and Lou Ann was only beginning to try to pull them apart to get to a common core, and that was a long process that ultimately might not provide a solution anytime soon …or she hated to admit it, but maybe not ever.

She renewed her original plan to revisit Joe Moreno and pulled into the too-familiar Spark parking lot and pulled in a space away from Moreno's car.

Lou Ann interlaced her fingers and pushed them forward in a warmup for another bout with Moreno now that she knew more about him. She especially wanted to ask him about the stranger accosting him in his office, but that would implicate Chastity, and Lou Ann didn't want to do that.

Ding-Ding! She was ready to enter Moreno's arena.

Lou Ann opened the unlocked front door and widened her eyes to adjust from the sunny outside to the club's cool dimness.

A woman wearing ripped jeans and a white midriff blouse Lou Ann had never seen before, strode toward Lou Ann with her loose blond hair tapping her bare shoulders.

She halted in front of Lou Ann blocking her progress.

"May I help you?" she demanded.

"I'm here to speak with Joe Moreno."

"He's busy."

"Tell him Investigator Lou Ann Jasinski is here to see him."

The woman turned her back on Lou Ann and yelled,"Hey, Joe! Someone's here to see you."

"We're not open!"

"Excuse me," Lou Ann said to the woman who was still intent in blocking her, so she walked around her.

Heel!

Moreno bolted out of his office.

"Investigator Jasininski, I've said and done everything that you've asked so far. But I have a business to run. I have nothing more to offer. You've spoken to my employees, and by now I'm sure you've tracked down George. I even gave you footage!" Moreno threw up his arms. "I'm done." He sucked in a deep breath and lowered his arms. "Look. This is a nightclub, and drugs happen. We can't frisk everyone, and drugs can easily be stashed in…uh…unconventional places."

That part was true.

Moreno lowered his voice. "I'm sorry."

Moreno turned, walked back into his office, and closed the door.

"I'll see you out," the woman said.

"That won't be necessary. I'm quite familiar with this place."

Lou Ann walked out the door and hurried around to the back door of Moreno's office, pressing her ear against the door.

Remarkably, she could make out the sound of papers rustling.

High heels click-clacked in the background. It had to be the same woman.

"Gillian! God dammit! I told you to lock the front door. What've she'd run into Maurice?"

Moreno slammed his desk.

"I'm sorry, Joe. I tried to stop her before Maurice showed up."

"You got damn lucky this time! Now, what are you going to do *now*, and going forward when we're here alone?"

"Lock the door."

"Yeah!"

"Good girl. Now open wide."

Open wide?

"One for you. Two for me."

"Oooh," the woman moaned.

Moreno clicked his tongue on the roof of his mouth.

"Good, huh?" a man's accented voice asked. "You like it pure, huh?"

Is that the heavy envelope that hit the desk?

More crinkling.

Footsteps approached the back door.

Lou Ann ducked back.

The footsteps retreated.

Lou Ann slowly exhaled through her nose.

Another envelope thwacked.

"For others."

A combination lock clicked twice, once, four times.

More rustling.

"Gracias, my friend. See you next month."

Moreno's office door closed.

Shit!

Lou Ann dodged around a corner.

A man swaggered to a Beemer that hadn't been there when she parked.

He walked to the driver's side, his face in perfect position.

She winced, and luckily a truck rumbled by, muting the click her cell's photo.

Got you!

29

"Congratulations to you and Ian," Shelly cheered.

"What?"

Everyone knows about us already?

"The letter Administration received from the young guy's parents. Awesome!"

"Oh. It was only my second day. Dr. Hottman is the one who deserves the applause."

"Okay. You completed all those nursing clinicals. It's not like you walked in here unqualified. Enjoy the praise."

"I did what any of us do every day. We take care of families. You would've done the same."

"It's not that we wouldn't do it. It's how you did it."

"Thanks. But today's another day."

Shelly playfully punched Joanna's shoulder. "Yee-haw."

Joanna shoved the thermal lunch tote into the break room fridge.

"Oh, you brought lunch today," Ian said behind her.

Joanna whipped around, nearly bumping noses with him.

"Harry packed it for me."

The words flew from her mouth.

"Harry? Who's Harry?"

"My uncle."

"Your uncle packs your lunch?"

"Yes. And he's awesome. I live with him and my Aunt Lou Ann."

There, she said it.

"I didn't mean it that way. He is awesome and he cares for you."

"He does, and he always has. He wanted to make sure I have an energy snack in case I don't have time for lunch."

"Smart guy."

"I'll share."

150

"I don't want you running out of energy."

Joanna winked. "Don't worry. I won't. Bring it on!"

"I plan to."

She and Ian hurried to check out rounds.

Joanna buzzed through her shift, and shared her lunch snack with Ian.

She kept looking at her watch and making sure it synched with the ED digital clock.

Bing. Her watch alarmed—ten minutes to go.

She whizzed into a seat at the computer and her fingers tapped across the keys while she completed the remaining shift notes.

"You're making me dizzy," Ian teased. "And you even shared your lunch snack with me."

"I need to get out of this hospital on time."

"You're certainly on course!"

"I need to get home to babysit my niece so Harry and Lou Ann can go out tonight. They rarely get to do that, and Lou Ann scored wrestling championship tickets."

"Wow! I hear it's sold out."

"Are you wrestling fan?"

"I wrestled in high school and college. It went by the wayside in medical school and during residency. But I miss it. I fool around with it at the gym."

Joanna eyed him. No wonder his muscles strained against his scrubs.

"What time are your aunt and uncle leaving?"

"Eight."

"How old is you niece?"

"Thirty months."

"I like babies."

Long pause.

"Can I stop by tonight?"

"Ummmm."

"It's okay."

"How about I text you?"

"I'd like that."

"I'd like that too."

Joanna stood closest to the locker room and shifted from one foot to the other. Thankfully, the shift was mild compared to the last two days, and the shift report ended without delay.

Joanna rushed away.

She skidded into the locker room, tossed off her scrubs, jumped into her jeans, and ducked into her shirt. Her work clogs banged into her locker and she traded them for sneakers and tied them on.

She waved to Shelly. "Gotta go!"

"Hot date?"

"Date with my niece."

"I thought otherwise."

"You would!"

Joanna jogged out of the locker room and smacked into Ian.

Ian rubbed his nose.

"Oh! I'm so sorry!

She touched his nose. "I was in such a hurry, I wasn't looking."

"It's okay. Go on."

Joanna pointed at Ian. "I'll text you."

"I'll be around icing my nose."

"Oh, no."

"I'm kidding. See you later…maybe."

She grinned. "Maybe. I'll fill the ice cube trays just in case!"

Joanna skidded her car into the driveway and parked on the grass, not obstructing Lou Ann's or Harry's vehicles, since she wasn't sure which they would take to the wrestling match tonight.

Who would have guessed Ian was a former wrestler!

She rushed out of her car and into the house.

"I'm home!" she called.

Lou Ann came out carrying Joley Kay.

"Joley Kay is fed, and so is Isabelle. Take a deep breath. You're right on time. Harry and I are going to grab something at the arena. Leftovers are in the fridge. I love you, and thank you."

"My pleasure."

Joanna opened her arms wide. "Come here, you!"

"Jo-Jo!" the baby cheered.

Lou Ann surrendered Joley Kay to Joanna. "You be good, young lady!"

Joley Kay nodded.

Harry came out wearing dress jeans and a brown and beige plaid button-down shirt.

"Woo-hoo! Look at you!" Joanna gasped.

"I even shaved again."

"Everything okay?" Joanna ventured.

"Back to work tomorrow."
"That's fantastic. I'm so happy! Have a great time."
Lou Ann kissed Harry. "We will. We should be home by eleven."
Joanna smiled. "Good to know."

30

Lou Ann and Harry left their firearms at home so they sailed through the arena security. Lou Ann gave the two complimentary tickets to the arena ticket taker, and she and Harry pushed through the turnstile.

A hostess examined their tickets.

"You're in A gate, row two, seats 25 and 26. Great seats! You'll be right in the middle of the action. Have a good time."

"Thanks."

"Wow! He gave you primo seats!"

"I know! And I was going to walk away."

"I'm glad you didn't."

Harry and Lou Ann stopped at the closest vendor to their seats and got two cheesesteaks, fries, and two large sodas. The fries sizzled and cheese oozed from the long, thick bun. The rare indiscretion was worth it.

They settled into their seats.

Harry's eyes went huge. "Best seats!"

"I had no idea!"

A spotlight shone on an entrance.

The audience roared and shot to their feet, applauding. Lou Ann and Harry followed along.

Chastity stood in the center of the ring wearing a tuxedo, her blonde-streaked hair slicked back into a cascading ponytail. She held a microphone to her red-lipsticked mouth.

"Give it up for the reigning champion, Gorilla George!"

Gorilla George swaggered into the arena draped in a white fur-trimmed, red velvet cape slung over his massive shoulders revealing red silk trunks. A thick, gold-and-jewel-studded championship belt covered his waist. He stomped in his Americana red, white, and blue-striped and star-spangled boots to the delighted audiences' screams. And when he victoriously raised his arms, his biceps bulging, the crowd cheered even louder.

He entered the ring and growled.

The spotlight traveled to the opposite ring entrance.

"And introducing in this corner, The Monster."

The Monster entered the arena, cloaked in a green cape with black sequined spiders that billowed out to reveal dark green trunks. His green-spidered boots matched his cape.

"Boo! Boooo!" the crowd chanted.

The Monster waved his fisted hand at them and then entered the ring where he poked his finger at Gorilla George.

"Boo! Boooo!"

The Monster grabbed Chastity's mic.

"Boo! Boo! To you too!"

"Hey! You don't grab her mic or her!" George waved his arms beckoning The Monster toward him. "You come after me!"

"I'm going to shove that mic up you know where!" The Monster bellowed.

The black and white striped referee jumped over the rope.

"That's enough. Don't make me kick you out of here," he admonished The Monster.

"Yeah, yeah, yeah!"

Gorilla George removed his cape and belt, and The Monster removed his cape.

The bare-chested men glared at each other and flexed their muscles.

The bell rang.

Lou Ann leaned against Harry. "Oooh!"

Harry's eyes sparkled at the impending collision between Gorilla George and The Monster.

"I didn't think it was going to be this violent."

Harry laughed. "It's showmanship."

Gorilla George leapt up and drop-kicked The Monster to his back.

Enraged, The Monster kipped-up and body-slammed Gorilla George.

Lou Ann covered her eyes. "Oh, no!"

"It's been less than five minutes, Lou Ann. You're missing all the action."

Lou Ann peeked through her fingers.

Stunned, Gorilla George began to crawl away.

The Monster jumped on Gorilla George's back and began to bend his legs back.

"No!" Lou Ann screamed.

George tossed The Monster off his back. He ran to the rope, bounced off it, backflipped, and landed smack on top of The Monster.

The crowd roared.

Lou Ann jumped out of her seat and whistled.

She plopped back in her seat.

"I had no idea you could whistle like that!"

"He got right up!"

"Yes, he did."

"I don't like that Monster."

"You and the rest of the crowd."

Joanna reached for her cell while Joley Kay napped in her lap. She stared at the screen and then scrolled to Ian's contact info.

Just do it!

She texted him.

Want to come over?

A string of response bubbles appeared.

Sure. 20 min K?

K. See you then.

That was it. There were no further texts.

Joanna set down her cell, noting the time.

Joley Kay opened her eyes, yawned, and stretched.

"Aren't you awake just in time?"

She rocked out of the den chair with Joley Kay.

"Let's both get freshened up, because we've a visitor coming."

The baby studied her.

"It's true. And girl rule number one: we have to look our best without looking like we tried."

Joanna stopped in her bedroom and grabbed a clean shirt and then proceeded with Joley Kay to the nursery. She put the baby in the crib and then Joanna changed into a clean shirt.

"No drooling on this one!" she warned Joley Kay.

The baby grasped the crib's side rails and rocked back and forth.

"Now for you."

Joanna changed Joley Kay's diaper, put her in a clean dress, and brushed her baby-fine hair.

"I think a bow would be too much. Remember we want to look

natural."

She picked her up and went into the bathroom, flicked on the lighted mirror, and with her free hand applied a thin coat of mascara.

Joanna held up Joley Kay to the makeup mirror.

"I think we're about right, don't you?"

The baby pointed to their reflection.

"I'm glad you agree."

The doorbell rang.

"It's go time."

Joanna took a deep breath and, with Joley Kay on her hip, she answered the door.

Ian stood on the other side while holding a pizza box.

"I brought dinner."

"Yay! Come in."

Ian walked inside. She eyed him without being too obvious. He was wearing jeans just tight enough without being too loose, and a yellow polo shirt, and not the dark blue one he had on at the end of the shift. He'd shaved since. He tried just enough.

"And who's this?" he cooed.

"This is Joley Kay."

Joley Kay examined Ian and then turned her face against Joanna's chest.

"Sorry. She has stranger anxiety, but she just needs a little time to get to know you."

"Understandable."

"That pizza is smells heavenly. Ooh, how's your nose?"

"Still works," he joked.

Joanna pointed. "Kitchen's that way."

While Ian headed into the kitchen, Joanna poked her head out the front door. He'd walked her to her car, but she had no idea what he drove.

He must drive some fabulous muscle car.

But parked on the side of the road was a silver sedan, not even a Beemer. Maybe that wasn't his car.

Then Ian rushed back out.

"I got drinks too."

He went straight to the silver sedan.

That really was his car.

He retrieved a two-liter bottle of soda, clicked the remote, and headed back inside.

Ian winked. "You do have ice, right?"

She grinned. "Absolutely…just in case."

Ian set the soda next to the pizza, while Joanna retrieved plates and two glasses from the cupboard.

Joley Kay remained attached to her hip, peeking periodically at Ian.

Ian began to play peekaboo with his hands to his eyes.

The baby giggled.

"Looks like you're becoming fast friends."

"I don't know if it's fast, but I'll leave that up to Joley Kay."

"She's taking you in, and I bet by the end of this evening she'll consider you a friend."

"I'd like another friend…sort of."

"Am I your friend?" Joanna asked, risking an answer.

Ian cocked his head, and his hazel eyes definitely softened—a look that set her heart aflutter.

"Yes and no," he replied softly.

Best response she could hope for!

"Let's eat," Joanna said.

Ian plopped a gooey slice of pizza on each plate.

Joley Kay flapped her hands. "Me-me-me!"

Ian raised his brows. "Can she have pizza?"

"She likes to chew on the crust. I think that makes her teeth feel better."

"Crust it is."

Ian cut the crust off his slice and handed it to Joley Kay.

Joley Kay waved it like a victory flag.

"That was nice of you. Here, have another slice," Joanna said.

"I'm good with this one. I'm not much of a crust man, so win-win."

Ooh, definitely win-win.

They sat at the kitchen table with Joley Kay attached to Joanna's lap.

The baby drooled while chewing the crust.

"She looks happy," Ian said.

"She is a happy baby." Joanna hugged Joley Kay. "Aren't you, a happy gal?" she cooed.

The baby gave a drooly smile.

"So is she your niece on your mother's or father's side?"

Her brain scrambled for an answer she couldn't or wouldn't give.

"It's complicated."

Ian took a hefty bite of his pizza, and Joley Kay quieted, sensing tension.

Joanna searched for a response that would end his inquiry...for now.

"My mother died, and I have no idea who my father was. Lou Ann and Harry took me in and now they're my family."

There, she said it!

Ian's eyes went huge.

"I'm sorry," he offered.

Joanna toyed with her pizza and then bit off a piece.

Ian and Joley Kay continued chewing.

"Thanks for bringing pizza," she said, changing the subject that hung there without an ending punctuation.

"Happy to do it. I was selfishly hungry."

Joanna raised her slice. "Here's to your selfishness!"

Ian pushed a wide smile causing a sweet crinkle at the corners of those "Hotty" eyes.

The weighty moment thankfully shifted away.

Even Joley Kay resumed gumming her crust.

Two slices remained in the pizza box.

"Do you mind if I save a slice for Lou Ann and Harry?"

"Sure." Ian leaned back in his chair and rubbed his belly. "I'm stuffed."

Joanna eyed his six-pack abs.

If he was stuffed, it sure didn't show.

Joley Kay dropped her slimy crust.

Ian chuckled. "Apparently she's done too!"

Joley Kay baby-smiled at Ian.

"You're officially in!" Joanna teased him.

The baby held out her messy hand to Ian.

Without hesitation, Ian grasped her finger.

"Ooh, I didn't have a chance to wash her hands."

"No problem. We'll wash our hands together." He smiled at Joley Kay. "Right?"

The baby slapped the table.

Joanna suddenly saw the other side of "Dr. Hotty" and, saw that like her, he put on his mask every day to conceal who he rally was. They had that in common.

31

During the wrestling championship match, Lou Ann had searched for wrestling moves on her cell and rapidly became knowledgeable regarding Gorilla George's and The Monster's moves against each other which made her all the more glued to the match and to rooting for George to retain his title. Even Harry boo'd. Harry pumped his fist when Gorilla George slammed his opponent.

And then it happened. The Monster was down and not getting up. The referee called it.

Gorilla George retained his championship status!

Lou Ann and Harry jumped out of their seats and applauded and shouted with the crowd clearly for Gorilla George.

The ebullient crowd began to bump their way to the arena exit.

"Let's wait until the crowd disperses," Harry said.

"I'm with you. I hate to fight a crowd. Plus, with these great seats, it'll be a while before we can make it out of here. And then there's going to be glut of cars leaving the arena.

Lou Ann and Harry leaned back in their seats.

"That was awesome!" Lou Ann gushed.

"Now you're an expert on wrestling moves. I saw you looking at your cell."

"I'm no expert, but I have to say I've learned a lot."

"Amazing you're not hoarse."

"Did I go overboard?"

"At a wrestling match? You're kidding."

"I did have a great time."

Harry squeezed her hand. "Me too."

Then they spotted Gorilla George trotting toward them, and Chastity wasn't far behind.

Lou Ann stood. "Hey, George. Congratulations! I had an awesome time!"

"I'm glad."

"I almost didn't recognize you with your regular clothes. George and Chastity, this is my husband, Harry."

George shook his hand—Harry's hand swallowed in George's gigantic one.

"Nice to meet you. Your wife treated us okay. My fiancé and I are happy you both made it."

"And thanks for the great seats."

"Our pleasure."

"The crowd's dwindled. We'll walk you out to your car. Ours is parked in the garage too."

"Sure," Lou Ann said.

Harry was like a kid at Christmas. "Yeah, absolutely."

George and Harry traded wrestling stories while Lou Ann and Chastity walked ahead.

"The tickets were a godsend," she said to Chastity. "Harry is an FBI Special Agent and he was involved in a major drug bust where he had no choice but to kill one of them when the dealer shot first."

"He did what he had to do."

"But tonight he had an awesome time and for a couple of hours he could let it go, even though he was exonerated."

"I can tell he's good man, like my George. I never thought I'd get into the wrestling gig, but I love it too."

"It shows."

"I'm sorry I was so nasty to you earlier."

"Thanks, but I wasn't insulted. I was the one who cold-called on you. It turned out more than okay. I had a great time and learned a lot about wrestling."

"George and I love a rowdy crowd."

"And we got rowdy along with them," Lou Ann admitted.

Harry caught up to Chastity and Lou Ann before they all readied to cross the street to the parking garage.

Each looked both ways before crossing.

Laughter rang in Lou Ann's ears before she was tossed in the air and then free-fell to the asphalt, slamming to her back. She grasped for breath. Exploding pain followed.

"Lou Ann! Lou Ann!"

Is that Harry? He's so far way. Uh….

George pulled Chastity back to the sidewalk while Harry huddled over Lou Ann while she lay helpless in the middle of the road.

"Road rash. I'm okay, " Chastity called.

Harry's hand shook while he reached for the cell in his back pocket, all while hovering over Lou Ann, while he dialed 911.

"I'm outside the Clearwater Arena. My wife was just hit by a car," he shouted into his phone.

"We have your location. Rescue is on the way. Don't attempt to move her. Sheriff on the way, just around the block."

George stood in the road blocking traffic. "Get out! Move away!"

Sirens blared closer.

"Come on! Come on! Please come on."

"What the hell happened?" he called to George. "That white car swerved out of nowhere."

It wasn't a Florida plate. There was a star. Texas? Were they out for him and got Lou Ann instead? God, please no. Please no.

A sheriff's vehicle screeched to a halt and a Sheriff's deputy flew out of it.

The deputy's eyes widened and teared up.

He squatted next to Harry and Lou Ann.

"Tim," Lou Ann whispered in between agonized grunts.

"It's me. I'm right here for you. Don't move."

He covered her with a silver blanket.

"Rescue's on the way. Save your strength. We're all here for you."

"Ca-ca ca-car."

"Road's blocked. No cars. No car. We'll have it on security cams. We're going to get who did this to you."

Rescue vehicles flooded the scene.

"Lou Ann, we're going to put a C-collar on you. We'll do all the work. Once we get you in the truck, we'll give you pain medicine. Hang in there."

"Okay," she horsely whispered. "Harry."

"I'm right here."

"Where are you taking her?"

"Hampton."

"Lou Ann, baby. I can't ride with you because they need to focus on you. I'll see you at Hampton."

Another crew evaluated Chastity,

She shook her hands. "I'm okay. Take her. Take her."

"Miss, let us take a look."

"It's only road rash."

"I'll take her to the emergency room." George said.

"All right. Not being difficult, but just sign here declining transport."

Chastity signed the document.

"Harry, I'll drive you both," George said.

"Thanks, but I'm okay. I'll drive there."

Harry climbed into the rescue vehicle. "Baby, I'll see you at Hampton."

He kissed her on the forehead and his tear dropped on her cheek.

"I love you."

"Love too," she mumbled.

Harry jumped out of the Rescue vehicle.

The Rescue vehicle pulled away with its lights strobing and its siren blaring.

Harry stood in the middle of the street with his hand held toward the Rescue vehicle speeding away.

32

Joanna's cell rang. It was Harry. They must be on their way home. She had to tell Ian to leave. It would be too hard to explain why he was here. She'd feign fatigue—that they'd both have to get up early.

"Hey, Harry. How was the wrestling match?"

Silence except for Harry's heavy breathing.

"Harry?"

"Lou Ann's been hit by a car. They're taking her to Hampton. I gotta go. I don't know when I'll be back. Take Jolie Kay to Suzy's in the morning."

"Harry!"

He hung up.

She grabbed Ian and burrowed her head against his chest. Sparks shot out of her brain and her heart felt like it was going to explode from her chest any second.

"What's wrong? Something bad happened."

"Lou Ann was hit by a car. They're taking her to Hampton!" she blurted.

Joanna pushed out of Ian's embrace.

Even Joley Kay went silent.

"I gotta go! I gotta go to Hampton!"

Joanna spun in circles, panting.

"Joley Kay. I gotta grab Joley Kay."

"Stop a second. Take a deep breath, or you'll hyperventilate. I'll drive," Ian said.

"No! No! Car seat. Joley Kay's car seat is in my car."

Ian held out his hand. "Give me the keys. I'll drive. Get the baby."

A flood of tears streamed down her cheeks.

The baby's eyes got huge.

Stop. Or you'll scare Joley Kay.

164

Joanna sniffled back the tears, wiped her wet cheeks with the backs of her hands, and cleared her throat.

Then she picked up Joley Kay and hugged her close.

"We're gonna go for a ride.."

The baby wrapped her arms around Joanna's neck.

Ian held up Joanna's car keys.

"Let's go," he said.

Harry gripped the steering wheel until his knuckles blanched. He stared straight ahead. His heart vibrated in synch with the car's engine.

Did he run a red or breeze past a stop sign? He had no idea. No one had hit their car horn or yelled at him. He must be driving automatically.

Get ahold of yourself. You don't want to kill anyone. Not anyone good, anyway.

He stopped at a red light. He was paying attention, after all.

He eased his grip on the wheel and pale pink flushed to his nail beds.

Honk! "Come on, pal! Let's go!" the driver behind him shouted.

Harry hadn't noticed when the light turn green.

He stepped on the accelerator and glanced in the rearview mirror. He'd left the annoyed driver two blocks behind.

He swerved at the blue hospital sign and rocketed into the Emergency Room parking lot space. The engine had barely died down when Harry leapt from the vehicle. He swatted the door shut and ran into Hampton ED.

Harry banged on the locked ED entrance.

"Hey!" the woman behind the admission desk yelled.

Harry froze and then whipped around.

"I'm sorry! I'm sorry! My wife! They brought her here. A car hit her!"

The woman rushed out from behind the admissions desk.

"Sir, it's all right. Who's your wife?"

"Lou Ann Jasinski."

"Okay. Come sit with me, and I'll find out what's happening."

Harry flopped into the chair facing her desk, his eyes laser-focused on her computer keystrokes.

"Okay. Rescue brought her in. The emergency doctor is seeing her now."

Harry bolted from the chair. "I have to see her now!"

"You can't go in there...yet," she qualified. "I'll let them know you're here, and the doctor will be with you soon as she can. You want your wife stabilized. You want her to get the best attention. Right?"

Harry nodded. "I'll go wait over there. But please let her know I'm here."

The woman picked up her phone and tapped four digits.

Must be the extension.

"I have Lou Ann Jasinski's husband here." She glanced at him.

"Harry Boxer," he announced.

"Harry Boxer," the woman said.

"Uh, huh. I'll tell him."

"Mr. Boxer. They're still assessing your wife."

"Assessing?"

"Yes. They'll keep you updated."

He had no choice. His whole experience at the hospital was interviewing suspects, and then when Joley Kay was born.

*Joley Kay. Joley Kay. She's not going to understand. *I* don't understand.*

George walked through the ED waiting room while holding Chastity's hand.

Harry stood from the waiting room chair.

"Harry, how is she?" George asked.

"I don't know. They won't let me back in there."

"I need to get Chastity set."

"I understand."

George sat at the admission desk with Chastity.

"My fiancé got road-swiped by the same car that hit Lou Ann Jasinski—Investigator Jasinski—Death and Homicide Investigator with the Sheriff's Department."

Oh, God. He didn't even tell the woman that. Lou Ann was foremost, his wife.

"Oh, my" the woman said. And then looked at Harry.

He wanted to yell that it wasn't important what she did for a living right now.

He swallowed hard. It was all his fault. That car was meant for him!

George filled out forms and then the ED door opened.

Harry jumped up.

"Chastity Bancroft," the nurse called.

"Go, Chastity."

"Nurse! Nurse! How's my wife, Lou Ann Jasinski? Please! I gotta know. Please!"

"I'll check for you. Come this way, Ms. Bancroft."

"It's only minor road-rash. I need my friend, Lou Ann, taken care of first."

"She is. You're not interfering with that. We'll take a look at you." The nurse looked at Harry and George. "It's busy tonight. It might be a while."

The ED door closed behind Chastity.

George sat next to Harry.

Neither spoke. They didn't need to.

Ian parked Joanna's car in the staff garage lot. He squeezed her hand and then let her go.

Joanna opened the back seat door and unbuckled Joley Kay from her car seat and lifted her to her chest.

"I'll get the door," Ian said, and he shut it.

They rushed to the hospital, taking the overpass connecting the garage to the hospital.

For the first time, Joley Kay felt heavy in her arms, but she kept up with Ian.

Joanna with Joley Kay, and Ian entered the ED.

"Harry!" Joanna cried.

Harry stood with slumped shoulders.

"Da-da."

Joanna hugged Harry with Joley Kay attached to her hip.

"Da-da! Ma-ma!"

Harry held out his arms. "Come here, beautiful."

"Ma-ma!"

"Mama's here. She had a boo-boo."

Harry and Ian locked eyes.

"Harry, this is Ian…Dr. Hottman. I work with him."

"Nice to meet you, Dr. Hottman," Harry said.

They shook hands while Harry held Joley Kay.

"I was at your house when you called Joanna. I drove. I'm so sorry what's happened."

Harry didn't ask for an explanation. His mind was surely as muddled as hers, and more so.

"A huge man stood. "I'm George. Your parents were at my wrestling match. We were crossing the street from the arena when a car came out of nowhere. No one had time to react."

"Joanna and I will see what's happening."

"Thank you, Dr. Hottman."

Ian nodded. "We'll be back."

Joanna and Ian swiped their hospital IDs at the secure ED entrance.

Joanna waved to Harry before the ED door closed, locked, and clicked behind her.

33

"Hi, Hannah," Ian said to the woman in scrubs.

Ian opened his hand to Joanna.

"Joanna, this is Hannah, the ED attending caring for Lou Ann. Hanna, this is Joanna, who's an ED nurse on the day shift with me. Lou Ann Jasinski is her aunt."

"Nice to meet you under the circumstances. How is she?"

"Lou Ann just got back from CT. Her brain scan is negative for any head trauma. No chest, abdominal, or pelvic trauma."

Joanna drew a deep breath. "Thank God."

"Initial X-rays later confirmed by CT, indicates that your aunt has a left tib-fib fracture. Given the reported speed of the car that careened into her, she's lucky to be alive and to not have sustained massive trauma. Her face and left side are bruised. She's received Morphine for the pain so she may be groggy. Jason Mills is in seeing her now."

Ian turned to Joanna. "He's the best orthopedic surgeon at Hampton. State and nationally recognized, too."

"I'm relieved Rescue brought her here."

"Come, she's in room two."

Hannah led Joanna and Ian to Lou Ann.

"Hey, Jason," Ian said.

"You're here early."

"I'm here with Joanna, ED nurse...and *friend*. Lou Ann Jasinski is her aunt."

Lou Ann blinked her drowsy eyes. "Joanna," she called softly.

"I'm right here."

"As Hannah explained, Lou Ann sustained a left rib-fib fracture. I'll be taking her to the OR shortly. She's a little drowsy from the pain meds so I would feel better if her husband can cosign the consent," Dr. Mills said.

"I'll get him. He's in the waiting room," Joanna replied.

Joanna emerged from the main ED and into the waiting area.

Harry read Joanna's puckered face. It was bad news

He pressed his feet against the floor to steady himself and pushed to his feet while clutching Joley Kay. His chest burned around his heart.

"Lou Ann's stable but drowsy. She's asking to see you before she goes to surgery."

"Surgery!"

Joanna placed her hand on his shoulder. "Yes. The orthopedic surgeon has to fix her left leg fracture. Everything else was negative. Her face and left side are bruised." Joanna clutched her hand to her mouth and nodded. She lowered her hand. "Lou Ann's going to be okay. She has the best doctors and nurses taking care of her as well as the top surgeon."

"Take me to her."

"Mr. Baxter, the baby can't go back there."

George stood. "I'll take her so all of you can be with Lou Ann."

He held out his massive arms.

Joley Kay clung to Harry.

"I'm going to be right back, princess. This is George."

Joley Kay wiggled in Harry's arm and screeched.

"I'll stay with her," Joanna said.

"No. All of you need to be with Lou Ann. Let me try with the little one. I'm actually good with kids."George opened his palms. "Come here, darling."

Red faced and with tear streaks on her cheeks, Joley Kay glared at George.

George pouted.

Joley Kay sucked in her snotty nose and examined his face.

George cast his eyes down.

The baby wrinkled her face.

George looked at her and wiggled his fingers.

Joley Kay smiled.

George beckoned to her with his hands.

Harry surrendered her to George.

"Wow, not even a whimper!"

George winked. "I told you I was good with kids."

He gently bounced the baby.

"Go, I got it," George said.

Harry sneaked away with Joanna.

Joanna swiped her ID at the entrance door and Harry followed her into the belly of the Emergency Department.

Patients on stretchers readied to be jockeyed into the next available rooms.

Nothing moved fast for patients in an emergency room unless they were critically injured...like Lou Ann. But soon her room would be available.

"Mr. Baxter?"

"Yes."

"I'm Dr. Hannah Fulton, the emergency room doctor taking care of your wife."

"Thank you, doctor."

"She's in room two. She's stable at the moment."

At the moment?

Harry nodded.

Ian chatted with another guy in scrubs, but stopped talking with him when he saw Harry.

Ian beckoned to Harry.

"This is Dr. Jason Mills, the orthopedic surgeon who's admitting Lou Ann. Dr. Mills, this is Harry Baxter, Lou Jasinski's husband. I'll let you two talk."

Ian walked away while Harry and the doctor shook hands.

"Lou Ann sustained a fracture of the bones in her left lower leg... her calf," Jason Mills said.

"Is it the tibia, fibula or most likely both?" Harry asked.

"Sorry, I'm not used to explaining in plain language. Are you in the medical field?"

"No, but I've been here before on multiple occasions interviewing subjects. I'm an FBI Special Agent. I'm only saying that because I'm fairly familiar with injuries and trauma. However, not involving my wife."

"I understand. I'll be in the operating room with your wife, Lou Ann, for quite a while putting in pins and plates and the like. I'll take you to the surgical waiting room now, and I'll be out as soon as I'm finished. We'll talk afterwards. But do you have any questions right now?"

"No. I just need to see her before surgery."

"Absolutely."

Harry gulped and headed toward room two.

The last thing he wanted was for Lou Ann to know he was panicked.

He sucked in a deep breath and walked into her ED room.

"Harry."

Her voice teetered between a whisper and a gritty hoarseness.

Joanna stood vigilant next to her while holding her hand.

Lou Ann managed a quarter of a smile.

Harry leaned over and gently kissed her forehead, half afraid he'd hurt her.

"My face…looks really bad…huh?"

Harry smiled. "No. It's bruised, but you're still the most beautiful woman in the world."

Lou Ann let out a hoarse giggle. "Liar."

He took her other hand.

"I'm a wishbone," she joked. "Don't let go. I like it."

"Are you in pain?"

"Nuh. Morphine. Second thought, let go. I need my cell."

"Honey, I don't know where it is."

She pounded the mattress beneath the tangle of IVs.

"Cell," she insisted.

"Aunt Lou Ann, don't. You're going to rip out your IVs, and you're gonna need them. They'll have to stick you all over again."

She collapsed in the bed.

"Cell. Photo. I need photo."

Ian shrugged.

"Do you want a photo of all of us?" Joanna asked. "I have my cell."

It was weird request, but then again she was probably high on Morphine.

"No," she huffed, because they didn't understand.

Lou Ann blinked. "Photo-man-shakedown-Spark."

"Spark nightclub?" Joanna asked.

Lou Ann nodded.

A woman entered the room.

"I was one of the Rescue crew who responded to your accident. I grabbed your cell. It's in this plastic bag. The glass is shattered, but it's yours."

"Thank…you!"

Lou Ann ripped open the plastic bag.

Harry reached for the bag. "Stop, Lou Ann! You're going to cut your fingers."

She yanked the bag back.

"Lou Ann, give me the bag with the cell."

"No! Photo. Important, Harry. I show you."

"The photo's gone. The cell doesn't work."

"I got hit for it."

"I'll get a pair of rubber gloves," Ian said.

He went to the room's cupboard, retrieved the gloves, and gave them to Harry.

"She might not be able to focus at the moment," Ian said. "Joanna and I will leave while Lou Ann gives you her cell's password."

"Good idea. Thanks...Ian."

"No problem. It might work. She's adamant about some photo."

After Joanna and Ian left, Harry put on the rubber gloves and took the shattered cell out of the plastic bag.

"Password. I promise you can change it when I get you a new phone."

Lou Ann recited the four-digit password.

"I'm in. But the screen is hard to see."

"Go photos."

"Okay."

Harry's eyes went huge.

Unbelievable.

Even through a cracked screen, the photo Lou Ann took outside of Spark looked exactly like the drug trafficker he killed on that boat.

34

Lou Ann went to surgery feeling relieved. No wonder she'd insisted on me seeing that photo on her cell. They'd both stirred the proverbial hornet's nest and she paid the price. It was an intended hit job for the both of them. But Lou Ann stepped in the line of fire before he had. If only he'd walked in front of her and Chastity. George would've dented the car and they'd be okay.

Harry stopped with Joanna and Ian in the ED waiting area to pick up Joley Kay. It was close to midnight, and Joley Kay must be exhausted.

But George was wide awake and Chastity sat next to him. Joley Kay snored in George's arms.

"She conked out."

"I see."

George stood while cradling Joley Kay and transferred her to Harry's arms.

"Thanks for watching her."

"Anytime."

"How are you, Chastity?" Harry asked.

"Just like I said, minor road-rash. But George insisted. They cleaned out the road grime, put on some antibiotic cream, gave me a tetanus shot, and Motrin. I'm good to go, but unfortunately Lou Ann is not."

"Not for a while anyway. They just took her to surgery."

"We'll both be praying for her," George said.

"Thank you, and I appreciate that, and I'm sure Lou Ann knows you are."

"Anything we could do for you?" George asked.

"No. You've been a tremendous help."

"I wish I'd seen that coming and so we would've stepped in

front."

"I know. I would've done the same."

"Yeah, but you'd be flattened," George joked, then shook his head."All joking aside, Lou Ann is a strong woman. She's a fighter."

"You got that right on both accounts."

"Take Joley Kay home and yourself too. Lou Ann will be in surgery for a while, and I'm sure she'll be sedated afterwards. Plus, you and Ian need to get up early. I'm staying," Harry said.

He had a point. Lou Ann would sleep post-op. And it would be best for Joley Kay to sleep in her crib.

"All right. But if anything changes call me."

"I will, sweetheart."

Joanna kissed Harry's cheek, and Harry handed her Joley Kay who snuggled in Joanna's arms.

"Thanks for everything, Ian," Harry said.

"I'll make sure Joanna and Joley Kay get home safe."

Joanna waved to Harry. "Bye."

"Bye."

Ian set his hand on Joanna's shoulder. "Let's go."

Joanna turned to look at Harry.

He nodded. "I'll be fine. Go."

Ian opened the surgical waiting room door and Joanna with Joley Kay left Harry behind.

"Maybe I should stay."

"I promised to take both of you home. Besides, you can visit Lou Ann tomorrow when she'll be awake."

"It's already tomorrow."

"All the more important for you to get a few hours of sleep."

Joanna hoisted slumbering Joley Kay over her shoulder and walked with Ian to her car in the garage.

"Why is it so dark? I can't make out my car."

"The parking garage lights are out. Strange."

Her heartbeat bumped. "Let's go back. Something's wrong."

Was this tied to Lou Ann? What was with the photo? Was someone spying on them?

She tightened her grip on Joley Kay.

"Just a minute," Ian said.

A beam of light shot from his cell.

He clicked Joanna's car remote and the car's headlights flashed and a honk followed.

"There! Second row. Let's go."

"No! I hear footsteps. Let's get out of here."

Ian glanced sideways.

He heard them too.

"Turn around and walk fast back to the hospital," Ian whispered.

Joanna stuttered a breath, whipped around, and speed-walked back toward the hospital's entrance. Joley Kay flopped in her arms, unaware.

"Hey, you!" a man yelled in the dark.

Ian pushed Joanna from behind.

"Run!"

35

Ian slammed open the exit door from the garage that led back to the hospital and ushered Joanna through the door while she clung to Joley Kay.

The parking garage light flashed on.

"Wait! It's security. Power's back on! It's okay now."

"Ian, I don't feel comfortable."

The security guard approached. "Hi, Dr. Hottman. Didn't mean to frighten you or the young lady with the baby."

"Oh, James. I had no idea it was you."

The security lights' switch flipped off at the fuse box, and I was trying to restore the lights when I saw car headlights flash and heard a honk. I knew someone was there. I just didn't know it was you. Odd time for anyone to be in the staff section of the garage."

"A friend sustained injuries tonight so that's why we're here so late."

"Sorry to hear that."

"Working overtime?" Ian asked James.

"Mortgage. Kid's college tuition. You know."

"Gotcha." Ian beckoned to Joanna. "Let's get you home before anything else happens."

"Drive safe, folks," James said, and then disappeared among the night shift cars.

Ian opened the back door and Joanna buckled Joley Kay into her car seat and then jumped into the passenger seat of her own car.

Ian slipped into the driver's seat and pressed the button to lock all the doors.

He started the engine. "What a night! Are you all right?" he asked.

"I'll be better once my tachycardia subsides."

Joanna peered into the back seat.

"I can't believe she slept through everything."

The house security lights flashed bright when Ian drove Joanna's car into the driveway.

"Home," he said softly.

"Thank God, because I didn't think we'd make it here."

"Which one is your house key?"

Joanna pointed to the silver one on her key ring.

"While you get the baby, I'll open the door."

"Thanks. Kind of hard to do with her sacked out in my arms."

Ian eased the driver's door shut and headed to the front door while Joanna unstrapped Joley Kay from her car seat. In a few hours she'd walk her and her car seat over to Suzy's house before leaving for the hospital.

Ian unlocked the front door.

Joanna left the hallway light on when she rushed out, so they weren't completely in the dark.

Isabelle bumped her wet nose against the back of Joanna's calf.

"There you are. I'm so sorry we left you so quickly."

Isabelle trotted into Lou Ann and Harry's bedroom and returned to whine in the hallway.

"They're not coming home tonight, but I'm here."

Isabelle lay down outside the bedroom.

"She's convinced something's wrong," she said to Ian.

"Dogs are sensitive like that."

Ian squatted next to Isabelle and petted her.

"It's okay," he soothed her.

Isabelle buried her snout in her paws.

"She'll stay that way tonight. While I attend to Joley Kay, can you check if she has water in her bowl?"

"Sure thing."

Joanna changed Joley Kay's diaper and slid her out of her clothes and into her nightie. It was blessedly like dressing a rag doll. She laid the baby in her crib and slid up the side rails. Still nothing. Joanna leaned over the baby to make sure she was breathing, and was comforted to hear her steady in-and out.

Hopefully Joley Kay would continue to sleep. But Joanna doubted she'd get any rest. Sleep would surely be futile for her in the remaining hours.

Joanna turned to find Ian standing in the doorway of the nursery.

"She's really out," he said.

"Thankfully so."

"I refreshed Isabelle's water bowl."

"Thanks. It's there for her, but I doubt she'll leave her post. I'll leave Joley Kay's door open in case she wakes up crying."

Joanna tiptoed out of the nursery.

She and Ian exchanged worried looks.

"I don't want to be alone here."

"I'll stay…on the sofa in the den. We have get up in four hours anyway, and we both need some sleep."

"Thank you."

Joanna fetched a pillow and a blanket from the linen closet and handed them to Ian.

He set them on the sofa.

"I'll check to make sure all the doors are locked."

"I already set the alarm."

"Okay. All set then."

Ian kissed Joanna on the cheek and settled on the sofa.

"I'll keep my door open." Joanna paused. "I'm afraid to close it. I've never been here alone overnight."

"I'll be right here."

36

Harry shifted in the surgical waiting room chair, alone. He stood and paced. Lou Ann had been in surgery for two hours. His heartbeat lurched. Maybe there was a complication or her injury was far more extensive than expected. Harry raked his fingers through his hair.

The door to the waiting area groaned open and Lou Ann's surgeon emerged.

It was over.

Harry stopped pacing.

He studied Dr. Mills' face carefully. But he couldn't immediately read him. The doctor wasn't smiling. Neither did he seem overly concerned. All Harry cared about was whether Lou Ann was okay.

Jason Mills approached Harry.

"Mr. Baxter?"

"Yes."

"Your wife is in the recovery room. The surgery went well."

Every muscle in Harry's body sighed.

Harry held his hand out to the surgeon. "Thank you, Dr. Mills."

The men shook hands.

"You're welcome. I'll see her tomorrow."

"It's already tomorrow."

"That it is. Get some rest. Then in the afternoon," Jason Mills said, finally with a smile.

"Can I see her now?"

"She's still sedated, but no other patients are in the recovery room. I'll let the nurse know."

"Thank you again."

Jason Mills waved. "No problem."

Then the doctor left, leaving Harry alone once again.

Harry looked up and whispered, "Thank you, God."

A nurse entered the room.

"Mr. Baxter?"

"Yes, that's me."

"Come with me."

He followed the nurse down a deserted hallway.

"She's still recovering from anesthesia, and she's received pain medicine, but she is rousable."

The nurse pressed the button outside of the double doors and they swung open.

There she was! Beneath a white hospital blanket. IV pumps blinked at her side.

He rushed to her.

Her swollen, bruised face crowded her closed eyes.

"Lou Ann…honey…it's me."

She licked her lips and then opened her mouth.

"Harry," she whispered.

"Rest. I'm right here."

He leaned over and kissed the top of her head.

"Love you," she mumbled.

"I love you too."

A nurse slid a chair next to Lou Ann's bed.

"Sit."

"Thank you."

Harry sat.

"Baybee?"

"She's with Joanna."

"Mmmm."

The cardiac monitor over Lou Ann's head of the bed beeped at a slower and more even rhythm as her chest rose and fell.

Harry took out his cell from his back pocket. He promised Joanna he'd call her once Lou Ann was out of surgery. He hoped she was asleep by now, and he didn't want to wake the baby. So he texted her. She'd get it in the morning.

Joanna's cell pinged.

She picked up the phone that lay next to her and read Harry's text.

She clutched the cell to her chest.

Yes!

She texted back.

"Thank God."

She could finally close her eyes.

37

Joanna rolled to her side to find Isabelle lying next to her bed.

She leaned over the side of the bed and petted her.

"How did you know?"

The dog must've sensed the sudden quiet calm after Harry's text.

Joanna jumped out of bed. Her alarm hadn't gone off yet.

She peeked in on Joley Kay, who was wiggling in her crib, not fully awake but trying to be.

She decided to check on Ian next, before Joley Kay called for her attention.

Joanna found Ian folding his blanket.

"You're awake."

"Yep."

"I didn't want wake you last night, but Harry texted that Lou Ann's surgery went well."

"That's wonderful. I knew she'd pull through."

Joley Kay's cries echoed into the den.

"I need to go to her."

"I'll get the coffee started," Ian said.

"Great. You can shower in my bathroom, and I'll take one in Lou Ann's bathroom once I get Joley Kay changed and dressed. Then I'll take her and Isabelle to Suzy's house across the street. Suzy cares for both of them while we're all at work."

"Sounds like a plan."

Joanna returned to the nursery.

"Good morning!" she cheered. "Is someone ready to get up?"

Joley Kay gurgled a smile and thrust her legs.

Joanna picked up Joley Kay and hugged her and then readied the baby for her day.

"Are you ready to go see Suzy?"

Joley Kay waved her arms. "Jo-Jo."

Stab in the heart. She and Ian needed to leave for their shift soon or they'd be late.

She tossed Joley Kay's diapers and change of clothes in a diaper bag and then rushed to the kitchen to get Joley Kay's and Isabelle's provisions.

On her way past the bathroom Joanna heard the shower running.

She filled Joley Kay's sippy cup with milk and grabbed Isabelle's kibble, tossing it into another bag.

"Let's go to Suzy's, Isabelle."

Joanna rushed out the front door with Joley Kay, two bags, and Isabelle in tow.

"Oh. No. It's so early." Normally Lou Ann or Harry dropped Joley Kay and Isabelle at Suzy's.

She sighed a relieved breath. The lights were on at Suzy's.

Joanna and Isabelle looked both ways before crossing the street to Suzy's house.

Joanna rang the doorbell.

Suzy opened the door.

"Joanna?"

"Yeah. I know Lou Ann or Harry usually drop her off, but Lou Ann is in the hospital and Harry's with her. I need to get to the hospital and we...I...was up late and I'm sorry, but I haven't fed her or bathed her. Here are her and Isabelle's things."

Joley Kay held out her hands to Suzy and Isabelle walked into Suzy's house.

"What happened?" Suzy asked.

"Lou Ann was hit by a speeding car."

"Oh, my God!"

"She's out of surgery and Harry stayed at the hospital."

Suzy took the baby.

"Don't worry. I have plenty of supplies for both Joley Kay and Isabelle so they can stay as long as needed. Let Harry know. I'm sure he'll need sleep when he gets home. And please let Lou Ann know that they're fine and safe here."

"Thank you, Suzy. Bye-bye, Joley Kay."

"Bye-Bye, Jo-Jo."

Joanna kissed the baby's sweet face.

He chest throbbed all the way across the street.

At the front door she turned and waved to Suzy and Joley Kay and they waved back.

Then she walked inside the house and closed the door.

Ian walked into the living room, his hair wet and his skin smelling of fresh flowers.

"Sorry about the girly body wash."

"I'm not. It was actually refreshing." He teasingly pointed at her. "Just don't tell anyone."

"Your secret is safe with me."

Joanna rubbed her cheeks.

"Yeah. I have an electric razor in the car and a change of clothes in my locker. You don't like the rugged, tired look?"

"Rugged, maybe. Tired? I'm getting used to that look."

"Coffee's ready. Cream and two sugars, if I remember correctly."

"Didn't know you noticed."

"Of course I did, while I stood patiently behind you at the coffee pot in the break room."

"That was you tapping your toes?"

He waggled his brows. "You noticed."

"Go shower, and I'll do the rest."

"The rest of what?" she ventured.

"Breakfast to go, of course."

"Humph. Covered coffee mugs are in that cupboard."

"Got it."

Joanna quickly showered and changed, securing her wet hair in a ponytail.

They'd surely have all eyes on them when they both showed up with wet hair.

She walked into the kitchen to find two covered coffee mugs and two freshly microwaved and wrapped breakfast sandwiches.

"Here's yours. Here's mine. Here are your car keys. I'll meet you at the hospital." He winked. "See ya!"

"Why's your hair wet?" Shelley asked Joanna while they changed into their scrubs for their day.

"I didn't sleep well because a car hit my Aunt Lou Ann last evening and she was in the OR for a tib-fib fracture until after midnight."

"Oh, no!"

"Jason Mills performed the surgery, and she's doing well."

"He's the best."

"I'm sure she's on the orthopedic wing by now. My Uncle Harry texted me when she was in the recovery room. I'll check where she is in the computer, because I'm anxious to see her when I get a chance."

Shelly hugged her. "We'll all cover for you."

"Thanks. It'll be change of shift up there too, so I'll wait until mid-morning."

"You let me know. I'll take care of things. I'm sure all the attendings and nurses will understand."

Joanna didn't mention Ian's involvement and definitely not that he spent the night at the house, albeit separately. The last thing she needed was a bunch of gossip.

Ian walked out of the men's locker room clean-shaven and wearing crisp scrubs. That electric shaver clipped away a full day's plus of stubble.

"Hey, his hair's wet too," Shelly said.

Joanna shrugged and scooted away.

The outgoing team mingled with oncoming one.

Stan Farkas sniffed. "Smells like flowers. Is that you, Ian?"

"Yep."

Hannah, the night attending, approached Joanna and Ian.

"I hear your aunt is doing well."

"Yes, and thanks for taking care of her."

"I have grave news to tell you."

Joanna's breath seized. "My aunt has a complication."

"No. She's stable. But James, the parking garage security guard, was found early this morning unconscious due to a skull fracture. He's in the ICU."

Joanna and Ian exchanged knitted brows.

"We just saw him shortly after midnight when we left the hospital while my aunt was in surgery."

"I don't know how long he'd been there. One of the staff went to his car to fetch something and that's when he found James," Hannah said. "The Sheriff's Department has been notified. Complicating matters, the garage lights were off during the night."

"Joanna and I were leaving the hospital when the lights at the fuse box were tripped according to James. They were back on after he fixed the problem."

Joanna clutched Ian's arm and whispered in his ear. "It happened, again!"

"We have an electrician checking the system," Claudia announced.

The outgoing and oncoming teams buzzed about James and the parking garage."

"People! Simmer down!" Claudia called.

The teams hushed and gathered closer.

"As you may have heard, and I confirm, that James, our parking garage security guard, was attacked sometime early this morning. He suffered a fractured skull. Our neurosurgery team immediately responded. James is now in the ICU. Both the Sheriff's Department and Clearwater Police are providing security. Our two day-shift security guards will ultimately alternate shifts. Please arrange to go to the garage in numbers to ensure that everyone reaches their vehicles safely." Claudia continued," However for now we have patients to take care so let's attend to our shift reports."

The teams concluded the transfer rounds and quietly departed.

Joanna pulled Ian aside.

"It's my fault James was attacked. Whoever did this wanted to send Lou Ann a message to not mess with whatever she was investigating. I was supposed to be the target. Not James."

"We have to get to Lou Ann," Ian said.

"And to Harry," Joanna added.

"And I'll make sure you're not left alone under any circumstances."

Lou Ann blinked awake and looked down at the cast surrounding her left leg. Then she remembered that white car broadsiding her. Being airborne, and incredibly in pain. Then smack onto her back and being pushed against the hot asphalt.

How long had she been out?

Was anyone else hurt?

Her heart monitor blipped faster and faster.

"Harry!"

Harry stirred in the chair next to her. "What? What?"

He opened his eyes as if he were seeing her for the very first time, tossed off his blanket, and rushed to her.

"Lou Ann, baby! You're awake!"

Wrinkles rippled across Harry's forehead. "Are you pain?"

"I'm okay. The pain medicine is working. But my face feels tight. How bad does it look?"

"It's swollen and bruised, but less so than last night."

Lou Ann's heart monitor beeped faster and faster.

"Chastity!"

"She's all right. She was treated for road rash, and was discharged from the emergency room last night."

Lou Ann took a deep breath. "That's good. I'm so relieved!"

A nurse rushed into the room.

"Your heart rate monitor alarmed, but looks like your heartbeat is back to normal."

The nurse reset the monitor.

"Do you need more pain medicine?" the nurse asked.

"No, I'm good. Thank you."

The nurse left, but a woman in scrubs and with a doctor's badge entered.

"Good morning. I'm Hannah Fulton, the emergency doctor on duty when you arrived. You look much improved since last night."

"That's because I've had the best doctors and nurses."

Joanna and Ian rushed into the room.

"You're awake!" Joanna cried. She pointed to the man in scrubs who also wore a doctor's badge. "This is Dr. Ian Hottman. I work with him in the emergency room. We were both here before you went to the operating room."

"Hmmm. This *is* Dr. Hottman?"

"Yes."

Lou Ann would interrogate him later. Priority one was to get out of here and pursue her investigation.

"I'm happy you're recovering, and according to Dr. Mills, your surgery went well," Ian said.

"Boy, it's getting crowded in here. You must be quite popular," Dr. Mills said as he entered the room.

"I'll leave you with Dr. Mills, Dr. Hottman, and Nurse Stemple," Dr. Fulton said.

"Thank you, Dr, Fulton," Lou Ann said.

"I echo the sentiment," Harry said.

"Okay, Dr. Mills, when can I get out of here?"

"You just got here." Jason Mills grinned. "And I just got to know you."

"Nothing personal," Lou Ann joked.

"No offense taken. Let's see how you're doing." Dr. Mills approached Lou Ann. "Your vital signs have been A+ and your bloodwork this morning is normal. And I did have to put in a few screws and plates to stabilize your fracture."

"I hope there weren't any spare parts left over."

Dr. Mills chuckled. "None that I'm aware of. The cast will stay on for quite a while and you'll require some rehabilitation such as physical therapy. You'll need crutches, and we'll take care of that before you go home. So the short answer is that you can't leave yet.

For now, can you wiggle your left toes?"

Lou Ann wiggled them.

"Perfect."

She needed out of here and get to the man she captured on her cell. She was certain he was the key to her investigation. But how to do that with a cast? Harry! And Tim Farmer! She couldn't involve Glenda because it was Glenda's niece. Too close. She couldn't compromise the investigation surrounding the deaths of three innocent young people. She refused to add anymore victims.

"Dr. Mills, Harry, Ian and I need to speak to you outside," Joanna said.

"Okay," Dr. Mills said.

While Mills, Ian, and Joanna headed out of the room, Lou Ann tugged Harry's shirt.

"The cell photo."

"I saw it."

"I need to get out of here."

"You heard Dr. Mills. It's best you stay here."

"No!"

"Lou Ann, I'll be right back."

Damn! She was stuck in this bed. But not for long.

38

Joanna pulled Harry aside. "We need to get her out of here. Ian and I were nearly attacked last night in the staff parking garage when someone tripped the lights. Luckily, the security guard fixed it and then Ian and I were able to leave safely. But this morning the guard was found unconscious and suffered from a skull fracture. Probably because he intervened. I was targeted as message to Lou Ann or to you, Harry. I'm not sure. Maybe both of you. The security guard tragically took the brunt."

"That's awful and evil. The cell photo that Lou Ann took while investigating at Spark—he looks like the drug trafficker I killed. Lou Ann needs protection."

"Absolutely," Ian said.

"Can you please let me into this huddle?" Dr. Mills asked.

Ian explained the dire situation to him.

Dr. Mills's face tightened. "It's too soon to discharge her."

"Home health!" Joanna suggested.

"I have to agree. We should at least give it serious consideration, Jason," Ian said.

Mills propped his chin on his palm and paused.

"Dr. Mills, Lou Ann is in danger and potentially other people, like the security guard, could be hurt. Please," Harry pleaded.

"Ian and I will help you with securing a home health nurse," Joanna said.

Dr. Mills shook his head. "I'm uncomfortable but yet comfortable with this decision. Nothing like this has ever happened before."

"You haven't had a patient like Lou Ann before," Harry quipped.

"True. I'll arrange for home health, but it probably will take the better part of the day to make the arrangements. However, she will need to come see me post-op."

189

"Agreed," Harry and Joanna said at the same time.

She was unable to get out of bed to join the gathering outside her room. It was about her, and she hated that she couldn't participate. But she'd put her proverbial foot down—her right one. She would not spend another night in the hospital.

Her room's door eased open. The conclave had apparently broken up.

"I will discharge you later today," Dr. Mills said.

"I know that's a difficult decision for you, but it's for the best for everyone involved."

"We'll also set in motion the arrangements for a home health nurse."

"I'll check in on you and report your status to Dr. Mills," Ian added.

"And I'll be there too along with Harry. Between the three of us, we'll make sure you won't be alone," Joanna added.

Lou Ann wasn't a baby, but she did need help, initially. But she'd keep that to herself to avoid spoiling her discharge. Plus, Harry had his own obligations. And she had two good hands, and along with her exceptional aim, she could fire her gun at any intruder. She'd be more than fine.

"I deeply appreciate the care I've been accorded here, and I'm grateful for all the plans surrounding my discharge today."

Dr. Mills took a deep, conflicted breath and then nodded. He pointed at Lou Ann. "And this doesn't negate your post-operative follow-up with me."

"Understood," Lou Ann said.

"Great," Joanna said.

"Also Joanna and I will be in the ED. Let us know how we can help," Ian said to Dr. Mills.

Joanna kissed Lou Ann's head. "I'm only two floors away."

"I know."

"And you're not rid of me," Harry said.

"I wouldn't have it any other way."

She couldn't believe it. She was finally home. She was practically an expert at using crutches even before she left the hospital.

Dr. Mills, with Ian's and Joanna's help, had speed-ordered a wheelchair, and to Lou Ann's wrinkled horror, a bedside commode and, yuk, a bedpan.

Harry had picked up all the medicines Dr. Mill's prescribed at the pharmacy.

In fact, everyone had gone out of their way to bring her home.

Except for the crutches, she'd make short-order of the rest of the stuff.

Harry parked as close to the front door as he could, while Lou Ann remained reclined in the passenger seat to accommodate her bulky cast.

"I'll be right back. I need to unlock the front door, disable the alarm, and open the door."

Lou Ann watched Harry fuss over her.

She'd assert her independence as soon as she could to relieve him of his duties to her. He had a job, and so did she. Damn this cast!

Harry returned to the car.

"All right. Alley-oop."

Harry scooped Lou Ann up out of the car and carried her into the house.

"Damn, you got heavy!"

Lou Ann chuckled. "It's the cast."

"Uh-huh."

Lou Ann smacked Harry's shoulder.

"I'm joking. My back is fine."

He carried her to the bedroom where stacked pillows for her head and legs were placed especially for her comfort.

"Harry."

"What?"

"Do I tell you how much I love you?"

"Pretty much."

He laid her gently on the prepared bed as if she would break.

"Comfy?"

"Very much so. Thanks."

"I'll go get your antibiotic and a pain pill."

"I'll have one of each please, garçon."

Harry grinned and bowed.

"Would madame like something to drink?"

"I guess a cocktail is out of the question, so ginger ale will do."

"Fine choice, madame."

While Harry left to fetch her requests, Lou Ann stared at the bedside commode. She sighed. If she was alone, she could end up stranded on the bathroom floor. Then someone would have to rescue her. Nope. The commode would have to do…for now.

Harry returned with a bedside tray.

"Today's special to start with is an appetizer consisting of an antibiotic capsule with a pain pill on the side. The entree for this evening is a turkey sandwich and, as requested, a glass of our finest ginger ale. Enjoy."

He set the tray across her lap.

"Might you join me?"

"Don't mind if I do."

Harry left and once again returned with the exact same menu minus the medicines.

He sat next to her and picked up his glass of ginger ale. "Cheers."

"Cheers"

They clinked glasses and proceeded with their dinner.

"Harry, what about Joley Kay?"

"I'll pick her and Isabelle up from Suzy's once you get settled."

"That's not what I mean. I'm scared that she'll be scared when she sees my face and this cast."

"She can't live at Suzy's, and she's going to have to see you. It will be worse if she's told to stay away. She won't understand."

"I get it."

"Eat your dinner."

She'd eaten her dinner with Harry next to her. The antibiotic tasted tinny and the pain pill bitter despite the ginger ale and the sandwich. But she needed both. The pain pill took the edge of the discomforts of the day, including the early discharge and the mechanics of settling in at home. She'd only required one pill. It was effective and yet didn't make her drowsy.

Her palms started to sweat and her throat went dry anticipating her daughter's cries when she saw her mama in this kind of condition.

Harry would be back with Joley Kay and Isabelle any minute now.

The front door opening echoed into the bedroom.

The baby giggled and Isabelle barked, both happy to be home.

Now she'd spoil it for both of them.

Isabelle romped into the bedroom and her paws skidded to halt.

Isabelle eyed Lou Ann.

If Isabelle reacted this way, surely Joley Kay would squirm away from her.

Isabelle slowly approached Lou Ann.

"Hey, girl. It's me."

The dog licked Lou Ann's hand and settled at her side.

"Thank you, my sweet girl."

Her other sweet girl hadn't made her appearance yet.

Maybe Harry was preparing her.

"Mama's in here," she heard Harry say. "She has a boo-boo."

"Boo-boo?"

"Remember when you fell down and got a boo-boo?"

"Uh-huh."

Wow, new vocabulary.

Harry entered the bedroom while holding Joley Kay.

Joley Kay reached out to Lou Ann.

"Uh, oh. Mama boo-boo."

She didn't cry. She didn't pull away in horror!

Harry set Joley Kay next to Lou Ann.

Joley Kay tapped on Lou Ann's cast.

"Careful, princess," Harry warned his daughter.

"It's all right. It doesn't hurt. She's just exploring."

Joley Kay examined Lou Ann's bruised face and pointed at it. "Boo-boo."

"Yes, mama has a big boo-boo."

Joley Kay took Lou Ann's hand and kissed it.

"Thank you. All better now."

"Mama play."

"Mama can't play right now."

Joley Kay scooted to the edge of the king bed.

"Hey, where are you going?" Lou Ann called.

Harry grabbed the baby.

He tapped her nose. "You little wanderer."

"Bear!" Joley Kay demanded.

"You want your bear?" Harry asked.

She nodded.

"Okay, let's get your bear."

Harry left the bedroom only to return with Joley Kay clutching her bear.

"Here, Mama."

She dropped her favorite stuffed bear next to Lou Ann.

Harry smiled. "Satisfied?" he asked Lou Ann.

"Satisfied doesn't begin to describe how I feel." A tear dribbled down Lou Ann's swollen face. "I'm beyond words."

39

Joanna glanced at the ED clock and confirmed the time on her watch. One and half hours until end of her shift. It had been an unusually slow day in the ED, making the passage of time pass much slower. Lou Ann was home by now, and thankfully the arrangements made before Lou Ann's discharge went smoothly.

Joanna had one last important thing to do, call Kaylee. She should've done that at the time of the accident and then when Lou Ann was in surgery. But everything cascaded at seemingly lightning speed. Perhaps she'd be angry that neither she nor Harry contacted her.

Joanna dodged into the break room, and fortunately she was alone.

She double-checked Greek time before dialing Kaylee's cell.

"Hey, Joanna. What's up? Strangely, I was just thinking about you guys. How is everyone? Joley Kay must be into everything. I can't wait to see her and all of you. You have to come to Greece. How's Ian?" Kaylee innocently prattled on.

"Stop, Kaylee."

Pause with both Joanna and Kaylee breathing into their phones.

"Lou Ann was in an accident. A car hit her."

More pause.

Kaylee's anger seeped through Joanna's cell.

"I'm so sorry, Kaylee. It happened so so fast."

"When?"

"The night before last. She had surgery yesterday in the wee hours and, uh, she got home today."

"Today, your time. You're telling me she left the hospital twenty-four hours later."

"It's complicated. It was for her safety."

"Safety?"

"Yes. She was working on three related deaths when she was intentionally hit by a car. Her surgeon, Ian, and I arranged for home health. Plus, Ian is going to check on her even after she's home." Pause. "Are you mad at me?"

"No. Yes. I don't know. My head is spinning. I'm on my way."

Kaylee hung up before Joanna could explain further. But then a phone call couldn't address everything that happened and was happening. It was better this way.

Ian walked into the break room.

"Are you okay?" he asked.

"Sort of. I just called my sister who lives in Greece. She's on her way."

"From Greece? Your sister?"

"Yes, and yes, my adoptive sister."

"Both were true. But she and Kaylee had a bond—a sisterhood—that she wasn't ready to divulge. She'd leave the description of their relationship as simply "sister."

"Wow. Not that I ever wanted to meet Kaylee during a tragedy, but just the same, I look forward to meeting her."

"She looks a lot like me."

An understatement.

How was she going to explain this?

Joanna's secret past was about to burst open.

Joanna stood next to Ian at change of shift report and pressed her feet into the floor to thwart her fidgeting. Ian seemed distracted too, and recapped the uneventful shift more succinctly than usual.

She was out of her here.

Ian hurried to Joanna before she dodged into the women's locker room.

"Wait for me. We'll walk out together for safety. Plus, I'll follow you to your house so I can check on Lou Ann."

She leaned in to kiss him, but quickly pulled back, stifling the urge.

They were already the butt of gossip.

"I'll meet you at the ED exit to the parking garage," she whispered.

"Okay."

Joanna whipped off her scrubs, tossed them in the hospital laundry bin, and changed into her jeans and shirt.

"I heard about your aunt. I'm so sorry," Shelly said.

"Thank you. She's recovering. I have to hurry home."

"I understand."

Joanna hugged Shelly and bolted out of the locker room.

Ian was already waiting for her.

He held out his hand. "Shall we?"

Joanna looked around and saw no one.

They'd dressed so quickly that they were the first ones at the exit to the garage, so she accepted his hand.

They'd parked next to each other, making the trip quickly and alone.

Joanna jumped into her car and Ian into his, and he followed her out of the parking garage and then all the way to her house.

Joanna pulled into the driveway next to Harry's car. Lou Ann's car stood painfully empty and silent. Ian parked on the side as he'd done before.

He was still an outsider to the family, but increasingly less so.

Joanna waited for Ian to hop out of his car, and they walked to the house where she unlocked the door and, after Ian entered, she set the alarm.

"It's just me," Joanna called. "And Ian," she added.

"Come on back. We're in the bedroom," Harry called back.

"I'll wait in the kitchen," Ian said.

"I'll check if it's okay," she reassured him.

Joanna entered the bedroom to find Harry and Joley Kay snuggled next to Lou Ann.

"Jo-Jo," Joley Kay squealed happily.

"Hi, princess. I see you're with mama and dada."

"Mama have bad boo-boo," Joley Kay announced.

"She sure does. And I'm sure you're making her so much better."

"Uh-huh."

"That's her new phrase," Lou Ann said.

Joanna leaned over Lou Ann and kissed her head.

"Kiss-kiss." Joley Kay puckered her tiny lips.

Joanna kissed Joley Kay's cheek and got a wide baby grin as her reward.

Then she kissed Harry's cheek.

"Looks like the whole gang's here."

Joanna sat on the side of the bed.

"I called Kaylee."

Harry grimaced. "I totally forgot."

"So did I. She obviously was shocked and a bit angry. She's on her way."

"I'm relieved," Harry said.

"I know it's a long trip, but I am and always will be happy to see her," Lou Ann said.

"I'm glad, and I'm sure Kaylee is anxious to see you, and she'll see how well you're recovering."

"Maybe my face won't look so monstrous by the time she arrives."

"I don't think you look like a monster," Harry said. "And obviously neither does Joley Kay."

"Count me in," Joanna said.

"Oh, I have to call Glenda about the investigation."

"Glenda knows, and so does Tim Farmer. Both came to the hospital when you were in surgery, and Tim was at the scene too. You may not remember."

Lou Ann shook her head. "No, I do remember Tim being there. I'll call Glenda. I refuse to be bumped from the case."

"Lou Ann, you just got home and, although necessary, way too early. You won't be back on duty for some time."

Lou Ann scowled. "Says you. Bring me my laptop!"

Joanna eased out of the room and hurried to the kitchen, where Ian was having coffee.

"I heard," he said.

"You have to do something about her! If she keeps this up, she'll delay her healing and worse not heal properly."

Ian stood, scooting back the kitchen chair. "Joanna, I'm here strictly in a professional capacity for your aunt. She's stubborn and a fighter. But I'll try to talk to her."

Ian grinned and then kissed her, again this time on her cheek. Which was perfectly fine with her. Her lips weren't ready, and her body might never be."

He tapped her on the nose. "But for you, I'm here strictly on a personal level."

No fireworks, but plenty of sparklers.

"Thank you on both accounts."

"Take me to her."

Ian walked into the bedroom along with Joanna.

"Wow. Looks like you're surrounded," he said. "Can't get that many in a hospital room."

"I'm better off here in my own home." She flipped her hand toward the bedside commode. "As you can see I have all the accoutrements at my disposal."

"For now," Ian said. He nodded at her. "Compromise."

He was all right . She liked him.

Ian examined her face.

"Less swelling. Should be resolved, more or less, within two weeks."

"More or less, huh?"

Ian smiled. "Compromise, remember?"

"Humph. I'll consider it."

"Progress."

Ian next examined her left casted leg.

"Your toes have good circulation."

She wiggled her left toes.

"For the finale," she joked.

Ian took out his cell out of the back pocket of his jeans.

"I'm texting Dr. Mills about your progress. Done."

"Harry, I *need* my cell."

She wouldn't divulge to Joanna or Ian about the photo of the man. He raised his eyebrows at her.

"Lou Ann, your screen is cracked. Remember?"

She played along. "Oh, that's right."

"While Joanna and Ian are here, I'll go buy you a new cell."

Lou Ann managed a surreptitious wink.

"While I'm out, I'll get dinner. Chinese?"

"Sounds good. My usual." Lou Ann looked at Ian. "You like Chinese?"

"I do."

"Well, you're staying for dinner, so put in your order."

"Kung Pao," he said.

"You heard him, Harry."

"I'll be back soon with a new cell and dinner."

After Harry left, Joanna picked up Joley Kay.

"Let Mama rest."

"Mama have bear."

Lou Ann hugged Joley Kay's bear to her chest.

"Thank you, and I'll take good care of bear for now."

"Do you need anything before we leave you alone?" Joanna asked.

"Nope. I'm good."

"I'll be just across the hall in Joley Kay's room."

"I'll be fine, but if I need anything, I'll let you know."

"That goes for me too," Ian said.

Lou Ann gave them a thumbs-up.

"Can you close the door? I want to take a nap before dinner."

"Sure. But you'll call if you need anything, right?"

Lou Ann nodded. "Right."

Joanna left with Joley Kay in her arms and Ian followed.

The bedroom door eased shut.

She was finally alone. Although they were all well-intentioned and fawned over her way too much, she'd been starting to worry that they'd never leave.

Lou Ann stared at the door and waited for Joanna to pop back in, but she didn't.

Lou Ann scooted a bit toward the edge of the bed for her nightstand.

Her arm banged against the nightstand's drawer handle. Damn! Lou Ann grimaced waiting for Joanna or Ian or both to burst into the bedroom at the handle's metallic ping.

But they didn't.

She scooched again. Suddenly and alarmingly weightless and about to pitch over the edge of the bed, she flailed her hands and grabbed onto the mattress to pull herself back. Shit! She almost fell off the bed. Then Joanna and Ian surely would storm into the bedroom like the cavalry.

She reached as far as her arm could reach and—eureka!— her fingers just clawed over the drawer handle.

She pulled the door open inch by inch and pawed inside the drawer until she located her shattered cell phone.

There it is! Come on. Come on. Got it!

She flipped the cell onto the bed, screen side up.

The photo of the this man after he'd left Joe Moreno's Sparks office appeared behind the spider-cracked glass. Her new cell would show a clearer photo since thankfully she'd saved all her data, including photos, in her cloud. She'd eavesdropped on their heated conversation and paid for it. But she wasn't done with the shakedown stranger or with Moreno.

But given her injury, she'd need help to rein them in. If Harry declined to do it, she'd have to resort to plan B.

40

"I'm back with a new cell and Chinese," Harry called.

Lou Ann tossed her cell back into the nightstand drawer, but it bounced off the edge and landed on the floor.

She was supposed to be resting instead of plotting her next move.

The bedroom door eased open.

"Hey, you're awake. Did you get enough rest?"

"Yep."

Harry sat on his side of the bed and handed Lou Ann her new cell.

"We'll review your iCloud-stored files after dinner."

"Absolutely."

Harry was all in.

"Harry, can you get my crutches? I need to get out of this bed. I don't want have a clot form and travel to my lung."

Wrinkles creased in his forehead.

Harry brought her crutches to her side of the bed.

Crunch.

Ummm. He stepped on the smashed cell.

He leaned over and picked up what remained of the smashed cell.

"I thought you were resting?"

"I did for about ten minutes, but I had to study the photo."

"We'll get a better look after dinner, because I'm as perplexed as you are. That can't be the same guy. He's dead."

"Apparently he has a look-alike. Hmmm. Where did we see that happen?"

"Point taken."

Who would have thought that Joanna and Kaylee—two unrelated girls—could have looked so eerily alike?

Joanna peeked in the bedroom and then at the crutches.

"Why don't you set up some plates? Harry and I will be there in a few minutes," Lou Ann said.

"Umm. Okay."

Joanna hesitated and then left the room.

"We'll scrutinize that photo later when we're alone," Harry said.

"Yeah, I don't want to alarm Joanna or Ian, especially because of their close call in the staff parking garage. And then the security guard was attacked. We need to tread carefully. We can't risk anyone else getting hurt, or"—Lou Ann's stomach tightened—"murdered."

"Thanks for dinner," Ian said.

"And thanks for checking in on me," Lou Ann said.

"No problem. You're doing remarkably well despite leaving the hospital early, albeit necessarily."

"I'll walk you out," Joanna said.

Ian waved. "Goodnight everyone."

"See you, Ian," Harry said.

Joanna and Ian stepped out into the cool evening.

She walked with him to his car, and they stopped in front of the driver's side.

Ian leaned in and pressed his lips to hers.

Joanna's heart jackhammered in her chest, and she held her breath while Ian's mouth lingered on hers. Then her mind buzzed to a halt, and she pulled away abruptly. Joanna shuddered. Otto and his cretin entourage—and even Newell— were the last to invade her mouth. It was a horrible reflex!

"Hey. I'm sorry," Ian apologized. "It's too soon, I know, but I couldn't help it. I...didn't mean to make you uncomfortable."

"Don't apologize. I could've pushed you away earlier. It's not about you, Ian."

Confusion colored his face.

"I understand you need more time to consider where we're going."

"I want to go a little slower."

"Take your time. It's okay. I'll wait. Unless, at any time you don't want me too."

Joanna took his hand. "I want to go forward."

"Okay, we'll slow down." He grinned. "It's worth the wait. You're worth the wait."

Joanna grazed her lips against his lips. "Thank you. Don't go anywhere."

"Not planning to."

* * *

"Where are they?" Lou Ann asked.

Harry peeked out the bedroom window.

"They're out by his car. Still talking. Once Ian leaves, I'm sure Joanna will go back in her room. And Joley Kay is fast asleep. We should be good."

"All right, I've accessed my cloud and wait....There! My photos are transferred."

Harry leaned over Lou Ann's shoulder.

"It's not going to go faster this way. I'm searching for the photo."

Harry strained his eyes at the cell's screen while Lou Ann scrolled through photo after photo."

"Stop," he called.

"I see it too."

Lou Ann zoomed in on the stranger's photo.

"Still unbelievable. They're identical. If they are twins, they're were working different angles. And now that I killed his brother, he's going to be really pissed. With the other two in the hospital, your guy is going to run out of his supply soon unless he hooks up with someone else."

"And he's going to need a hell of a lot of money soon, like money from Joe Moreno, who's getting his cash from club-goers, who'll pay for whatever drug they're selling, and whoever innocently dies from an unsuspecting overdose, well," Lou Ann slapped the mattress, "that's the risk of business."

Harry bolted out of bed. "I'm going down to Spark."

"And I'm going with you."

Harry shook his head. "No, babe, this is a running sport and you can't run, and no way am I going to risk losing you. Be honest. You know it's not possible. I would have given anything to not have this happen to you. But it did. And you're alive, and you're going to stay that way."

Harry's agent cell rang.

He entered a code.

"Baxter."

He clutched his cell.

"Affirmative."

He looked at Lou Ann.

"I've got to go. The two injured drug traffickers escaped from the hospital. They're out there."

Harry ran out of the house. Thank God Joanna and Ian were still by his car.

"Joanna! Ian! Get in the house, now!"

"What's happening?" Ian asked.

His tightened face mirrored her frozen shock.

Harry's bellow surpassed his ire when she and Kaylee returned after absconding with his car for a joyride. He hadn't been angry then either. He'd been in full panic.

"Lock your car doors, Ian. We need to go back inside right now! Something's terribly wrong."

"Okay," he said, with an exhaled low whistle following his anxious affirmative.

He pressed the car's remote and the doors beeped into locked position.

They rushed toward Harry, who stood sentry at the open front door.

Joanna and Ian darted inside past Harry and then Harry returned inside, shut the door, locked it, and set the alarm.

"What's happening, Harry?" Joanna blurted, afraid of the answer.

"I need to leave right away, and I can't leave Lou Ann alone."

"Why?" Joanna begged.

"Something happened that I urgently need to take care of."

Joanna shook her head. "That's not an adequate answer."

"That's all I can tell you at the moment."

"No!" she insisted. "You don't get to march us back in here for nothing."

Ian's eyes grew huge in the silence.

"I had to kill a man on a drug boat or he and his three traffickers would have killed us. The two who were injured were taken to a Tampa trauma unit. They just escaped after punching a guard and shoving nurses. I need to track them down."

Joanna tugged on Harry's sleeve. "Not alone. Please don't go alone."

"No. My partner, the State Police, the Sheriff, and police units, and more, are forming a dragnet. We'll get them. But I need you to stay here, not only so you can watch over Lou Ann and Joley Kay, but also for your safety."

"I'll be here all night," Ian said.

"Good man. Thank you."

Harry returned to the bedroom to get his last-minute gear.

"I don't need a babysitter," Lou Ann said.

"It's for their protection and Joley Kay's."

Harry reached into the under panel of Lou Ann's nightstand, took out her pistol, loaded it, and handed it to her, along with additional ammunition.

"You're not the babysitting type."

"I'll be ready," she said.

"Me too."

He leaned over, kissed her, and left.

41

After Harry skidded out of the driveway, Joanna peeked into the nursery where Joley Kay baby-snored, blessedly unaware of what was happening. She left the nursery door open.

Lou Ann was next on her rounds.

"Hey. Wow!"

"Yes, it's loaded, and the safety is on. So you and Ian can go to sleep now, separately."

"Separately is not the issue. The loaded gun is."

"No, *the gun* is my issue."

She could shoot from anywhere and at any position and not miss.

"Harry left me in charge," Joanna said.

"Oh, he did? Really? Is that why he gave me a full loaded gun plus ammo? Who's here to protect who?"

Lou Ann and Joanna traded glares.

Joanna's eyes began to mist. "I can't lose you. I can't lose Harry. I'd be utterly lost."

Lou Ann beckoned to Joanna. "Come here. Lay your head on my shoulder."

Joanna crawled into bed and rested against Lou Ann.

"You're okay. I'm okay. Harry chases after people for a living, and so do I, and we've been doing it since way before you came. Yeah, it can be scary for you, me, and Harry. But Harry and I have done this for years, so we have that going for us."

Lou Ann kissed Joanna's head.

"Go. Make Ian comfortable, because no one is going anywhere for a while."

"Okay. I love you."

"I love you too. And my job as a mother is to protect my family, including Ian, who I can tell is absolutely ga-ga over you, which isn't hard to do."

"I told him I want to go slow."

"Is he pressing you?"

"No. I let him kiss me briefly and that's where we are, and he's fine with that."

"Good. Let it develop at your pace."

"I haven't told him or anyone at the hospital about the details of my past. Don't be upset, but I've been talking with Kaylee, and she said the same thing. But I do need you."

Lou Ann stroked Joanna's hair. "I know, and I'm not upset. I'm happy you and Kaylee have each other."

"Speaking of Kaylee, she'll be arriving tomorrow."

"I'm sure this situation will be resolved before she arrives."

Joanna got off Lou Ann's and Harry's bed.

"Goodnight, *Mom*."

"Goodnight, sweetheart."

Joanna handed Ian a pillow and blanket and led him to the sofa in the den.

"Thank you," he said.

He fluffed the pillow and set it at the far end of the sofa.

They sat together on the sofa, silence between them.

Ian rested his hand on Joanna's.

"Get some rest. I'll be right here by the front door, and I'm a light sleeper—a consequence of staying awake in the ED, including overtime. He grinned. "And I have supersonic hearing."

"We have that in common."

Joanna swallowed past the dry lump growing in the back of her throat.

She 'd memorized Otto's footsteps as they approached her locked cell door, and followed by his vile cadre of men waiting to take their turn with her.

Ian squeezed her hand. "Are you all right?"

"I'm just on edge," she explained, keeping her tortured past filed under "secret" along with all the sordid details in the section of her brain marked "Do not open."

Neither did she reveal Lou Ann's loaded gun because there was no point in thickening the tension surrounding this bizarre evening.

And she wouldn't blame Ian if after tonight he'd never return and probably even avoid her.

Ian huddled on his makeshift lookout point and waved to her.

"I'll leave my door open."

It wasn't an invitation for him to join her, but he'd settled in, and she doubted he took what she said that way.

Joanna tiptoed down the hallway so she wouldn't wakeup Joley Kay.

She peeked into the nursery one last time to find Joley Kay in the same position she'd left her.

Joanna took a deep breath and then spied on Lou Ann, whose eyelids fluttered.

She turned to head toward her bedroom when Lou Ann said, "I know you're there."

Nothing gets past Lou Ann.

42

Randall Ranger jumped into Harry's car just as Harry began to pull away.

"You're getting slow," Harry said.

"Fast enough to get in," Ranger said.

Harry hung a sharp left out of the field office.

"That the fuck happened?" Harry groused. "They were cuffed to their beds."

"FHP, police and sheriff units are casting a wide net."

"Let's hope they have big nets."

Harry hurried along the street to the hospital.

Red and blue strobes formed a ring lighting up the evening sky.

Ranger set their blue strobe on the dashboard of the FBI-pool black sedan.

A Sheriff's deputy waved them over to the locked-down hospital entrance.

Harry parked the car at the tail end of the caravan of law enforcement vehicles, and he and Randall exited the car to meet two policemen who waited at the rear of their vehicle.

"Baxter and Ranger, FBI," Harry announced.

"Come with us. They're ready for you," one of the policemen said.

Harry and Randall followed the policeman to the hospital's guarded main entrance.

"Baxter and Ranger," the policeman said.

Two sheriff deputies nodded and let them through.

The hospital's entrance doors clicked shut.

"Glenda…Assistant Sheriff Martinez," Harry corrected himself.

"Agent Baxter. Agent Ranger," Glenda acknowledged them. She raised her eyebrows at Harry. "Please tell me Lou Ann is not about to come through that door."

"I won't have to because she's standing guard at the house, along with Joanna and Dr. Ian Hottman, who is an ED physician who works with Joanna. He was visiting with her when all this went down."

"Visiting, huh?"

"Yes, thankfully so. I believe someone was following them the other night in the staff parking garage at Hampton."

"Where the security guard was attacked?"

"Same."

Glenda's stoic expression vanished.

Lou Ann's at home, locked and loaded. Even with a bad leg she can shoot the dick off of a mosquito."

Glenda nodded. "Best sharpshooter we have."

Then she resumed her "commanding" face.

"We're going to the third floor," she said.

She halted before the elevator bank.

"Deputy Timothy Farmer was pistol whipped and two nurses were brutally beaten. All are in intensive care. The patient unit has been evacuated, and all patients and staff have been moved and are presently being guarded by my deputies and the police."

Harry's brain scrambled. "Tim Farmer? Lou Ann's Tim Farmer?"

"Yes. He fought hard, but ultimately was overtaken. But he saved the nurses' lives. Lou Ann trained him well."

"I'll let her know when I can."

The elevator door dinged open and Harry, Ranger, Glenda and two sheriff deputies entered.

After the doors closed, Glenda pushed the third-floor button and stepped back, joining the rest of them while the elevator ascended in silence.

Harry, Ranger, Glenda and the accompanying sheriff deputies exited the elevators to an eerie ghostly unit.

The usual buzz of the nurses' station stood still and silent, and the computer screens were blank, as if in homage to the violence that engulfed the place of healing.

While white-hooded crime scene techs with knee-high footed coverings circled the hospital room's carnage, photographing the room and collecting specimens, Harry and Ranger took the stairwell to the second floor where the unit was temporarily relocated.

They walked past closed patient doors and nodded to the sheriffs and police crews standing guard.

"This is Agent Ranger, and I'm Agent Baxter we're here to interview the third-floor staff."

Harry and Ranger proceeded unimpeded to the combined second and third floor nurses' stations and displayed their FBI badges.

"We'd like to speak to the third-floor staff. Is there a place we could do that?" Harry asked.

"Yes. My name is Jenna Sands, and I was the third-floor charge nurse this evening."

"Ms. Sands, I'm deeply sorry for the tragedy that occurred here this evening."

Jenna momentarily looked down and then at Harry.

"Thank you. I can lead you to a conference room."

"We appreciate that."

Harry and Ranger followed Jenna.

She unlocked the conference room door. "It's empty tonight and private."

Empty was the theme this evening.

A long, dark wood table sat in the middle of a desolate room surrounded by too many empty seats surrounding it. The interview room at the field office was a quarter the size of the room, and a tenth the size of prison interview ones. Even the conference rooms at the field office weren't as big. Harry scanned the room, amazed how uncomfortable he was in the expansive space.

"We use this conference room mainly for presentations, etc, because of its size. I don't have anything smaller or more private."

"This is fine, thank you." Harry cocked his head. "Can you stay for a while to talk with us?"

"Sure. I'm way out of my elements tonight anyway."

Harry, Ranger, and Jenna sat at the end of a table that could easily accommodate twenty-five people.

Harry folded his hands on the table while Ranger sat back cross-legged with a notebook and pen in his hands.

"I'm going to ask you a few questions."

Jenna glanced at Ranger and then back at Harry.

"I imagine this may seem intimidating, but it's important for us to get contemporaneous notes," he reassured her. "Take your time answering. Often after such a shock, it may be hard to recall everything. No pressure."

"Okay." Jenna leaned forward. "But I want them caught and severely punished for what they did to Nancy, Millie, and Deputy Farmer!"

"You said *them*."

"Yes, them, the two of them."

Jenna pulled back. "I'm angry. I'm scared."

"Understandable," Harry replied softly.

Although he wanted to go straight to the two unknown evil interlopers, Harry refocused to an orderly chain of questions.

"When did you come on shift?"

"I got here at 6:45pm, as usual. Shift turnover starts about then. I'm the charge nurse from 7pm-7 am."

"How many nurses are there per shift?"

"We're usually full up and my nurses are rarely floated to another unit, so a full staff on our postoperative and surgical unit consists of eight nurses."

"Regarding the two drug traffickers, did the same nurses care for them?"

Jenna squeezed her hands into fists and then sucked in a deep breath.

"Yes. Nancy Chang and Millie Ford are the two nurses who cared for these individuals, and were attacked tonight."

"Do you need a few minutes?"

"No, I want to go on…for them and Deputy Farmer." Jenna eased her tight fists. "So Deputy Farmer arrived to relieve Deputy Reiss at our change of shift. The deputies would stand guard outside the room the men shared for containment purposes. The shift change occurred uneventfully, and Nancy and Millie went inside for their normal rounds and to check the mens' wounds, et cetera—normal postoperative care—with Deputy Farmer protectively present. I saw them all go into the room.

The deputy had the keys to the cuffs and always carried a gun just in case. Also the individuals were shackled to their bed. We normally don't do that, but given their violent behavior, we continued with the shackles. While Deputy Farmer stood guard with his gun, Nancy and Millie's plan was to change the individuals' dressings and managed their IVs, same as on dayshift. And as per protocol, the men had been unshackled—not at the same time—and the deputy would accompany each of them to use the bathroom. They were also checked for any complications resulting from being shackled and then shackled again. They were scheduled to be transferred tomorrow morning to the prison infirmary, and then once they were deemed medically stable enough, placed in regular cells. Am I talking too fast or confusing you?"

"No, you're doing fine."

Ranger nodded.

Jenna cleared her throat and continued. "Then two men wearing hospital scrubs asked what room the men were in because they were there to provide physical therapy. But the weird part was that physical therapy typically takes place during the day shift. I inquired about that, and they said they were very busy during the day and the men were the last ones on their list."

Jenna stuttered a breath. "God forgive me, I let them pass."

Harry placed his hands on Jenna's balled fists.

"You didn't know."

Alarm gripped Harry. How the hell did these scumbag imposters get hospital scrubs?

When Jenna's curled fingers eased, and Harry slipped his hand from her hers.

He needed to get a description of the evil imposters.

"Can you describe what the two men looked like?"

"One was tall and bulky…muscular., about your height, and with curly black hair. The other was a bit shorter," she pointed to Ranger " but muscular too. Uhhh. And brown hair, straighter, and parted on the side."

Jenna's eyes misted and she sniffled.

"And I and several nurses heard some thuds coming from the room and failed to notice that Nancy, Millie, and Deputy Farmer never came out of the room. By the time I approached and entered the room, the 'physical therapists' were gone and so were the men. Deputy Farmer was bloodied, and moaning, slumped against the far wall. And both of his guns were missing. I found Nancy crying, her face bloody and crawling toward the door while Millie huddled in a corner, shaking and with her head down. Her scrubs were bloodstained. The shackles and the men's patient gowns were tossed on the floor and they were gone. I called the hospital rapid response team and 911."

Jenna pressed her hand across her mouth and kept shaking her head.

"Jenna, where do staff get their scrubs?"

"There are both men's and women's locker rooms on each floor, and you need a code to get in." Jenna gasped. "Oh, no!"

Ranger stopped writing in his notebook and looked at Harry.

They needed to end this fast, and go through every locker room stat because these monsters must have followed someone into the locker room and could have injured or killed the person they followed to get those scrubs.

"Jenna, how would we get in these locker rooms?"

"I have the codes for the women's ones on this floor and the third floor, and the nursing supervisor has the codes for all the locker rooms."

"Can you get the supervisor for me?"

Jenna bolted from her seat.

"Yes, and yes."

Harry and Ranger rushed out of the conference room and followed Jenna.

They halted at the nurses' station.

"I need the nursing super, stat!"

"Right away," one nurse said.

"Follow me," Jenna said.

She led then to the second-floor women's locker room and entered the code to open the door. It clicked.

"Anyone in here?" she yelled.

No answer.

They entered, and Harry and Ranger scanned the room and then walked throughout it. Nothing was disturbed as Harry had expected, but he and Ranger would still to go through everything as fast as they could.

"Thanks, Jenna."

"The nursing supervisor should be here by now." she replied.

And when they arrived, a woman in scrubs and a lab coat and carrying a clipboard was already waiting for them.

"These are Agents Baxter and Ranger, and they need your immediate help to get access into the locker rooms."

"Yes, I'm apprised of the situation. I'm Gwen Ives. Let's go!

"We need to narrow our focus to the men's locker rooms," Harry said.

"I thought the same."

"This is a large hospital, but given the proximity to the room on the third floor, I need to start with the second, third, and fourth floors."

"Absolutely," Gwen said.

They gathered at the second-floor men's locker room and Gwen gave them access.

Harry's pulse quickened.

Harry and Ranger ran through the locker room.

Nada

"Next," Harry said.

Gwen led them up the stairwell to the third floor, where all the action was happening at the end of the hallway.

Glenda waved at them, but Harry couldn't stop. He'd get to her as soon as could. Instead he nodded his head and gestured an umpire swipe. He'd explain later.

Gwen rushed to the third floor men's locker room.

Could this be it? He shifted his thoughts. *Too close.* Still they needed to look just in case.

Again, another code. Another unlock. Nothing.

The three bolted up the stairwell to the fourth floor and Gwen unlocked the men's locker room. A soft moan met Harry's ears, and based on the wide-eyed look on Ranger's face, they'd found the breach.

Harry and Ranger squatted next to the man in scrubs.

"Sir, we're here to help you. What happened to you?"

The man held his head.

"I came to get scrubs cuz I was late for my shift. Two men pushed the door open before it closed after me. One punched me in the head, and I don't remember after that cuz I passed out."

Gwen spoke in her cell. "I need rapid response in the fourth floor men's locker room!

The man was hurt, but alive.

Ranger pointed to the shelves covered with tangled, and obviously pawed through pairs of scrubs.

"Did you see the men who broke in and assaulted you?"

"No one I know. Bulky. One with black curly hair raised his fist. Then the ear-ringing punch. Both white men."

Harry and Ranger waited until the rapid response team arrived.

This latest information not only fit the timeline, but also the description of men who'd come to break out their criminal gang members at any cost. They were out there now, ready and willing to take down anyone who happened to blunder into their path.

Harry knew exactly where the men on the loose were heading.

He and Ranger exchanged knowing glances.

"The docks," they said at the same time.

Harry and Ranger rushed out of the fourth-floor men's locker room, ran down the stairwell steps, two at a time, and bolted out of the third-floor stairwell door. In contrast to the huddled group of nurses and patients on the second floor—except for the gaggle of law enforcement spilling out of the room, now designated as a crime scene—the remainder of the floor was eerily devoid of nurses and patients.

Glenda stepped away from the crowd and raised her arm to flag them down.

They met halfway down the hallway, huddling out of earshot from the crime scene's buzz.

"Where have you been and what do you know?" she pressed.

Harry brought her up to speed on Jenna's interview, the successful breakout of their criminal subjects by fellow gang members posing as physical therapists in scrubs they'd obtained after assaulting a hospital employee. Most important, they were out and armed and dangerous. Plus, they now had Tim Farmer's gun.

Glenda's eyes got wider while she listened to Harry's report.

"Ranger and I have to go," he said. "We're confident they're headed back to Tampa Bay's intercostal waterways where they had an unfortunate (for them) encounter with both of us and the Coast Guard. Their boat's been confiscated, but they'll kill to steal another.

"Here's what you need to know before heading out," Harry continued. "The hospital's security footage showed two individuals wearing black hoodies pulled over their faces and jeans— believed with some confidence to be our escaped subjects based on physical description. The video showed them sliding into and speeding away in a reported-stolen black Nissan Rogue from a local, closed dealership, with the rear plate replaced. Then the unidentified driver and guy in the passenger seat picked up the two imposters and our two escaped subjects."

Glenda continued, "The crime scene crew has wrapped up processing the room. Multiple Bolos have gone out. Now get out of here. I'll handle the media and the press conference warning the public."

"I have every confidence that Ranger and I will be at the next presser confirming that we've captured the scumbags."

He nodded to Ranger and said, "Let's roll."

43

Lou Ann's cell blared an urgent matter. Joanna and Ian burst into Lou Ann's bedroom with their cells blasting the same emergency beeping message.

They looked at each other dumbfounded.

Lou Ann swallowed hard. Harry had left over an hour ago, and she was sure it was to deal with that emergency whatever it was.

Lou Ann grabbed her crutches and headed into the den.

"Quick! Turn on the TV!" she called to Joanna.

Joanna and Ian ran out of the bedroom.

The TV would be on before she managed to hobble into the den.

She wielded her crutches faster and faster, but when she stepped into the den, Joanna and Ian were already glued to the TV.

Glenda appeared on the screen.

She searched for Harry among the law enforcement agents lined up behind Glenda. He wasn't there. He ran press conferences. Something had gone terribly wrong.

Glenda stepped up to the microphone.

"Good evening. I'm Glenda Martinez, Assistant Sheriff of the Pinellas County Sheriff's Department.

"As you may know, three days ago, FBI Special Agents and Coast Guard officers responded to a foreign vessel in Tampa Bay waterways that contained fifty pounds of Fentanyl, and an unknown substance which is presently in the process of being identified. Two of the suspects were shot and killed during that response due to their lethal threat to all officers. Two of the four perpetrators were injured in gunfire and taken to Tampa Area Regional Trauma Center, and were recovering from their injuries when two unknown individuals aided their escape, and in the process dealt severe injuries to a sheriff deputy and two nurses, all of whom are presently in guarded

216

condition in the intensive care unit along with a surgical assistant, who was found injured in a hospital's men's locker room.

"The escaped perpetrators were last seen wearing dark, hooded sweatshirts and jeans when they, along with the imposters got into a stolen black Nissan Rogue with Florida license plate RWS556Q, joining an unknown driver and front seat passenger.

"Please do not accost these individuals as they are considered armed and dangerous, and please secure your vehicles and your homes.

"Above are the perpetrators' mug shots. I have every confidence that all our law enforcement colleagues will cooperate in surrounding and capturing these dangerous individuals in a timely fashion. I have no further information at this time, and as the situation unfolds, we will call another press conference. Thank you."

Glenda walked away despite the throngs of media chasing after her.

Lou Ann stared at the screen while Joanna and Ian remained silent.

They all jumped when Lou Ann's cell rang.

"It's Harry!"

She gripped her cell.

"Where are you?!"

"Ranger and I are pretty sure where these criminals are going. We're driving now. Do not go outside, and for God's sake, Lou Ann, do *not* intervene. Protect everyone in the house and keep them inside and away from any windows."

Harry paused.

There was something else critical that he needed to say.

"Tim Farmer was the deputy attacked."

Her heart pounded against her chest.

"He's stable, along with the two nurses and surgical technician. You trained him well."

She trained him, but she couldn't protect him.

"Lou Ann?"

"I'm here. We just saw Glenda's press conference. We didn't see you."

"I had to take off. I gotta go. I love you."

Why did he have to say that?

"I love you too," she responded.

She ended the call and stared at the screen.

Those three words could be the last ones they ever exchanged.

44

Harry eased the their vehicle along the street leading to the Tampa docks—the same ones where they'd returned with two dead and two injured drug traffickers.

The headlights from a car behind them grew brighter as it closed in on their tail.

Harry and Ranger unholstered their pistols.

The car behind them moved to the left and began to pull up next to them.

Harry released his gun's safety.

But the car in question, a blue Hyundai with a young couple, passed their purposely creeping-along vehicle, and continuing to the stop sign ahead, where it turned right, away from the docks.

They put their pistols back in their holsters and continued their mission to the docks.

Harry's cell buzzed.

It was from the Coast Guard.

"Quiet out here," the official said. "Nothing in. Nothing out. Mild chop. That's it. Will continue to patrol."

"Thanks."

Harry shook his head.

"Nada, huh?" Ranger asked.

Harry shook his head.

"They may have gone to another dock," Harry said.

Harry's cell buzzed again.

"You're popular. I'm hurt."

"Well, you're not married to a Homicide and Death Investigator who's neck deep in drug-related deaths."

"She have a sister by any chance?"

"Nope."

"Damn."

Although he'd shown up for a rematch, and he'd counted on them showing up with more reinforcements to wreak revenge on him for killing one of their own—their leader. According to the Coast Guard, they weren't in the waters...yet. But they wanted him.

Game on!

The Coast Guard had no further updates to offer.

Harry temporarily abandoned his urge for a showdown with the trafficking gang.

He inspected the vehicle's every mirrored angle.

Although they'd received no reports of them in the water, they didn't need to be in the water to circle him like sharks.

Ranger's cell buzzed.

"Finally,"

"Yes. I'll tell him. We're circling back."

"That was Glenda. They found the Nissan Rogue abandoned in an industrial lot behind...guess where? Spark. It's being towed for processing."

Harry called Lou Ann.

"What's up?" she asked, sounding panicky.

"Ranger and I are at the docks. They're a no-show. But law enforcement has recovered the stolen Nissan in an industrial lot behind Spark—and we're on our way there. They had to have commandeered another vehicle, but none have been reported stolen...yet."

"That's because it hasn't been stolen. Run any vehicle registered to Joseph Moreno."

"Brilliant."

"Of course. I'll be running the same. See you soon."

"Back at you."

It was their code for "Come back alive."

45

Lou Ann set her crutches against the den's sofa.

"Joanna, can you bring me my laptop? I left it on my bed."

No way was she going to sleep. She'd work the whole night if she had to, just as she'd done in the past.

Joanna returned with Lou Ann's laptop.

"Thanks."

Joanna shrugged and returned to her spot next to Ian.

Ian leaned against Joanna and poked his head around to ask Lou Ann, "What's the plan?"

"The criminals who escaped with the help of their gang dumped their vehicle that they'd stolen. It's where they dumped it—behind Spark nightclub—the nightclub where my superior's niece was poisoned—as in intentionally overdosed—and there were two other victims too. There's someone at Spark who I believe is implicated in drug trafficking. What may have looked like money in his pocket by aiding intentional or unintentional drug addiction, it has gone very bad for him, and he doesn't have a way out once he's in, other than death."

"Tragically, I get it. Drug addiction consequences—including overdose and death—pour into every ED in the nation. It's unstoppable at this point. We have to cut the head off each of those snakes, one by one. Problem is, they just regenerate. We need to change the nature of the snakes."

"That's a lot of snakes, but I believe, as we all should believe, that nothing is impossible. That being said, I'm going to scan vehicle registrations starting with the big guy at Spark, Joseph Moreno."

What she wouldn't give to jump in her vehicle and shoot straight over to Spark. But she'd have to leave that to Harry.

Meanwhile, she'd have to work fast from her temporary office, a sofa.

Her fingers hovered over her work laptop, where she could access vehicle registrations and stolen stolen vehicles.

Lou Ann narrowed her eyes.

The database listed vehicles registered to four Joseph Morenos—two in St. Petersburg, one in Tampa, and one in Clearwater.

She steepled her fingers and rolled the tips.

He might be living at any of those addresses.

She closed her eyes to prompt her recollection of when she parked in Spark's lot for that first interview. Moreno got out of a vehicle. *What was it? What was it?* She repeated to herself.

Corvette? That was one of them, but that didn't make sense as a getaway. Hmmm? Ah!

"Silver sedan!" she yelled.

Joanna and Ian sprang to attention.

"BMW!" Her enthusiasm melted. "No."

"No, what?" Joanna asked.

"A Beemer wouldn't fit six individuals: driver, passenger, two enablers, and two escapees."

Lou Ann snapped her fingers. "They got to know that. They've split up!"

She pushed her brain harder.

"Not reported stolen. Therefore, easily taken,"she thought aloud.

She picked up her cell and called Harry.

He answered on the second ring.

She didn't give him a chance to speak and risk losing track of her newborn theories.

"I remember Joe Moreno getting out of a silver Beemer, but not one that could handle six people. They've broken up in a 'divide and conquer'."

"I got the same results."

BANG!

"Harry! Harry! No!" she wailed.

46

"Shit!."

Harry and Ranger exited their damaged vehicle with their pistols ready and crept along next to the incapacitated car.

The car's tires sat, punctured and quickly losing air over a rigged metal strip.

The dark industrial lot was the perfect place to set up a trap and they drove right across it.

Air hissed out of the tires, but no bullets pinged against their barricade.

Harry and Ranger whipped toward the groan of hinges, followed by the echo of a lid slamming, releasing the stink of rotting garbage. A shadow raced away from the dumpster and disappeared like the devil in the night.

Harry and Ranger returned to the grounded vehicle while keeping their pistols on alert.

Harry called the field office.

"We're behind Spark Nightclub in an industrial area. All four of our vehicle's tires have been flattened, and the vehicle is unusable. We request a replacement and a tow."

His cell's pinging would pinpoint their location for assistance.

Harry and Ranger sat in the dark vehicle with darker than dark surrounding them.

"I'm pissed. And so is my gun," Harry said.

Then he called Lou Ann.

She answered on the half-ring.

"Harry?!"

"I'm here, in the lot behind Spark with metal spikes in our tires. Someone popped out of a dumpster, clearly to take a peek at his handiwork. It's overly quiet now, but our backup is on the way."

"All I heard was a bang!"

"Yeah. Surprise. Surprise. I couldn't call earlier."

"I get it, but terror reigned."

"I'm sorry."

"Don't be. You need to be alert for yet another trap. How much longer?"

"This time of night? Five, ten minutes tops. I want to stay on the phone, but I can't."

"Don't want you to."

Lou Ann ended the call before he could.

Lou Ann's cell rang. Her first thought that it was Harry again, but her screen said it was Glenda.

"Yeah, Glenda. I know about Harry. We spoke. Field office has responded."

"Joe Moreno is dead. Shot in the head."

"When?"

"Some time this evening."

Lou Ann was speechless with relief.

"Lou Ann?"

"Yeah."

After the shakedown conversation she overheard, she wasn't shocked.

"It was coming. He had no other way out."

"Agreed."

Lou Ann itched to process the scene. She could do it. It wasn't impossible. The list of victims at Spark's grew. And that didn't include Moreno. He paid the price of "business". But she'd seek justice for Gloria, Elizabeth, and Tyler, who she'd speak for because they deserved to rest peacefully. The only positive aspect was that Spark was out of business, hopefully forever.

"I have to tell you something, and I know this will be difficult. I don't want to hurt you."

"Hurt me? Come on, Glenda."

"A silver Beemer is being tailed."

"That's great. That's the vehicle."

"We're also following another suspected vehicle, a black FORD F 150. Lou Ann, that truck in question is registered to George Mason, the bouncer at Spark."

Her heart skipped a beat.

"Why?"

"He was seen peeling out of Spark's lot after Moreno's exit door alarmed."

"Do you honestly suspect George of murder?"

"Listen to me. I know you and Harry were friendly with him."

"Why would George do that?"

"You and I know that people do things that we didn't think they were capable of."

"No. That's not George. What motive?"

"We need him to come in to interview him. He may have left a crime scene, one that he may have committed."

"No. He may have had words with Moreno, but he wouldn't have killed him. It's possible that when he left Spark, Moreno was alive."

And then she blurted the very words that could end her career.

"Glenda! You're wrong. George came to my rescue. He stayed at the hospital with Harry despite his girlfriend was being evaluated and eventually discharged." Lou Ann's hands were balled into fists. "He held my daughter, for God's sake. This man is not a murderer. I know him. And I should, because I'm the Homicide and Death Investigator here."

Glenda hissed between clenched teeth.

Lou Ann bowed her head. That was her death knell.

"You do NOT want to go there, because I'm the one who appointed you. Remember that. The investigation has to go on."

Both women paused.

"I apologize. Do what you need to do, but I do ask you to keep me apprised of the situation."

"Absolutely. Look, anything is possible. The problem is probability. We need to bring him in. You are aware that if he comes your way, you have a duty to call us."

Lou Ann had no choice but to say, "Yes."

"Go rest. We're on it."

We're?

"Looking forward to having you back," Glenda said, clearly tossing her a bone.

"So am I."

So-am-I.

Red and blue strobes lit up the dark lot while Harry and Ranger sat vigilant in their incapacitated vehicle.

"Shit! Something's going down at Spark. We gotta go," Harry said.

"Let's leave a note on the windshield saying,"Be back soon," Ranger said with dark humor.

Harry opened the door. With the four tires completely flattened, the car door scraped the concrete forcing him to crawl out.

Then the passenger door let out a loud scrape.

Ranger.

"My knees!" Ranger complained.

Whether they stayed in the car, or made their way through the shadowy lot, being ambushed was a risk. But the field house would track them, alive or dead.

So they'd hoof it.

The vehicle would need to be towed, and a replacement would find its way to them.

With their guns drawn and ready to play cat and mouse, Harry and Ranger stole across the asphalt to where they'd entered it— where they drove right into a trap.

They stared at the dumpster where a shadowy figure in a "Jack-in-the-Box" move popped out and raced away.

There could be another one or more watching them, using the one who got-away as a distraction.

Harry gestured to Ranger to ease around the dumpster while Harry stood facing the giant container.

A gang could fit in there, easily overwhelming the two of them.

Harry raised his finger, alerting Ranger, and then he kicked the dumpster, waiting for "rats" to spring at them.

Harry whipped his head around ready to fire at the shadow leaping out from behind the dumpster.

"Rawoo!"

Only a cat.

Everything looked big in the dark.

While Ranger stood at one end of the dumpster and Harry at the other, they lifted the weighty lid.

But the only thing they encountered was rotting trash.

"Let's get out of here," Harry said.

They released the lid, and it rebounded once before slamming shut, leaving a cloud of ashy dust.

Harry and Ranger rushed out of the lot, following the beacon of flashing lights, and found a trail of responding law enforcement vehicles lining the entrance to Spark.

Harry and Ranger walked up to the lead sheriff vehicle.

"Agent Baxter and Agent Ranger," Harry said to identify them. He and Ranger holstered their guns, and both showed their credentials.

"We're responding to where the Nissan Rogue was dumped in a back lot two blocks south of here with potential criminals still in the area. A makeshift tack strip flattened our vehicle's tires so we knew they or at least someone remained in the area. One popped out of dumpster, but we canvassed the area and didn't find anyone else lingering. What's up here?"

"Owner of the place was shot in the head," the deputy said. "Found in his office in the back after an alarm went off."

"We're going to head on back," Harry said.

The deputy nodded.

Harry and Ranger walked to the back of Spark where all the action buzzed and found another sheriff's vehicle, CSU van, and another van marked Medical Examiner, and an ambulance.

Glenda stepped away from her conversation with the ME and flagged down Harry and Ranger and the three gathered in their own circle.

Harry started, "We were in the lot where the stolen Rogue was dumped when we were temporarily ambushed. One popped out of a dumpster, but upon our canvassing, we found no others. We saw the strobes from the lot and here we are. Looks like the owner, Moreno, took a header."

"Yes. But I've got an urgent matter you're not going to like."

Harry's skin prickled. "Not going to like" encompassed multiple meanings.

"It's about George."

"George. What about him?" Harry's brain whirred. "Is he injured?"

"No. He's a suspect on the run."

Harry's thoughts collided.

"After Moreno's office back door alarmed, one of responding deputies, who was in that area, witnessed a black FORD 150 speeding past him. He was able to grab the plate, but his priority was to enter the breached office. He discovered Moreno fatally shot, and then he ran the plate of the 150. It's registered to George."

Harry shut his eyes to internally process the bizarre and nonsensical information.

"No. I can't go with that."

It was his first gut instinct.

Glenda placed her hand on Harry's shoulder while Ranger remained silent.

"You know I need to bring him in for questioning. Given your relationship with George, I can't have you there during the interview."

Harry pressed his lips together and nodded.

"There's our replacement vehicle. We're back in the game. Let's roll, Baxter," Ranger said.

"We all have a long night ahead of us," Glenda said, her eyes empathetic.

"That we do."

Harry and Ranger turned and walked away.

"That we do, partner."

47

Ranger made a hard right while peeling out of Spark's lot causing Harry to swerve shotgun.

Harry clutched his cell before it surrendered to gravity.

"Man, does this car have pickup!" Ranger boasted.

That's what happened when he traded the wheel with Ranger.

But at least they'd canvass the docks from Tampa to Clearwater with lightning speed to cut off the drug trafficking gang before they were long gone, and before these evil-doers could then take great pleasure to shoot at the Coast Guard.

Harry's cell rang with "unknown caller" displayed across his screen.

He raised his finger to Ranger gesturing for him to slow up.

George's panting voice chopped over Harry's cell.

"Harry, I didn't do it."

Harry took a breath.

"Do what, George?" he carefully probed.

"Moreno, I found him there. I gotta go."

"Wait! Where are you going?"

But it was too late. George hung up.

Harry called George back, but he was sent to George's voicemail.

"George, call me back. I want to help you."

Harry stared at his cell.

George wasn't going to call him back. The man was no fool.

He had to get to him before Glenda did.

Lou Ann's and Joanna's cells rang at the same time causing both to startle upright in the couch.

Joanna's eyes went huge. She bolted off the couch and ran out of the room, leaving Lou Ann and Ian to exchange confused looks.

Lou Ann stared at her cell's screen. It was Harry!

"Harry! What's going on?"

"George called. He told me he didn't do it."

"I believe it."

"He's made a big mistake. I told him I'd help him."

"You can't promise that and neither could I because we're too close. Glenda would block us. I know I would. He can't avoid it forever. The longer he stays away, the greater the consequences."

"I know it's hardest for us both, but if he calls…."

"Yeah," her mouth said, but her heart opposed.

"Ranger and I are circling around and expanding our net to cover more docks. The Nissan Rogue is out and perhaps the silver Beemer by now. A speeding getaway boat is likely our target."

Tires skidded in the background and swishing came from Harry's cell.

Lou Ann's chest suddenly grew too small for her heart.

"Harry! Harry! Are you there? God, no!"

"I'm here. Ranger took another of his breakneck curves."

"He's driving?"

"Yes."

Screech.

"Stop sign!" Harry yelled.

"Sorry about that, Lou Ann. We're heading toward the Clearwater docks."

"Hey, slow up, dude. We may want to start tiptoeing," Lou Ann heard Harry addressing Ranger.

"Let me know about George," Harry said.

"I will."

After she'd hear him out.

Joanna returned to the den.

"That was Kaylee. Her jet just landed."

"So I finally get to meet your sister," Ian said.

Joanna glanced at Lou Ann for a reprieve, who only covertly cocked her head, her signal that it was up to Joanna to own the truth before Kaylee arrived to force the issue.

"I think you're going to really like her. She looks exactly like me."

She handled her own reprieve, temporarily.

Ian smiled. "That settles that."

Joann'a stomach clenched.

It was far from settled.

But she trusted Kaylee to ease Ian's shock and worse, the feeling that he'd been betrayed—intentionally lied to.

She wanted to tell him in bits and pieces, but what happened to her and Kaylee weren't bits and pieces, but huge chunks.

"Ian…"

"Yeah."

"Are you thirsty?"

He shrugged. "Maybe some water."

"I'll go get it."

Lou Ann stood with the help of her crutches.

"I'll go with Joanna," Ian said.

"No, Ian. I need to move around. And I have two good hands."

"Okay. You should."

Joanna reached for three bottles of water.

"Ian's a good man, and you and he are increasingly in a growing relationship. I see how he looks at you and you at him. Take it from me, don't ruin what is meant to be."

"He'll leave me. Not right away. He's not like that. He'll distance himself from me, and I'll be left alone."

Lou Ann pitched toward Joanna and hugged her.

"You'll never be alone."

Joanna pressed her head against Lou Ann's shoulder and sobbed.

"I'm sorry I lied to you and Harry about who I was."

"That's past and gone."

"I caused you both pain. I can't do that to Ian."

"It made no difference to us because we loved you. Do you have the slightest doubt in your head, or in your heart?"

"No."

"Okay. Wipe your tears. Wash your face. Kaylee's coming, and Ian is waiting for you in the other room."

Joanna swiped her palms against her wet cheeks and drew in a cleansing breath, and then went to the kitchen sink and splashed cold water on her face, extinguishing the heat of her worries.

She grabbed a towel and dried her face. She paused a few seconds before grabbing the water bottles and headed back to Ian.

"Here you are," she said.

Ian examined her face.

She needed an excuse…fast.

Joanna squeezed her eyes shut, faking an incoming sneeze.

She opened her eyes and breathed a quick breath through her nose.

"Sinuses."

"Let me see," Ian said.

Joanna waved her hands. "I'm fine."

Ian stared into her eyes. "They are watery."

"It will pass. It always does."

"Just never noticed it."

"Nothing that an antihistamine can't fix." Joanna sniffed through her nose. "See? Better already, doctor."

"I'll order maxillary films tomorrow."

Joanna shook her head. "That won't be necessary."

"Guest today. Doctor tomorrow."

"Okay," she said, pacifying him for the moment.

Lou Ann hobbled into the den.

"Feeling better?" Lou Ann asked Joanna.

"Much, thanks."

Lou Ann raised her eyebrows. "You should look into that."

"That's what I told her," Ian said.

48

A silver Beemer eased past an intersection leading to a Clearwater boat slip.

Harry leaned closer to the front windshield, his eyes sharp, his mouth dry, his veins overflowing with adrenaline. *They had them!*

Ranger slowed the car to park one block away.

Harry ran the plate, confirming their target. It was registered to Joe Moreno, the now dead Joe Moreno.

"Ready to walk it?" Harry asked.

"As ready as you are."

They holstered their guns, slipped extra ammo in their gunbelt, and padded their Kevlar.

They were set. The question was how set were their targets.

Harry and Ranger exited the vehicle in almost slow motion and without as much as a squeak of their shoes.

They slinked down an alley, taking cover against walls of businesses that had long since closed for the day, and into the early evening.

Waves slapped the still docks.

Harry peeked past the edge of a building.

Moored boats bobbed in the dark waters.

The Beemer stood waiting, its engine still humming.

From Harry's angle, two were in the front seat, and he could only make out one head in the back. Either way, they were outnumbered, but not outsmarted.

Another head popped up in the back seat.

Four on two.

They hadn't boarded a boat and apparently weren't ready to deploy, but he'd put in a call to alert the Coast Guard regarding the suspected vehicle's location.

"Special Agent Baxter and Special Agent Ranger here at Clearwater docks. Have eyes on suspected silver BMW," he softly spoke in his cell while keeping eagle eyes on the idling Beemer.

"We'll patrol."

"We'll signal when they make their move."

The car stopped idling.

Either they were made or their targets were about to flee.

Harry and Ranger pressed against a wall, ready to fire.

None of the subjects in Moreno's stolen BMW got out. No boat came to pick them up and no boat was commandeered.

Harry called Glenda, and spoke barely above a whisper into his cell.

"Glenda, Ranger and I found them at Clearwater docks, definitely four, parked in Moreno's stolen silver BMW. They're waiting for something or someone. I'm also requesting reinforcements from the field office."

"We're on the way," Glenda said.

The BMW's engine roared to life and the car jerked in reverse.

Harry and Ranger dropped to a squat behind a building.

The sedan sped away.

"Shit!"

Harry and Ranger took off to their car a block away.

They jumped in with Ranger at the wheel. Harry needed both hands free.

He called Glenda.

"They sped off heading west. We're in pursuit."

"We've two of our own rounding the docks."

Harry shoved toward Ranger and looked in the rearview mirror.

"I see them too," Ranger confirmed.

"Off to the races," Harry said.

The suspects drove into the downtown area where, unlike the quiet of the docks, people congregated in outdoor dining and strolled along the sidewalks, hindering their pursuit. To complicate matters, the cars pulling in and out of the bustling downtown area further stymied them.

"Go down this block and we'll try to cut them off," Harry said.

Ranger slipped their vehicle down the less-populated block and circled around.

"There they are! They've parked. What the hell?"

Harry stared at the car, left cockeyed and quiet in a rushed haphazard parking job.

They eased their vehicle behind the suspect's stolen BMW, and two sheriff's vehicles with flashing strobes approached from in front.

Their targets were caged in. It was over.

Harry and Ranger exited their vehicle with their guns drawn, and the two sheriff deputies were equally prepared for the takedown.

They all surrounded the vehicle.

No response from the trapped targets.

"Get out of the car now," the deputy commanded through his bullhorn.

Guns clicked, anticipating the takedown the hard way.

Nothing.

No suspects got out of their vehicle. Neither did they resist.

Harry didn't see them in the vehicle. They were ducking, and waiting to ambush once Harry, Ranger, and the deputies got closer.

He knew this trick.

Harry raised his hand, halting their encroachment.

Something was off.

The BMW didn't rock an inch.

Harry karate-chopped the go signal.

Harry, Ranger, and the deputies surrounded the BMW with their guns drawn at every window.

Nothing!

All four of them ripped open the car doors, ready to fire.

Harry kicked the Beemer."Ah, fuck! They're gone!"

"They're on foot, or their own picked them up, or they've carjacked or are planning to," Harry theorized out loud.

Two more sheriff vehicles arrived, plus two more from the field office.

Glenda hopped out of one of the sheriff vehicles. "What the hell happened?" she demanded.

"We had eyes on them and then they sped away into crowded downtown, where they knew we would have to slow our pursuit. After going down a one-way street we circled to find the vehicle. Apparently before we got there, they bailed," Harry recapped.

The responding law enforcement agents gathered.

"We need to split up and canvass the area, and we need to stay abreast of any reported stolen vehicles," Harry announced.

Dammit! It was the second time they were duped.

Glenda waved her hand. "I agree."

"Ranger and I will take west."

"'I'll go east," one deputy said.

"North," the other deputy claimed.

Glenda pointed "We'll cover the south."

They had all quadrants covered.

The probability that his targets would be on foot was nearly nil.

They'd already split up, making their capture that more difficult. Now he'd have to locate two different escape vehicles, and he had no idea of the makes, models, and plates, unless a report was filed in the next few minutes, an actual takedown during at this time of night it would need a "Hail Mary" pass. But even if that information surfaced, they could be anywhere, and that stuck in his craw.

49

With Harry gone, the plan was to get through the night.

But the pillow and blanket Joanna gave to Ian for a makeshift bed on the couch, waited neatly folded in one corner and her bed remained cold. They were all on edge. Plus, Kaylee was on her way. No one was getting any sleep tonight except Joley Kay.

Innocence was bliss.

"I'm sorry you're losing sleep," she said to Ian.

"Don't worry about it. I'm used to it."

"This is what you get when you stay for dinner at this house!"

Ian chuckled. "Dinner at my parents' house frequently ends up in chaos."

Joanna perked her ears. She hadn't a chance to ask him about his family, so involved with her own. She planned to ask about his family during their first dinner date this weekend. But he just offered her a sneak preview.

"Your parents live locally?"

"Yes, in St. Petersburg."

Joanna smiled. "What kind chaos would be there?"

"My mother is always worried that the dinner she prepared wasn't tasty enough, or was overcooked, undercooked, et cetera, despite my father rolling his eyes and saying it tasted fine to him, and then he would salt it, causing my mother to be more insecure. And then there's my older sister with her two hellions, who'd shove their dinner around on their plates and then take off from the table, which would cause my mother more distress, piss off my father, and cause my sister and brother-in-law to yell at their kids. And that's just Sunday night dinner. Don't get me started on Thanksgiving."

Joanna laughed. "Sounds like fun."

"You'll see."

Joanna widened her eyes at the increasingly obvious prospect of where she and Ian were headed. She wasn't ready to meet his family and jump through microscopic hoops to hide the gritty details of her past. She could just hear their disapproval.

"Let's just stick to our dinner date for now."

Ian grinned. "A wonderful place to begin."

Lou Ann left Joanna and Ian to themselves in the den.

Plus, she needed her own privacy to gather her thoughts and the evidence she'd gathered during her investigation of three young persons' tragic deaths, including Glenda's niece. They were all connected, and Moreno played a central role. The bastard would do anything to keep his nightclub business booming, including addicting his unsuspecting young patrons. The music. The dancing. The spiked drinks. And surely the open users in bathrooms and in hallways. He had them coming back for more and more.

She heard that conversation between Moreno and the goon whose photo was safely in her cell's cloud.

Moreno couldn't talk anymore, but the goon in her phone could, if he hadn't met the same fate as Moreno. But that shitbag had friends —friends who brutally beat Tim Farmer and the two nurses to spring out two of their own.

Lou Ann shivered. They tried to get to her, to run her over. She expected to be a target, but not Joanna or Ian, who thankfully escaped harm, but the parking garage attendant did not. These assholes seriously injured four innocent people.

She pounded her fists against the mattress.

Come for me, you cowards! Come for me!

Joley Kay whimpered in her room.

Lou Ann grabbed her crutches and headed to the nursery to calm her baby. The little darlin' probably needed a diaper change.

She swung on her crutches to the open door to find Joley Kay standing, gripping the crib's side rails, and rocking from side to side.

"What's the matter, my sweet baby? Come to mama."

Joley Kay's whimpers turned to red-faced screams.

Lou Ann leaned her crutches against the crib, picked up Joley Kay, and hugged her to her chest.

"Did you have bad dream?"

Joley Kay squirmed and pointed to the nursery window.

"Bad! Bad!" she cried.

A large shadow breezed past the window's curtains.

Joanna and Ian rushed into the nursery.

"I heard Joley Kay screaming!"

Lou Ann handed Joley Kay to Joanna. "Take her. And you and Ian get down in the hallway. Stay away from any windows.

"No," Ian said.

"Lie down, Joanna." He pushed Joanna with Joley Kay against the hallway wall.

Lou Ann didn't want to call and take any resources away from or distract the FBI, aka Harry, or Glenda and the department. They were hot on the trail to nab those killer traffickers. She could handle herself like she'd done for years.

"I'm going with you," Ian announced.

"Have you ever fired a gun?"

"No."

Ian wasn't a coward. Lou Ann mentally shrugged. He wasn't going to stay back.

"Follow me."

Lou Ann swung her crutches and faster into her room, grabbed her duty belt and holstered her loaded gun along with a magazine. As one of the best sharpshooters in the department, the extra ammo was the only insurance policy she needed.

Ian's eyes got very big. "Shit! There's a lot of stuff on that belt. That's got to weigh a ton."

"Yep."

She hadn't worn the full duty belt since her promotion to homicide. But with her crutches and cast slowing her down, she needed every tool.

"Come here, Ian."

Lou Ann handed Ian one of her off-duty pistols.

"This is loaded. You have six shots—six bullets. See this red handle here?"

"Yeah," his normally confident voice now shaky.

She reached for the gun back. Firearms quick start 101—not!

"I could do it. So, this red handle."

"That's the safety. Important—safety on, safety off."

"Got it. I have six bullets. Safety on. Safety off," Ian repeated.

"Good. Now steady it with both hands. This is how you cock it. When you squeeze the handle here and the safety is off, you'll discharge the first bullet. Then all you need to do is squeeze the handle every time you need a bullet until all six are spent. The casings each time you fire are hot and fly out to your right."

"Got it."

This time he said it with more conviction.

"When and if you *fire*, upon my command, go for critical mass—the chest. Hitting an arm or leg would be purely accidental. Don't go for small moving parts like hands and legs that are pumping. Critical mass, remember that."

Ian nodded.

"We're going to go outside. Stay behind me. Don't fire or point the gun at anything or anybody until I tell you to. If I shout *get down*, go to your belly, cover your head, and pray. It's okay if you stay back."

"No. I'm ready. Let's go."

Lou Ann and Ian moved to the hallway.

"No, Ian, don't," Joanna pleaded.

"Joanna, Ian and I are just going to go outside to check things out."

"Those 'things' are not big shadows."

"It's going to be okay."

"Then why do you and *Ian* have guns?"

"For just in case," Lou Ann tried to reassure her.

Joely Kay whimpered.

"Joanna, take Joley Kay to our bedroom and lie down next to the bed." Lou Ann smiled at Joley Kay. "We're going to play a game now." Joely Kay stopped whimpering. "You and Auntie Joanna are going to hide," Lou Ann placed her finger to her lips, "very quietly. And then I'm going to try and find you."

Joley Kay grinned, anxious to play the game.

"One, two, three, go!"

Joanna grabbed Joley Kay and did as Lou Ann instructed.

When both were in place, Lou Ann closed the bedroom door.

Lou Ann and Ian proceeded into the kitchen and paused at the sliding doors leading into the backyard.

The clip-clip of paw nails against the kitchen floor tiles came from behind Lou Ann.

Isabelle trotted past Lou Ann and Ian and growled at the glass doors.

"Isabelle, no!"

But the dog's paws scraped against the glass.

Bushes rustled.

"Isabelle, stay," Lou Ann commanded.

Isabelle backed up, but continued her low growl.

"Good girl."

Lou Ann clicked open the sliding glass door lock. She paused and listened to the backyard bushes.

The rustling stopped.

Lou Ann tilted her head toward the sliding door, gesturing the "go" sign to Ian.

She eased the door open just wide enough for them to sneak through, and when she and Ian were through, she closed and it engaged the smart lock to keep Joanna and Joley Kay safely inside.

When Joley Kay was born, she and Harry doubled the security system. Both Harry and she were always at a certain amount of risk of criminals with a grudge finding out where they lived. But whatever was out there wasn't going to get through this sliding glass door, nor through the alarm- secured and smash-proof windows. Plus, with the film-proof window tints, people inside could see out, but no one could see in.

They began their rounds in the back yard.

Ian's breaths nipped warm and quick against the nape of her neck.

Crickets vibrated in their nightly concert.

A shadow rose huge from the bushes—the one she and Joley Kay saw through the nursery window.

Lou Ann crossed her hand to the right on her duty belt and took out her Taser.

Ian sprang out from behind her and trained the gun she'd entrusted him with onto the towering invader.

"Don't! It's me, George."

Lou Ann let loose of her Taser.

"George?!"

"Who the hell is this with the gun?"

Ian lowered the gun and put the safety back on.

"It's all right. I know him," Lou Ann reassured George.

"No harm, no foul, my man," George said.

More rustling came from the bushes.

"That's only Chastity," George said.

Chastity emerged from the bushes, diminutive next to George.

"Quick! We need to get inside," George instructed in a low voice.

Lou Ann pressed the code into the sliding door's outer keypad and after they'd all filed inside, she secured the inside lock.

George took a deep breath. "There's no time to explain. I didn't kill Moreno. And they're coming after you."

Harry's phone alarmed. It was from Glenda.

"What's happening?"

"Our deputy has just responded to a traumatized woman who was about to get into her car with her baby when two men pushed her and her baby to the ground and threatened to kill them if she didn't surrender the key to her car. She gave it to them and after the two men got into the vehicle, two other men came out the home's front bushes. They tossed the car seat out of the car and all four took off. She was too frightened to stand up to see which way they fled. The deputy is with them now. The suspects are now traveling in a black Toyota Corolla, license plate CJ72291, leaving the victim's residence, 691 East Sherwood Court. Neighbors came out and witnessed a black Toyota Corolla speeding due west."

"We're on it."

"I know that neighborhood," Ranger said. "There are multiple speed bumps and one-way streets in the suburban neighborhood, and to get out you have to exit onto US 19. From there they could get off any exit and and into other neighborhoods."

"Glenda, Ranger is familiar with the area. Keep all units quiet. We don't want them to dump that car and endanger someone else. They're getting desperate."

"Agree. We'll try block them in without them knowing we're there, and we'll strike when we've boxed them in."

"We're taking US 19 southbound," Harry said.

"We'll head northbound."

Harry and Ranger sped southbound.

Harry spied every black sedan, but thus far no black Corolla.

Caution signs to look out for the make and color of vehicle including the license plate blasted from every overhead digital sign along the route, so far no one had called the tip line. Despite the warning signs, motorists had seen so many that they automatically drove on without notice. But not everyone, and Harry still held hope a motorist had seen them, especially if the suspects carjacked car speeded past them or cut them off, pissing off at least one motorist who'd be more than likely to report them.

The evening summer traffic further hampered Harry and Ranger's search.

They'd not heard from any other units patrolling with the same mission.

Another alarm call.

"Baxter."

"Coast Guard. Two men fitting suspects description wearing

hooded gray sweat shirts and hobbling are getting into a boat that had just pulled into Clearwater docks. Black vehicle dropped them off and then sped off. In processing of seizing unknown craft and its occupants. That is all."

"Coast Guard is nabbing a boat that I'm positive the escaped injured subjects just got in. The Corolla sped away. Two down, two to go! We're heading toward the docks. With any luck, we'll run right into them."

Harry contacted Glenda.

"Coast Guard is seizing a boat at Clearwater docks. Corolla still at play. We're on our way to the area."

"We'll head north of the area, and I'll move units to south."

Ranger punched the accelerator. "That's enough! These shitbags have ruined my night of pizza, beer, and a double header. But nooo. I got to run around and chase these bastards," he groused.

"Once we nail these scum, beer and pizza is on me. Can't do much about missing the double header. Whole pie and a six pack?"

Ranger grinned. "Yeah. What are you gonna have?"

"My family."

50

"George, why were you and Chastity hiding in my back yard?"

"According to my neighbors and good friends, a Sheriff's Department vehicle was circling around my apartment complex, and then one of them got out and knocked on my door, demanding for me to come out. I knew they were searching for me, so I left my truck parked there so they'd think I was home to delay them. We had to get to you to warn you and protect you, so we took Chastity's car. We still thought they might've also marked her car, so we left it camouflaged under a creek bridge a mile from here. We dodged and hid from patrolling vehicles until we made it to you."

"Protect me from whom?"

"More like 'whoms'? When I arrived at the club upon Moreno's urgent request and found him dead, I squatted outside, waiting to get into my truck, when I heard one of the two killers say that you, Lou Ann, have a photo of one of them and they're going to get it and you."

"How do they know I have that, and how do they know where I live?"

"I believe they were behind sideswiping you, and then after, making their way to the hospital. They could have been hanging around disguised, trolling and eavesdropping on your conversation like when you told Harry about the photo. As far as knowing where you live, they probably followed you to your house after you left the hospital. Their branches are extensive."

"Did you know Moreno was dirty?"

"No. He stayed in his office a lot, and I thought he was working to grow the club. He paid me and the bartenders well, but skimped on the waitresses, telling them to move the drinks and food quickly so they'd make good tips. That's common in the business, but he was

243

constantly touching them. And if they were near his office for any reason, he'd make their life miserable and pressuring them to quit, and if they didn't he'd fire them. His office was off limits, except for me. He needed me around to be his gatekeeper. He'd give me a list of people to push to the head of line."

"Were they the same people?"

"Some, but others I hadn't seen before."

"Did you recognize the men who'd killed Moreno?"

George shook his head.

"They may have been there before but not when I was there."

Lou Ann grabbed her cell phone and brought up the photo of the man and showed the photo to George and Chastity.

"That was one of them," George said.

Chastity smacked the table."Oh, my God! That's the man who was in Moreno's office when I walked in on them."

Ian brought Joanna, who carried Joley Kay, to the kitchen table conference.

Joanna roved her eyes upward while assessing George. Lou Ann mused she'd initially done the same. George's hulk was overwhelming at first, but his gentle soul was in contrast to his brawn. But pissing him off was always ill advised.

"George, Chastity, this is my niece, Joanna."

Lou Ann would forever refer to Joanna as she would Kaylee, her niece by blood. For Lou Ann and Harry, she and Kaylee were no different. They were family and always would be.

"It's nice to meet you," George said.

"Same here," Chastity said.

"Likewise," Joanna responded.

Joley Kay reached her arms out to George

"Come here, my beautiful princess," George cooed.

"It's okay, Joanna," Lou Ann reassured her. "She knows him from the hospital."

Joanna and George's eyes met.

"I overheard you saying my Aunt Lou Ann is in danger."

"That's true, and it's why I'm staying here."

Despite the necessary exchange, tension still echoed around the normally peaceful kitchen. But peace was an iffy proposition tonight.

She needed to break this up.

"Let's move to the den and watch the news," Lou Ann said.

She looked at her cell. Harry hadn't called. But he was involved in the active pursuit of the gang and hopefully between Harry and all the reinforcements all this would end before the evening was over. These criminals couldn't evade the massive hunt for them. And although she more than appreciated that George stood ready to respond to any threats aimed at her, no one had come her way. Their house was a fortress by her and Harry's design. They were safe. And George? If she as much breathed that he was here, they'd come for him and Chastity as an accessory, and she wouldn't let that happen. He was innocent and she wasn't going to turn him in. Harry would understand.

Meanwhile, they'd all sit and let the evening unfold and deal with the consequences tomorrow.

Security lights flashed and bathed the outside of the house, the bright response pushing into the den.

Joanna rushed out of the den and to the front door and then spied through the peephole.

"Kaylee's here!" Joanna cried.

Although they'd talked and used FaceTime, she hadn't seen Kaylee since Joley Kay was born.

Kaylee waved and grinned, knowing full well that Joanna was on the other side of the door.

Kaylee's house key scraped into the lock.

The second the door opened, Joanna bear-hugged her.

"So good to be home! Hey, Lou Ann. Do you have company? There are two cars parked along the curb," Kaylee called.

The front door flew open and Kaylee suddenly slammed into Joanna. They toppled to the floor with Kaylee landing atop Joanna, both now in a shocked sandwich.

"What's happening?" Joanna whispered, her voice uncontrollably shaky.

"Shhh. Don't move," Kaylee whispered back.

Joanna peered through slitted eyes, pretending she'd been knocked unconscious.

A man wearing all black jumped over her and Kaylee, his foot landing on Joanna's hair, causing her head to snap back.

Footsteps scuffled in the hallway. And then bodies crashed against the walls. Glass cracked.

Joanna's heart pumped hard in her chest and her whole body shook.

Bullets!

Muted thunks followed.

Kaylee rose and grabbed Joanna's hand.

And just as they stood, a man grabbed Kaylee from behind, his large hands encircling her throat.

"No!" Joanna yelled.

She drew her hand behind her head and in bow and arrow maneuver, she shot her two fingers straight into the thug's eyes.

He whipped back and reflexively brought his hands to his stunned eyes releasing his grip on Kaylee's neck.

Kaylee swung around and kicked her assailant in the balls, and when he bent over helpless, protecting his eyes and scrotum, Joanna grabbed a lamp, snapping its cord from the electric outlet, and mustering her rage, she smashed the lamp's ceramic base over the bastard's head.

He crumpled to the floor.

Joanna kicked him in the head for extra insurance he'd not get up.

"Give me the cord," Kaylee called.

Together they tied the man's hands behind his back with the lamp cord.

Joanna grabbed her cell from the back pocket of her jeans and dialed 911.

"911."

"Men broke into our house. They're still here."

"We have your location. Sheriff's on the way. Can you get out of the house or to a safe area?"

"We heard shots, and I don't know who else is outside the house."

"Is there a closet you can access?"

"It's in our bedrooms, but they're in the hallway."

"I'm going to keep you on the line."

"Kaylee!" Joanna cried. No!"

"Who's Kaylee?"

"My sister."

Harry's heart squeezed.

The 911 call was coming from his home.

"They're there!"

Ranger hit the gas.

"They've got my family!"

"They'll have to deal with us!"

"I'll kill every last one of them!"

Joanna dropped the cell and ran after Kaylee, who headed into the hallway.

The family portraits that hung on the wall were ripped from their places, the glass smashed over the photos still in their frames.

Joanna's eyes went hysterically huge at the blood smears trailing along what was once cheery walls.

The man in black who had jumped over her lay motionless on the hallway floor, blood seeping from his sides, his hands bloodied.

Joanna stared at him. He looked her age, maybe even younger. What the hell? He was still breathing. But he was a criminal. Who shot him? Lou Ann?

Kaylee and Joanna ran into Lou Ann's and Harry's bedroom.

Lou Ann sat on the side of the bed with her gun aimed at a man, and he in kind trained his on her.

"Back away," Lou Ann instructed them.

Joanna and Kaylee slowly walked backwards out of the room.

Joley Kay! She had to get to Joley Kay!

The door to the nursery was still open.

Joanna would creep in there and get the baby out.

They'd have to run for it.

Help was on the way, but it might be too late.

Joanna backed into the nursery and turned around.

"Hello," the evil man said while holding Joley Kay, his hand over the baby's red faced and wide-eyed mouth, stifling her cries.

"Let her go!" Joanna cried.

"Oooh," he taunted. His eyes blackened. "Her child for mine."

"I saw him, your child. He's breathing, but he needs medical attention."

She guessed the young man bleeding in the hallway was this guy's son.

"Oh, he'll get it."

"Don't hurt the baby. She's innocent," Joanna pleaded.

"It's just business, along with payback."

"I'm a nurse. Let me see to your son," Joanna offered.

Anything to convince him to surrender Joley Kay.

The man paused.

His son stumbled into the nursery.

"Dad," he uttered.

Ian! Where is Ian? Where is everyone else?"

Lou Ann and the criminal glared into each other eyes in a game of chicken to decide who'd fire first.

His finger began to move on the trigger.

A split second, either way.

Lou Ann held her breath.

Go now!

She lunged at him and smashed her fist against his forearm, causing his weapon to wobble in his hand. His misfire hit the ceiling and plaster rained down on both of them. She yanked away the gun in his hand, and then picked up her crutch and walloped him on his head. He crumpled to the floor, unmoving. Lou Ann shook the flakes of white plaster out of her hair and tucked the criminal's gun into the back of her jeans. Now she had two firearms.

Joley Kay's screams were like a fire alarm in Lou Ann's ears.

Oh, my God! My baby! Nooo!

Lou Ann grabbed her crutches and speed-hobbled into the hallway. Glass shards punctured the bottoms of her bare feet, but Joley Kay was her life and soul, and she had to get to her—fast!

With her bum leg she rushed into the nursery to find Evil holding her baby, and Joanna and Kaylee accosting him.

Joanna kept her pleading eyes on Evil, while Kaylee shifted her weight side-to-side with her hands curled, plotting her attack.

Isabelle galloped into the room, growling through her bared teeth.

Evil aimed his gun at the dog.

"Isabelle! No!"

Isabelle's back was still up and she was still growling, but she obeyed Lou Ann and slinked back with her narrowed eyes laser-focused on the devil and his grip on Joley Kay.

Lou Ann's breath stuck in her lungs. His photo was in her cell—the one she took from her hiding place outside of Spark. George warned her that getting to her and her cell was the man in the photo's mission, no matter the cost.

Lou Ann aimed her pistol at the evil man.

"Joanna. Kaylee. Leave. *Leave!*"

This was between her and Evil.

Lou Ann needed to wrest her daughter from his grip, but she wouldn't further endanger Joanna, Kaylee, or Isabelle while doing so.

Evil held Joley Kay in front of him as a shield.

"Mama! Mama!"

"The photo for the baby."

Lou Ann aimed for his head, but she could miss and her daughter could die.

"Drop the gun," he ordered.

Lou Ann lowered her gun to the floor while hiding the gun tucked into the back of her jeans.

She slowly backed away while training her eyes on her baby.

"I'll get my cell. You can watch me delete the photo," she bartered with him.

"I changed my mind. You may have downloaded it or forwarded it already."

Lou Ann shook her head. "I didn't."

"I saw you show your husband my photo in the hospital. I'm sure he has a copy, if not others. So that's no good for me."

George had been right again.

"Doesn't matter now. Keep it as a token—a memory of me and this night," he taunted. "We'll be on our way now. Looks like I have a daughter and a son."

Lou Ann whipped out the gun from the back of her jeans and pointed it at the bastard who held her baby as a hostage.

"Wait there, you tricky mommy."

The evil thug pressed his gun against Joley Kay's head.

"One more step," he warned. "You shot my son, so it would be an even trade. I'll take the baby out before you even get off a shot."

"I'm sorry about that. He aimed at me at first and surprised me, and I'm sorry I shot first," Lou Ann lied to Evil. "But I didn't kill him. Just disabled him."

She had to choose her words carefully. Joley Kay's life depended on them.

Evil arched his brows. "What have you done with my associate?"

"Sorry about that too. That was also an accident."

"Seems like you're having a lot of accidents tonight."

"It happens."

She hoped he'd be her next accident.

She had to delay him. "Your son needs medical care. He's losing blood."

"I already discussed that with that young woman there, the nurse. She your daughter?"

"My niece."

He pointed to Kaylee. "What about the other one there?"

"Also my niece."

"Not as precious your sweet little daughter, huh?"

Joley Kay squirmed.

"Looks like your daughter is anxious to get out of here." The thug cocked his head toward his staggering son. "Let's go."

The snake Lou Ann had battered with her crutch swayed out of the bedroom.

The Evil cackled. "Ooh, I like you." His narrowed his eyes. "See you."

Lou Ann trained her eyes at the son she'd injured.

Marky-Mark! The guy on the sofa at Jade and Kelseigh's apartment.

"Mark," she called.

"Yeah, you got it right. Payback's a bitch!"

"How do you know her?" Evil prodded his son.

"She saw me at Jade's apartment on her interview tour."

Evil laughed at Lou Ann. "Wow! You really get around!"

Mark, the snake, who she should have finished off, and also Evil, who carried Joley Kay with a gun to her baby's head The devil incarnate started to walk toward the hallway exit.

If Lou Ann shot Evil in the back, the bullet could pass through him and into Joley Kay. She couldn't take the risk. But she wouldn't surrender. She had to rescue Joley Kay before they put her daughter in the car. Lou Ann's body burned with adrenaline. God forbid they managed to escape with her baby. Rule number one was to never let a captor take an abductee to another location. And Joley Kay was about to be kidnapped.

The terrorist trio turned left and toward the front door.

Lou Ann hobbled after Evil.

No fucking way were they leaving with her daughter.

She had to stop them, and she was ready to take a bullet for it.

Damn this leg! *Damn* this leg!

And then George popped out from the kitchen, bolted past Lou Ann, and ran like a bull who'd taken an arrow, out the front door.

Lou Ann raced behind him, smacking her casted leg every other stride.

The terrorists turned at the thunder behind them.

Gorilla George leaped in the night air, and with all his hulk, slammed into Evil, knocking the wind right out him, and while Evil struggled to breathe, he released his grip on Joley Kay. Lou Ann dropped her crutches. George grabbed the baby, tossed her into Lou Ann's arms, and proceeded to grind the devil into the ground.

Lou Ann hugged Joley Kay tight to her chest. The baby whimpered and her skin was hot. Lou Ann's tears dripped onto her daughter's head.

Thank you, George. Thank you.

George sat on Evil's back. "Eat dirt!" he growled.

The garage door squeaked open, and Ian and Chastity bolted out of the garage and both tackled the beaten scum.

Lou Ann's army sprang from every direction.

"Ready?" Kaylee asked Joanna.

"Let's roll."

Joanna and Kaylee raced out the front door.

They ran past Lou Ann, who blessedly cradled Joley Kay in her arms.

Joanna and Kaylee surrounded Mark, who collapsed, weakened before they could wrangle him to the ground.

Together they pinned him in case he resurrected, but all bets were that it wasn't going to happen.

All three of the perpetrators were now subdued.

"This is for pulling my hair," Joanna yelled at Mark.

"Fuck you!"

"Okay."

Kaylee grabbed Mark's leg and bent it back.

"What did you say to my sister?"

Mark grimaced and yelled, "Fuck you!"

Kaylee bent his leg further back.

"Shit!"

"Stop, Kaylee. He needs help."

"You're the nurse. But I'm not."

"Kaylee, no. Enough. Not a fair fight."

"Since when is any of this horrid night fair?"

"It's not."

"All right, have it your way."

Kaylee snarled at him.

"You make one wrong move, and trust me, you'll regret it."

51

Ranger skidded the car around the street corner and then rocketed to Harry's house.

"Stop! Harry yelled.

Ranger slammed on the brakes.

Harry ripped off his seatbelt and leaped out of the car.

Security lights flashed onto bodies that lay all over the front lawn.

Lou Ann! Lou Ann! Where was Lou Ann?

And then he saw her—a crutch under one arm and hugging Joley Kay to her chest.

He pumped his legs racing toward her at top speed, but his brain stuttered while he tried to process what had happened to his wife—the woman he would've given anything to save—and to the daughter they created together.

He wrapped his arms around them, kissed her lips and then laid his hand on his baby's head and then kissed his baby's head.

"I heard the 911 call. "Harry sniffed. "My heart froze."

"Babe, we're all right. Go see to the others." Lou Ann patted his arm. "Go ahead. We're safe now."

Harry turned and his eyes got bigger and bigger as he tried hard to take in everything around him.

His attention wandered around the bizarre situation.

George sat on a man, Ian was draped across a bruised man, while Chastity held down the man's legs, and Joanna and Kaylee subdued another suspect, blood on their hands.

If Harry hadn't seen this scene, he wouldn't have believed it.

Harry ran to Joanna and Kaylee.

"Don't worry, Harry. It's this guy's blood and not ours," Kaylee said. "But's it's nice to see you again."

Typical, badass, Kaylee.

252

"Likewise."

"He has a gunshot wound to his side. He needs medical assistance," Joanna said.

Sirens blared closer.

"An ambulance is coming along with a whole train of enforcement."

"Lucky you," Kaylee said to Evil's son.

Ranger ran up to Joanna and Kaylee and squatted next to Harry.

"Everyone all right?" Ranger asked.

Kaylee grinned at him. "We're all right, but this guy, not so much."

"Ranger, these are my nieces. And they can handle him until the ambulance takes him," Harry said.

Kaylee shot Ranger a thumbs-up sign.

Ranger nodded to her, and then Harry and Ranger took off toward Ian and Chastity.

"One hell of a good job, Ian, Chastity," Harry said. "But it's time for us to take over."

Ian held down the criminal while Harry snapped cuffs behind the man's back.

"What the hell happened to his face and..." Ranger looked closer, "missing teeth?"

Harry spied Lou Ann, who only had one crutch. Then he examined the criminal's face.

"Lou Ann," he answered.

Three sheriff vehicles and an ambulance screeched to a halt in front of the house.

Glenda exited the first vehicle and two deputies followed her.

She walked up the front lawn, scanning the aftermath from one end to the other, eyes widened as if deciding which pile up to approach first.

It had been the same for him.

Harry raised his hand to guide her.

Glenda strode to him.

"What the hell?" she demanded.

"Those are my thoughts exactly. Ranger and I—and all of you—were searching for the remaining two on the loose, only to find them here, plus an unknown third, at my home. But they're all subdued now. We've got to get this—this gang—off my lawn and into jail. Then we'll entangle the mess."

"Been in the house yet?" Glenda asked.

Harry shook his head. "I went to Lou Ann and Joley Kay first, and then here—and there."

"Understood."

Glenda directed the deputies to inspect the inside the house.

Glenda stared at the bruised and toothless man now cuffed.

"What's with that?'

"Lou Ann."

Ranger nodded.

"The woman is fierce, even with a cast."

Another ambulance arrived, and Evil's bloody son was gurneyed on one, while "Lou Ann's "handiwork" was loaded into the other.

Harry walked over to George, who was peacefully sitting on Evil.

"You can take me in," George said.

Harry shook his head.

"I know you have to. I'll explain later."

"Get... off... me, you... oaf!" Evil muttered beneath George's considerable hard-muscled weight.

"My...son."

"Your son's going to the hospital, and your other guy too, but no worries, you're all going to eventually meet up at the same place. Oh, there's your ride now," Harry said.

George held Evil down while Harry cuffed the criminal he'd spent the night chasing.

Harry and Ranger escorted Evil into the prison van that Glenda requested.

They pushed him in and secured the doors.

Harry banged on the backdoor of the van and it pulled away.

George stood and put his hands behind his back.

"Just do it, Harry."

Harry sucked in a breath, took out his cuffs, and squeezed them tight in his fists.

"Come on," George said.

This was all wrong.

"Don't make me wait."

Harry snapped on the cuffs.

"No!" Lou Ann yelled.

Glenda raised her hand at Lou Ann.

"He didn't do it! He saved Joley Kay."

Harry shook his head. "What?"

"He saved Joley Kay from that evil man."

"Glenda!" Harry said.

"He has to come with me," Glenda said, "and," she pointed to Chastity," her too."

Lou Ann caught Glenda's insistent expression.

"Still my case, and I'll meet you at the station."

"And I'll drive her there," Harry said.

255

52

Suzy ran across the street after the commotion of bodies, sirens, and vehicles had vacated Lou Ann's and Harry's front lawn.

Only a crime scene unit vehicle remained to process the house proper and their tow truck to remove and process the suspects's stolen car and the one that wasn't, who Lou Ann suspected belonged to "Marky-Mark." How he fit into this crime, other than being the Boss's son, was yet to be determined.

Suzy hugged Lou Ann and stroked Joley Kay's head.

"I don't know what happened, but I know it was bad. I couldn't come over earlier. I'm so sorry."

"Thank you."

Harry, Ranger, Joanna, Ian, and Kaylee sat on the stoop while CSU gathered evidence inside.

Lou Ann had never thought her house would be a crime scene.

Suzy's eyes saddened.

"You can't go inside, huh?"

Lou Ann shook her head.

She hadn't thought about where they'd go, until now. Once the house was processed, it would need to be cleaned.

"All of you can come stay with me. You know I have a big house to fill. I see your nieces, and especially Kaylee, who came all the way from Greece. I know you're all tired and stressed. Please."

Lou Ann hugged Suzy.

Lou Ann walked over to the stoop with Joley Kay and Suzy.

"Hi, Joanna and Kaylee. Kaylee, it's always wonderful to see you when you come. Although, not a wonderful night. Come to my house. I have more than enough room. You can take a shower. Have something to eat or drink, whatever your needs are. And a bed to lay your weary head."

"Thank you, Suzy," Kaylee said. Kaylee looked at the front door. "My clothes are in there."

"I've plenty of clothes. Perhaps not exactly your size or style, but clean."

"That's more than enough."

Lou Ann kissed Joley Kay on her head. "Go with Suzy. Auntie Kaylee is coming too, and Isabelle. Mommy and Daddy have to go to work, but we'll be back soon. I love you."

Joley Kay kissed Lou Ann's cheek. "Mama love."

Lou Ann's eyes misted. She'd just been inches from losing her baby.

Suzy held out her hands. "Come on, my sweet girl."

Thankfully Joley Kay went readily into Suzy's arms.

"Isabelle, go with Suzy and Joley Kay."

Isabelle trotted behind Suzy.

"Joanna?"

"I'll be there soon."

Lou Ann watched Joanna and Ian trade looks.

She decided to leave them to sort things out themselves.

Ironically, Ian was only going to spend a quiet dinner with them, and look what happened.

Lou Ann forced that nightmare of tonight to the back of her brain. She needed to function—to incarcerate the scum who'd terrorized them.

But first she needed to vindicate George and Chastity.

Joanna watched Kaylee enter Suzy's house. Suzy turned and looked back at Joanna and waved to her before going inside and closing the door.

"I'm so sorry, Ian, for everything that happened tonight."

"Certainly a night to remember, and most important to remember that we're all safe."

"You popped right out of that garage."

"Chastity and I hid there waiting for the right moment. And then it came. The element of surprise."

"I bet I'll never be able to get you to come to dinner again."

Ian rested his hand on Joanna's knee.

"What are we having next time?"

Joanna laughed for the first time tonight.

"Dinner for two in a restaurant—that is, if we're still on?"

"Absolutely."

"I'll walk you to your car."

The driveway suddenly looked desolate.

Joanna and Ian halted in front of his car.

Ian leaned against the front door and held out his hands.

Joanna leaned forward and kissed him.

"I'm going to head over to Suzy's house."

Ian nodded. "See you in the morning in the ED?"

"Absolutely."

Ian opened the front door, slid inside, buckled his seatbelt, and started the engine. He slowly backed away and then he turned the car around, stopped and waved.

Joanna waved back, and watched him drive away into the night.

She crossed the street and knocked softly on Suzy's door.

Suzy opened the door and beckoned, "Come on in."

Ranger parked the car at the Sheriff's Department Headquarters.

"This is better than our field office," Ranger said.

Ranger and Harry got out of the car, and Harry opened the back door, held his hand out to Lou Ann, and pulled her out and on her feet.

"I got it, Harry."

"I'll be your other crutch since one of yours is missing."

"I'm sure they'll find it in our bedroom. But it may have a few cracks in it."

"Looks like we'll have to get you a new one."

"Looks like it."

Lou Ann entered the lobby, and flanked by Harry and Ranger, she led them to the night officer.

'Good evening, Investigator Jasinski. Assistant Sheriff Martinez is waiting for you."

"These are FBI Special Agents Baxter and Ranger, who have been involved in searching for the drug traffickers."

Harry and Ranger showed their credentials, and handed over their firearms.

"Assistant Chief Martinez and her team are in interview rooms one and two on the fourth floor."

Hmmm. Her team.

"Do you need any assistance, Investigator?"

Lou Ann looked at Harry and Ranger.

"No, that won't be necessary."

Lou Ann, Harry, and Ranger walked to the elevator bank and took an elevator to the fourth floor.

Glenda stood at the outside of room one.

She beckoned for them to approach.

Lou Ann wanted to be inside the rooms instead of parked on the outside.

Good enough for Glenda, but not for her.

"George Mason is room one, and his accomplice, Chastity Bancroft is in two."

"I can vindicate both."

Glenda took Lou Ann's hand. "You've come here at night after everything that happened at your house to speak the truth. I have no intention of taking you off this investigation. I couldn't stop you if I tried. I've been listening to Mr. Mason's interview, and I've heard enough."

"Glenda, no."

Lou Ann wasn't going to leave until George and Chastity were released.

"Glenda, Moreno called George. He said someone had broken in. George raced over to Spark. Moreno was killed because he was part of the trafficking and was pocketing the money. George found him dead, but he overheard that I had a cell photo of the head trafficker and they were on their way to get me. George sped away in his truck, and ended up being pursued for leaving the scene of a crime scene that he didn't commit. He drove home, left the F150 as a decoy, and he and his fiancée, Chastity, took her car to my house to warn me and protect me. One of ours patrolled the area, so they ditched the car, and walked the rest of the way to my house.

The suspects arrived and parked. My niece Kaylee thought I had company. So she unlocked the front door and was ambushed. They shoved their way in, three of them. After one pulled a gun on me and I on him, I overtook him and hit him with my crutch, which splintered and broke. The head evil trafficker grabbed my daughter because I also shot his son—not fatally, but I grazed his hip. He was after the cell photo but decided against it because he claimed I already shared it, which I did with Harry.

He left taking my daughter with him I chased after him, but my leg hampered me. George ran out and tackled him, and while doing so George grabbed my daughter and tossed her to me. As you witnessed, Kaylee and Joanna—subdued one—and Dr. Ian Hottman, who was a guest in my house, and Chastity Bancroft subdued the other. I'll put all the details in my report. You have the wrong man and the wrong woman."

"Everything you just said is coming out in the interviews. They're wrapping up now. I had to do it, Lou Ann."

"I understand."

"They'll be released."

Lou Ann hugged Glenda.

"I'll need your full report by tomorrow."

"Yes. Assistant Chief Martinez, you'll have it on your desk by 4pm."

Lou Ann and Glenda laughed at Lou Ann's reference to her prior nemesis and superior, who demanded she hand in her report by 4 pm so he could go home.

"Eh, make it by 5pm..or...6."

"Out of habit, I'll stick with 4 pm. It'll keep me busy."

George and then Chastity came out of their respective rooms.

Lou Ann, Harry, George, and Chastity embraced in a group hug.

"Thank you, Lou Ann," George said with a tear in his eye.

Chastity sniffled. "Ditto."

"Let's all go home," Lou Ann said. "Oh, Chastity, let the deputy know where your car is. He'll give you a ride there."

"Joley Kay?" George asked.

"She's safe and hopefully asleep by now at my friend's house, thanks to you."

Lou Ann kissed George's cheek.

"Hug her for me, and get some rest."

Lou Ann grinned. "I promise."

53

Unable to sleep, Lou Ann finished her report at 3 am. She looked at Harry, who snored beside her. They weren't in their bed or in their own house, but she was grateful for Suzy's friendship and that they had a place to stay.

She eased out of bed, tiptoed along the hallway, and crept into the room where Suzy kept a crib for Joley Kay to nap.

Lou Ann gazed at her baby sleeping in a thankfully familiar bed. She leaned over and kissed her daughter's sweet-smelling head and prayed that Joley Kay would forget the horror of last night.

"You're safe, my baby girl. Mama and Daddy are here. Suzy's here, and Aunties Joanna and Kaylee. I love you."

Lou Ann tiptoed out of the room and left the door open in case Joley Kay cried out.

"Couldn't sleep, huh?" Harry asked.

"I thought you were asleep."

"I went to hug you and you weren't there. I figured you were checking on her."

Harry entered the nursery and looked down at his daughter.

When he turned around a tear ran down his cheek.

"I knew you were on the way," Lou Ann reassured him.

Harry bowed his head. "Not fast enough."

Lou Ann wrapped her arms around him.

"Although it seemed like everything happened in slow motion, I know it happened in a flash."

She pressed her lips against his and then combed her fingers through his hair.

"Don't. You got two of them and kept the others on the run. I had no idea. You had no idea. But Joley Kay is safe, so are the rest of us."

Harry sighed. "Yeah."

Lou Ann and Harry walked along the hallway and stopped at Joanna and Kaylee's temporary room, their door cracked ajar.

Lou Ann gently pushed the door open.

Joanna and Kaylee lay side by side in the same bed.

"They're in the same bed like when Kaylee first arrived from Greece. It took us time to get another bed for Kaylee. She was so pissed off at me for yanking her from Greece. But she liked you from the beginning."

"I was the safe one. She had a complex relationship with you at first because you represented the family she lost."

"I should've swallowed my ego and patched things up with my brother."

Harry rested his arm around her shoulder. "It wouldn't have prevented the car crash."

"But not the horrible nightmare that followed."

"Set it aside, Lou Ann. Joanna is one hell of a nurse, and Kaylee is set to take two law bars in two different countries."

Lou Ann smiled. "Kaylee always did everything big. She's indestructible!"

"And tonight, too." Harry squeezed Lou Ann's hand. "Has to be genetic."

"What about Joanna?"

Harry chuckled. "Genetic by association."

"Want to see what Suzy has in her refrigerator?"

"Since we're both up, I could go for a snack," Harry winked. "With you."

Lou Ann and Harry sneaked into the kitchen and Lou Ann opened the fridge.

"There's apple pie in here. I don't think Suzy would mind." Lou Ann shrugged. "It only would be two pieces."

Kaylee shuffled into the kitchen. "Did you say apple pie?" She scooted into a kitchen chair. "Couldn't sleep."

"Join the club," Harry said.

Lou Ann found three plates and silverware while Harry eyed the pie.

She cut three pieces.

"What do I smell?" Joanna asked while standing in the doorway to the kitchen.

"Make that four," Harry said. "Looks like we're going to polish off this pie."

They sat together at Suzy's kitchen table while eagerly consuming

Suzy's apple pie.

"I'll buy her another pie," Lou Ann said.

"You should get some sleep. You have a twelve-hour shift ahead of you," Lou Ann said to Joanna.

"I have to get up in another hour anyway. I'll consider this breakfast."

"You have a point. So do we," Harry said.

Lou Ann stood. "I might as well make coffee."

"I'll do it, since all I have to do is study. You guys have places to be. And I'll stay here with Joley Kay."

Lou Ann pressed her hand to her mouth and her eyes misted.

Kaylee pushed out of her chair, hugged Lou Ann, and sniffled. "It was all my fault. I unlocked the front door and opened it. Stupid me. I just stood there asking you if had company. And then they shoved their way in. Company from hell."

"No. Wasn't your fault, Kaylee. Please don't beat yourself up."

Harry joined in. "We were all fooled."

"I'm the one who was so happy Kaylee arrived that I hugged her at the open door," Joanna said.

"Now that we've all made our confessions, we have to be grateful we're sitting at this table and we have the day ahead of us," Lou Ann said.

"I'll start the coffee," Kaylee said, "because we're all going to need it."

"I'm off to the hospital," Joanna called.

"I'll text you if the house is ready—finished being processed." Lou Ann's words stuck in her throat. "I called a cleaning crew that specializes in cleaning up crime scenes."

Joanna stopped. "Oh. I thought the sheriff's department cleans everything up."

"No. It's at our expense."

"That sucks," Kaylee said.

Harry shrugged "That's the way it goes."

"Since I'll be here today, I'll keep on eye on our house," Kaylee said.

Our house. Kaylee said, "Our house."

Greece or Clearwater, Kaylee had a home—a family.

"Thanks, Kaylee," Lou Ann said, wanting to make sure she made Kaylee feel important—empowered.

The crew she knew would notify her, but she'd keep that to

herself.

Joanna waved. "See you guys in twelve hours."

Harry kissed Lou Ann. "I've a long day waiting for me at the field officeI. I may roll in at Joanna time."

"Do what you need to do, and I'll do what I need to do."

"Lou Ann…"

"What? My new crutch should arrive this morning. Then I'm good to go."

"Go where?"

"Where I may need to go."

Harry shook his head. "You can't drive like that."

"That's obvious. Who said I was driving?"

Harry sighed. "No one."

"Well, there you go. See you later."

"Later is the operative word."

"Yes it is. Bye, babe."

Harry hesitated and then walked out the door.

"You don't have any intention of staying here, do you?" Kaylee asked.

"Probably not."

Lou Ann's cell rang. It was Glenda.

"Yes, Assistant Chief Martinez."

"I need you to go to the apartment complex now. A deputy will be picking you up. I'll meet you there. We're bringing in two, Jade Anderson and David Montgomery."

"Yes, ma'am. On my way."

David Montgomery. No surprise there. But Jade? Then it hit her! Marky-Mark!

A Ford 150 swung into Suzy's driveway. It was George.

He couldn't be her ride. She was waiting for a deputy to pick her up.

Lou Ann hobbled out of Suzy's house.

"George?"

George got out of his truck. "Morning! As promised, here's a new crutch. Try not break this one."

Lou Ann laughed. "I think this one's a keeper at least for now."

"I got to hightail it out of here. With Spark closed, so did my bouncer gig. For the better. Wrestling full time for now. Gotta go work out."

George ran back to his truck and rode off.

Now she was more than set to go.

Lou Ann swung with her new crutch along, with the temporary one, into the house.

"Good morning, Lou Ann," Suzy said.

Lou Ann winced. "Sorry about your apple pie. We had an early morning snack. I'll get you a new pie today."

In between arresting two individuals.

"No worries. Glad you you enjoyed it. It was just sitting there anyway, and Joley Kay and I usually have oatmeal for breakfast."

"And here she is," Kaylee said, as she walked in holding Joley Kay.

Lou Ann kissed Joley Kay's cheek and playfully gave it a quick raspberry follow-up.

Joley Kay giggled. "Mama funny!"

"Yes, I am. Mama go now. You stay with Auntie Kaylee and Suzy. I'll come home soon."

"Okay."

"Her vocabulary is increasing ,exponentially," Lou Ann joked.

"Just wait. I'll teach her some Greek too. And so you'll know what she's saying, I'll tutor you too. So when you all come to Greece, you'll be experts!"

Lou Ann nodded. "Looking forward to it."

A sheriff's vehicle pulled into the driveway.

"There's my ride now."

Lou Ann stepped off the porch with her crutches and approached the sheriff's vehicle idling in Suzy's driveway.

She'd make it work. No pity.

But when she got closer, she couldn't believe it!

"Get in," Tim Farmer said from behind the wheel.

Lou Ann pumped her way to the passenger side and opened the door.

"When did you get out of the hospital?"

"A day ago."

A rainbow of deep purple and brown surrounded his eyes.

"I got a bum face and you got a bum leg—we're a hell of a pair. So let's get going and make some arrests."

Lou Ann slid into the vehicle and set her crutches to the back.

"I taught you well," she said. "Remember, anything can go sideways, including us!"

"That's not going to stop us," he said.

"Damn straight. Let's go, Farmer. We don't have all day!"

Tim Farmer backed out of the driveway, turned, and hit the gas.

Lou Ann leaned over and engaged the vehicle's flashing lights and siren.

She winked. "We'll be properly announced."

They zoomed past cars at time.

Tim laughed. "They probably thought we were after them and are wondering what they did wrong."

"The lights and siren do it every time. I never liked scaring people, but it's an occupational hazard. But then again, I don't mind scaring people who deserve to be scared."

"One look at us, and that's pretty frightening."

"Speak for yourself. We only have battle scars."

"You're right, as always."

"We'll heal, but these two suspects will have scars way beyond when ours will have healed, psychological ones," Lou Ann clarified.

Tim nodded. "Right again, Investigator Jasinski."

Lou Ann and Tim parked outside the apartment complex just as and Glenda and another deputy pulled up behind them.

"We're about to find out which one is ours," Lou Ann said.

Tim and Lou Ann exited their vehicle and met Glenda and the other deputy.

"Nice new crutch," Glenda said.

"George brought it over this morning. This one isn't splintered, and it doesn't have any teeth marks."

Glenda half-smiled. "Let's keep it that way."

"I'll do my best."

Glenda studied Tim's face.

"I got to hand it to you and Lou Ann."

"You and Tim call on Jade, and we'll give that creepy-peepy manager a ride."

Lou Ann, Tim, Glenda, and the deputy entered the complex and split to their respective assigned suspect.

"Jade fooled me. But then Marky turned on her from his hospital bed, hoping for a plea deal. At first I thought Jade and Gloria were good friends, and I felt bad for Jade and Kelseigh when Gloria was found dead. But then I recalled Marky-Mark arrogantly lounging on Jade's and Kelseigh's sofa. In hindsight, Jade interacted with Marky, but not Kelseigh. It was Jade who brought Gloria to the club, and Gloria's ex, Tyler, too. I imagine she brought a lot of young people to get them hooked and coming back to the club over and over again.

Like Mark, Evil had Jade on his payroll. Money is a great enticer, especially when someone is struggling to pay rent and college tuition. She trusted Mark. Would have done anything for him. Now they'll ultimately be in the same place—jail unit their trial. No graduation for her. No more nightclubs. No more boyfriend. Bad trade."

"I remember seeing them at headquarters, sobbing, and waiting to see you. She had me too. Turns out Kelseigh was genuinely mourning."

Lou Ann and Tim approached 16F, Jade's and Kelseigh's abode, and soon to be only Kelseigh's.

"Jade may know we're coming, and there's a high probability of a bathroom window escape. You do a door knock, and I'll go to the back of the apartment. Time it. Give me four minutes. It would've been two without this leg." Lou Ann glanced at Tim. "Go on four."

Lou Ann sprinted with her crutches. She'd become accustomed to moving at a stealth pace.

She hit the exit door, and emerged into the back courtyard, and then continued to the rear of 16 F. Yes! She looked at her watch. She made in three minutes. One minute to spare for getting into position.

Her watch beeped. Four minutes. Go time.

One foot and then another emerged from window. Then a torso. And Jade popped out.

Gotcha.

Lou Ann whipped out her crutch and blocked Jade. "Hold it right there, Jade. Going somewhere?" Lou Ann asked.

"Seriously. Get the fuck out of my way."

Lou Ann pushed her crutch harder.

"Seriously," she mocked Jade. "You're under arrest for drug trafficking."

Tim raced toward them and grinned.

"You don't have to say it, Farmer."

"Tim cuffed Jade, and he and Lou Ann flanked Jade while escorting her to their vehicle.

And just as they secured her in the back cage, Glenda and the deputy arrived along with handcuffed David Montgomery.

"Good morning, Mr. Montgomery," Lou Ann said.

"I didn't touch her. I told you that."

"Did or did not, doesn't matter. But our crime scene unit found a peep camera in Gloria's apartment, and on further inquiry and a canvassing of all female tenants, further peep bathroom cameras were discovered. You're charged lewd behaviors. See you in court. Take him away."

Lou Ann and Tim got in their vehicle and Glenda and the deputy got in theirs.

Both left the apartment complex in a better place, with Mrs. Stanko in charge, and with Kelseigh under her wing, as it should be.

54

Tim pulled the vehicle back into Suzy's driveway.

"It's been a day. I've missed working with you," Tim said.

"Same here. Stop by any time at HQ. We'll go out to lunch."

"I'd like that. Could use your sage tips."

"You're already exceptional without my further input. Proud of you. You're an asset, and that's how everyone sees it." Lou Ann winked. "That's all I'm going to reveal for now. Onward, Deputy Farmer."

"Onward to you too, Investigator Jasinski."

Lou Ann waved to Tim while he pulled away and he waved to her.

Godspeed, Tim Farmer.

Lou Ann marched up the stairs with her crutches. She'd miss these unique and surprisingly versatile weapons!

She'd just entered Suzy's house when her cell rang.

It was the ME, Dr. Barbara Kent.

"Hi, Barb."

"Hi. I've got some findings for you. First, David Montgomery didn't rape Gloria. Neg for type. But it's Tyler's semen."

"They must have had sex maybe in the car on the way to her apartment. He must have brought her home. I'm positive Mark, son of the head trafficker, and his girlfriend, Jade, laced their friends' drinks. But it took Gloria, Tyler, and Elizabeth time to die. And they obviously hadn't been users, or Fentanyl would have dropped them."

"Precisely. Gas chromatography/mass spectrometry identified a derivative of Fentanyl, but with sustaining intoxication before cardiac arrest. In my research and with colleagues nationwide, I learned there's yet another new drug called Rocket on the market today. Seems to be coming from the Caribbean and Mexico, but the lethal synthetic is spreading, with manufacturing increasing in the US. And it's available in liquid form and highly soluble in alcohol. Hence the spiked drinks at Spark. Gloria's vomit in the toilet tested positive, and Gloria's, Tyler's, and Elizabeth's toxicology confirm positivity for Rocket as well. It took Tyler longer to die due to his body mass, but Gloria and Elizabeth—who were smaller—died within the hour."

"Between me and the Sheriff's Department and Harry and his partner with FBI, and in conjunction with the Coast Guard, and of course George, we nabbed a ring. Harry sent the drugs seized on a boat to their lab. I'm betting it's Rocket because Harry hadn't seen this drug before. Rocket appears to be resistant to Narcan."

"Tragically, yes. But you can chelate it and provide cardiorespiratory support until it's renal- excreted. On the good side, if there is any, Rocket has a short half-life. I pray a new version with a longer half-life doesn't begin circulating. More research is ongoing in either event. Also, I've completed the autopsies, so I'm releasing them to the families. Worst part of my job."

"Thank you, Barb."

"All we can do is hope these young people were the last deaths."

May that be true.

"Are you ready, Harry?"

"In a minute. I'm straightening my tie."

The house had been cleared and cleaned. And she refused to let what happened in her home—those thugs—take away their home. She'd never let them win.

Joanna and Kaylee sighed.

"And they claim women take too long," Kaylee said.

Harry walked into the den.

"Come here," Lou Ann said.

She straightened his tie.

The doorbell rang.

Lou Ann glanced at the door cam. It was Ranger.

She disabled the front door alarm and let him in.

"You clean up well," Harry said.

"You, too. It's my funeral suit."

"Same here."

Lou Ann took Kaylee's hand.

Kaylee knew all too well about funerals.

Kaylee kissed Lou Ann's cheek.

"It's all right."

"We'll take two cars."

"Want to ride with me?" Ranger asked Kaylee.

"Sure."

Lou Ann and Harry secured the house, set the alarm, and followed Ranger and Kaylee.

Lou Ann took a deep breath. Joley Kay and Isabelle were at Suzy's, so she couldn't delay any longer.

Gloria's funeral was the first of the day.

They'd entered the funeral home where Gloria's body lay in a closed bronze casket covered with a spray of flowers.

Barbara sat in the second row with her hands folded in her lap.

Lou Ann nodded to her while she paused to greet Glenda, and Daisy and Richard, who were Gloria's parents, and who filled the first row.

Lou Ann hugged Daisy.

"I'm so sorry."

"I know, but you got who was responsible for her death."

Tears ran down Daisy's cheek. Richard gave her a handkerchief.

"I'm Lou Ann Jasinski. I'm an investigator with the Sheriff's Department."

She left out of Death and Homicide. It would only deepen their grief, and she assumed he knew anyway. Daisy did.

The priest arrived, and Lou Ann took her seat in the second row with her family, Ranger, and Barbara, and set her crutches down next to her chair.

Losing a child is gut-wrenching, no matter the age. It's so out of order. Lou Ann swallowed over the lump rising in the back of her throat. She came so close to losing Joley Kay to Evil. *May they all rot in hell. Sorry, God, that I feel that way. See to them all, because I no longer can.*

After Gloria's funeral, Elizabeth's and Tyler's funerals were next—the completion of a tear-filled trifecta.

While Lou Ann and Harry stood in line to console Daisy and Richard, Harry reached for his cell phone tucked inside his suit's breast pocket.

"Sorry, Lou Ann. I need to take this call," he whispered in her ear, and then he stepped aside.

At least he had the cell on vibrate only.

Lou Ann paused and stepped aside, letting other mourners pass.

Harry's eyes widened while he listened to the mysterious call.

He nodded grimly and ended the call.

"What was that all about?" Lou Ann asked softly.

"That was Freddie from the state lab. The unknown drug seized on that boat was something called Rocket, a new and fatal drug rivaling Fentanyl."

"Oh, my God. Barb identified Rocket in Gloria, Elizabeth, and Tyler's toxicologies."

Harry shook his head.

Lou Ann took Harry's hand. "Because we know what drug we're dealing with, along with Fentanyl, a new antidote is in the works. It's too late for these three young people, but we pray not for others."

"Amen to that," Harry replied.

Lou Ann walked with her crutches across the street to Suzy's house while still wearing her funeral dress.

"I'm so sorry for the parents who mourned their children today. Mine are grown and with their own lives, but they're still my children. I know their lives are changed forever, but you and Harry gave them resolution. Now their work begins. On a lighter note, Joley Kay played fetch with Isabelle all day or fiddled with her toes. I held her a lot today. She didn't nap, but she and Isabelle devoured their lunch. She's a happy baby. I'm not sure exactly what we do right. All she knows is that we love her."

Lou Ann hugged Suzy. "Thank you for everything, too numerous to count."

"I'll get her for you."

Isabelle bumped up against Lou Ann's leg.

"I know. You were so brave."

"Here she is," Suzy said while carrying Joley Kay.

Joley Kay reached her arms out.

"Mama!"

Lou Ann adjusted her crutches in her armpits and held her precious child.

"Bye-Bye Sooozy."

"Bye-Bye, Love. See you tomorrow."

Harry arrived.

"Hi, Suzy."

"Hi, Harry. She's been an absolute pleasure."

"Lou Ann or Joley Kay?" Harry joked.

Suzy grinned. "Both."

"I'll take the baby. You take the crutches."

"Deal. I can't wait to get a boot tomorrow."

Harry winked. "Save those crutches. You can't predict when they'll come in handy."

"I'll keep them readily available."

"Can I have one after tomorrow?"

"Absolutely."

The three of them plus Isabelle in tow walked back into the house that would always be theirs.

55

Ian opened the passenger side door for Joanna and then got in behind the wheel.

"So much has happened, but we are finally on our dinner date," Joanna said.

"Unbelievable, but thankfully so true."

Joanna laughed. "And you even came back to my house."

"You can't keep me away, no matter how hard you try."

Joanna rubbed her fingers together in loose fists.

You can't keep me away he said. But he may.

"Are you all right? You're suddenly so quiet."

"Just trying to figure what I want to order," Joanna countered quickly.

But she knew Ian was sure to ask at some point about Kaylee and how much they looked alike. But they weren't connected genetically, and they had nothing in common growing up. They hadn't even known each other existed until a few years back—a time neither could forget—and a time that guaranteed they'd never let go of each other, no matter the distance.

How could she divulge that without making Ian uncomfortable with her?

For the first time, she loved someone, the only male she trusted besides Harry. But Harry was like a father to her. She had no father, and her mother, a ling-time substance abuser, died from an overdose. Joanna couldn't recall a time when her mother wasn't high, because she never was. Joanna was better off on her own, until she wasn't—until she met Dr. Gerald Newell.

But this was not a story to tell over dinner.

Ian parked in the Italian House Restaurant lot and escorted Joanna from the car.

The restaurant was nice, and not a bit like the diner Lou Ann and Harry first took her to when she left the hospital, when they thought she was Kaylee. It seemed like yesterday.

"I can tell this isn't where you want to be," Ian said.

"Actually, I should've told you earlier. My family and I always go to a nearby diner."

"Okay, get back in the car. I'll cancel our reservations. Off to the diner. The one on Main, right?"

Joanna grinned. "Yes!"

Ian parked the car for the second time, this time at the diner.

"I bet they have the best food here."

"They do. My Uncle Harry would tease me, saying that they had the best mondo fries. So of course I ordered them, and the waitress looked so confused. Then Harry confessed that he made the name up. But the fries are out of this world and the burgers are so juicy."

"My stomach is already growling," Ian said.

They entered the diner and Joanna led Ian to the family's usual booth. Kismet! It was available.

Ian and Joanna slid into the booth.

The waitress approached. "Oh, hi, Joanna. Who's with you tonight?"

"This is Ian Hottman."

The waitress gave Joanna a wink. "Nice. What are you two having?"

"Two burgers, two fries, and two colas," Joanna said.

"Sounds good. I'll have mine medium."

"Medium for me too."

"The usual, huh?"

"Yep."

"You'll have to bring him back more," the waitress said.

"Most definitely," Ian piped up.

"I like him already," the waitress said.

"So do I."

Ian's eyes went big the moment their food arrived.

"Wow! Far better than the Italian place. I was trying to impress you."

"You don't need to impress me. It's not like my first day at the hospital. I decided you were a jerk before I even got to know you."

"People are sometimes not what they seem to be."

"Yep."

Oh, my God. I can't tell him.

Joanna focused on her meal—her heart pounding.

She polished off her meal and soda before Ian finished.

"You must have been hungry!"

"Uh-huh."

Ian finished his and left a generous tip.

The waitress smiled. "You two take care now."

"U-huh."

Ian and Joanna walked to the car. She held her hand away from his.

He escorted her into the car and then got in, but didn't start the engine.

Their eyes met.

"What's wrong, Joanna? Something's different. Did I say something wrong or act weird?"

Joanna shook her head.

"Then what is it? Tell me. You got pale and quiet."

"I...I.."

Ian reached over and took her hand.

"Kaylee isn't really isn't my sister. But she is."

"I don't understand."

She had to just say it. Get it over with. Kaylee had told her the right time would come. She couldn't keep evading him. And she already knew him well enough to know he wasn't going to retreat at this point.

Joanna couldn't stop her tears from overflowing.

Ian's wrinkled his forehead. "What can I do to help you?"

Joanna sniffled. "No-nothing."

She sucked in a stuttered breath. "Kaylee and I were trafficked by the same man when we were   seventeen. I was supposed to be sold to a man in Greece, but my trafficker—*she couldn't' bring herself to say his name*—thought I died, and I was switched out for Kaylee in her dead parents' car. They died in an accident, but Kaylee survived. We looked so much alike that she ended up in Greece. But the Greek man loved her and wanted to return the money he paid for her, but he was killed by our trafficker. Kaylee never got over it. She inherited his Greek estate, and that's where she lives and rushed here because Lou Ann was in the hospital. Our trafficker and his gang are dead. The groomer is now in prison after Kaylee, and I and many other girls testified to the horrors. I was afraid to tell you because I was afraid you'd decide I'm dirty and untouchable."

Tears streamed down Ian's cheeks. "I knew something was

different. Was off. Especially when I saw Kaylee. I'm so sorry that happened to you. But I do love you, and I'll do anything to help you. This is between us."

Joanna and Ian both wept.

Joanna sniffled. "So much for a first dinner date."

Ian leaned over, hugged her, and quipped, "Like the waitress said, Come again."

"Okay. I see a therapist so will you give me some time before our next steps. Because I would want those next steps."

"I want them too. I'll wait until you're ready. That's a promise."

"I thought you'd be nice and take me home and then run away."

"No. You're stuck with me. I wouldn't want to be anywhere else."

"Neither would I."

56

Kaylee carried her bag to the front door.

"I'm sorry I can't stay longer, but my studies call," Kaylee explained to Lou Ann and Harry.

"I understand. I'm so proud of the women you both have become."

"Truly unbelievable," Harry added.

Lou Ann and Harry hugged and kissed Kaylee.

A car pulled up the driveway.

"That must be my limo to the airport."

But what pulled up in the driveway wasn't the limo. It was Ranger.

"Looks like I made it on time for the bon voyage party."

"Hey, Ranger."

"Hi, Kaylee. Need a ride to the airport?"

A white limousine pulled up.

"I appreciate it, but my ride's here."

"Wow. A lot nicer than my car. Two of mine could fit unto that."

"It's over the top, but I like it that way. Look, Lou Ann, Harry, Joanna, and Joley Kay—and surely Isabelle—will be coming to visit me hopefully soon. You're welcome to come along. I've got lots of room on my jet."

"Um…sure."

"See you next month, Ranger."

"First name's Randall," he called while Kayla got into the limo.

"Okay, Randall. Later."

Ranger waved. "Yeah, later."

57

Two Weeks Later

"This is Rescue, We have young male down, found unresponsive by his parents. Intubated. Fluids on board. Multiple Narcan with essential no response. ETA five minutes."

"We'll be waiting," Ian answered.

Ian and Joanna and looked at each other.

"Rocket!" they called at the same time.

The next call Ian made was to ME Dr. Barbara Kent.

"This is Dr. Ian Hottman at Hampton Emergency Department."

"Is some one dead?"

"No. But I don't want him to be. I believe it's Rocket. I need your help."

"I'm on my way."

The End

www.ingramcontent.com/pod-product-compliance
Lightning Source LLC
Chambersburg PA
CBHW030424310726
48979CB00009B/1604/J